The
Picture
Makers

Also by Emily Ellison

Alabaster Chambers

First Light

Our Mutual Room:
Modern Literary Portraits of the Opposite Sex
(co-editor)

The Picture Makers

Emily Ellison

WILLIAM MORROW AND COMPANY, INC.
NEW YORK

Library of Congress Cataloging-in-Publication Data

Ellison, Emily.
　　The picture makers / Emily Ellison.
　　　　p.　　cm.
　　ISBN 0-688-09581-X
　　I.　Title.
　　PS3565.L619P5　1990
　　813'.54—dc20　　　　　　　　　　　　　　　　　　　　　　89-13927
　　　　　　　　　　　　　　　　　　　　　　　　　　　　　　　　　　　CIP

Printed in the United States of America

First Edition

1　2　3　4　5　6　7　8　9　10

For Lee Ella

Acknowledgments

Many thanks to the Atlanta Bureau of Cultural Affairs and the Mayor's Fellowships in the Arts for their support of this work; to Tina LoTufo, Patti Hansen, Bob Hill, Jane Hill, and Chuck Perry for their encouragement and suggestions; and to my editor, Harvey Ginsberg, for his kindness and good taste

Every human being is a colony.

—PABLO PICASSO

I learned from my own pictures, one by one, and had to;
for I think we are the breakers of our own hearts.

—EUDORA WELTY
On photographs taken for the Mississippi
Works Progress Administration from 1933–1936

The
Picture
Makers

Eleanor: 1984

⤸⟊⟋⤹

There's a breed of whale that has a heart the size of a Volkswagen. That's not so hard to imagine. Not for me. We've got people walking around in this family with hearts big enough to kill them. Take my father, Henry. If I were guessing the size of Henry Glass's heart, I'd guess: '56 Plymouth station wagon. That heart's so big and overloaded you can almost hear it pumping. You can almost see it too. I hate looking at pictures of my father. They tear me up. Especially these taken of him today. Today Henry turned sixty.

It doesn't feel like June the second. It's too cool and damp, and this morning when I go outside to meet Henry for our ride—the one we take every time I come home—he's wearing a shiny black windbreaker that used to be my brother's. While Henry waits for me, he throws rocks from the bed of his truck out onto a pile that was started some time back; he has big plans for these rocks, but what they are I've forgotten. Henry can never stand still. Cannot rest a minute. But he doesn't look as tired as usual and, for a change, not worried. Neither am I.

Normally, we are a matched set of first-class worriers. The kind that drives people crazy. I wish it weren't true, but I think about everything. Things that Will and Mama say don't even concern me, like what we're going to do with all those old people living in China (close to a hundred million, I've read) who are forced to retire at age fifty so the younger generations can have jobs. Like those babies in New York born to women addicted to cocaine. *There's not a thing in the world you can do about it.* I know that. But it doesn't keep me from waking up at three in the morning. Overpopulation, shaking babies, Henry. I worry about them all.

But this morning when I slowly hang one foot and then the other off my high old iron bed, I'm not thinking about a thing but a nice drive with my father.

First, we drive his old truck out on the west end of our property to check on the trees. This is the time of year when the peaches have a few more days left to hang before the picking. The migrants haven't arrived yet—bundled together the way they always are, thin and silent like pieces of fencing, on the backs of flatbeds and pickups, tired long before they ever start work. All my father's apprehension about too many cold days, or not enough, is over by June. All the spraying has been done, all the worry about drought. So he has about a week to run his truck up and down the rows of trees, and imagine. He gets out every few hundred yards and feels the fruit, smells it, cuts into a peach with his pocket knife, and wipes the juice from the blade on his sleeve. There are just these few days every year, before the work starts, when he has time to relax—the first time since February when he hasn't kept his eye on every cloud and insect and fungus that's crossed over these three hundred acres in middle Carolina, fearing disaster. I *know* where I come by my number one ailment. You get deep furrows dug between your eyes when your worries are as daily as weather.

I grew up riding over the ruts of this orchard with Henry. Watched the blacks and Indians pick our fruit every summer, wave flies and yellow jackets from their faces, drink water that sat hot and still in tin drums at the end of every few rows of trees. The poorest white women from town came out to our canning house and worked on the conveyor belts, sorting good produce from bad and losing the tips of their fingers. When I was little I'd play up under any one of those belts, and the water from the big vat that washed the fruit would drip on my head. Green itchy leaves stuck to my neck and to the backsides of my knees. I loved listening to the women talk. They passed conversation up and down the metal grids of the belt as swiftly as the rolling peaches. Appalachian words, spit out like seeds: *can, cook, wash, tote, youngins, men.* They'd stand there for hours—their hands swollen and wrinkled from the water and the fuzzy peach skin—until the lunch horn blew and the belt rattled and banged to a stop, and they'd jump down from their positions on boxes and crates to huddle in corners or outside under trees and eat lunches of dry cheese and biscuits and shiny little Vienna sausages.

I played there beneath them every summer until I was old enough to work. Once when I jabbed a stick up into the belt, and the stick was snapped in two and hit me in the eye, all the women scrambled to see about me. As soon as I had been passed among them and hummed over and known to be all right, one of them gave me the fiercest spanking of my life. Mostly they ignored me though, the way they would have their own children if their children had played there. When they did speak, it was with fingers coming at me, with pretend sharpness: *I'm going to box your ears. I'm going to skin you alive.* I knew the meaning of threats; it was their kind of love.

Their daughters work for Henry now, and their granddaughters. The younger women wear tight denim and Reeboks and their hair is pulled back in thick, loose ponytails; their mothers and grandmothers dressed in stretch knits and wore their hair in close perms they'd given each other or in high brittle hives. When the lunch horn blows today, the young women pile into their Camaros and Dodge Chargers and bring back bags of Hardee burgers and fries. At first glance, maybe, they look different, the different generations. But they're the same. The faces particularly, and the language. I've heard them talk. It's still men, children, cleaning, cooking. *In about two shakes I'm going to come over there and knock some sense into you. Hush, before I kill you, child.*

By the time I was nine, Henry had taught me to run the big water wheel that moved the fruit through the vat to the conveyor belt, and I stood high above the women, on a ladder, and grabbed as many leaves as I could before the fruit rolled below me. *Slow her down! Pick it up!* the women yelled up to me about the speed of the belt. And long before South Carolina law allowed, I was driving my father's truck out into the orchards, delivering water to the men. One thing I learned: I like my own money. Another thing I learned was nobody pays you when you stay home and help your mother with babies and laundry. I have to be outside.

But the summer I was sixteen, I got pulled in a notch. A mulatto woman was raped and strangled on our property. My father and I found her body early one morning, covered with blood and dew, in the weed-filled rut between two rows of our trees. He covered her with an old canvas tarpaulin and carried her to the bed of the truck. I remember something I kept wanting to do: take the tail of my shirt and wipe the sand off her narrow teeth. Even if you want to, it's hard to take your eyes off a dead person.

The woman wasn't that much older than I was, but she had three tight-faced children and she looked as old as my mother. After that I wasn't allowed out by myself in the truck during the weeks the migrant workers were on our property. Daddy set up an oak schoolteacher's desk for me in his hot dusty office. An old black oscillating fan blew so long on my sweaty blouse every day that I had a cold all summer. I sat there surrounded by glass and in view of all the others, the boss's daughter, answering the greasy telephone, typing their checks, and filling out the payroll.

I hate being cooped up like that.

That's why this morning my mind isn't on anything but getting out and breathing some fresh air. After we check on the trees, we decide to take a look at how the blackberries are going to be this year. We follow one of the old weedy logging roads out the back side of our woods and up this hilly, washed-out stretch where the berries grow thick and thorny as barbed wire on either side of the road. Of course checking on the trees and the berries is only an excuse for the two of us to get out in the truck. We love to ride.

We have left the others (the women: my mother and her mother, Gram) back at the house. I always worry about that. Every time I come home I feel like a piece of hemp stretched too tight for thinking about everybody. And every time my husband, Will, and I drive back down the interstate to Atlanta I go limp with sickness, worrying that I wasn't nice enough to someone. Mostly Mama. Since I was a kid I've been running out the back door behind my father, trying to get in the truck with him before she can yell. I like just the two of us bouncing over the ruts, hardly ever saying a word, just smelling the dirt and the air, watching him yank on his pants leg every time he pushes in the clutch to change gears. I'm ashamed to say I was always glad my mother was left behind, that there were always other children for her to watch and the house to keep her busy. It was selfishness. Meanness. I knew if she came along, I'd have to sit in the middle. I like the window. I want my own view. I want to be able to really look at anything that comes passing by.

This morning everything is wet from a drizzle we had last night. I slept with my windows open and could hear the rain pattering down all night and could smell it through the rusty screens. Henry and I track mud onto the floor of the truck; Mama is still in bed asleep when we pull out, trying to balance our cups of coffee.

I love this old Ford and all the other Plymouths and Chevrolets he has had before it. All of them with their torn upholstery and inches of sand under my shoes. There is always something rolling around in there on the floorboard causing enough noise to make any normal man goofy: a flashlight or a screwdriver or an empty Delco Remy box, a filthy coffee cup, a bottle of Maalox. Anything you can't find at the house, you look for in the truck, and it's probably there up under the seat with who-knows-what-else or falling out of the glove compartment with little fogged-up light bulbs and blunt-ended pencils and Gulf credit card receipts that are four or five years old. There's always a gauge broken or a handle missing or a window that won't go all the way down.

Mama's the one who knows cars. She'll say to him, Henry, have you had the oil checked in that thing lately? or, Henry, you have to watch the water in the battery, you know. And he'll tell her, Yes, he knows that, and he'll slam the door and bump off, with both of them knowing he's going to drive that truck into the ground. Run the tires off. He's done it. Come home with a flat without even knowing it. Drove thirty-six miles one time with the oil light lit up red as a monkey's hind end and didn't even stop to check on it. "Didn't you think that *meant* something, Henry?" Mama kept asking him that one time after they'd been told the engine block was busted. "Didn't you think that was a warning?" He might have (but he might not have) if he'd ever looked down.

How has the man survived? is what we're all wondering. I think that's partly the reason she always let me go off with him. She figured with an observant ten-year-old in tow he might be less likely to roll off a cliff or run over somebody. The theory didn't necessarily hold.

He forgot to pull the brake on one time when I was along, and he turned around to see his truck slowly picking up speed as it went backwards down a hill and crashed into someone's trailer. He went running after it, crying out in this pitiful voice, "El'nor!" And I went running after him, trying to tell him I was not in the truck but had been standing right there by his side all the time. The whole way home he was shaking so hard he had to keep pulling off to the side of the road because he couldn't keep his leg still enough to push in on the gas pedal.

There were other things too. The time he forgot to put the tailgate up on the truck and our old beagle fell out. "Dad, I don't think Sadie's back there," I kept saying, and we just kept flying. "Daddy, did you hear me? I don't think Sadie's in the truck." And by the time he stopped to check and said, " 'Nor, I believe the dern dog's gone," she'd probably been lost from us for fifteen or twenty minutes. We found her miles back down the road, stumbling in the ditch like some old lady on skinny legs who'd just been threatened or robbed.

I never honk at bad drivers in Atlanta because I always think, That could be Henry.

All those times I ran out after him to go for a ride, I think there was another reason Mama begrudgingly gave her approval. She must have let me go because in all the world that's probably where she'd most liked to have been herself, if it weren't for all she had to do, she—CoraRuth Jensen—riding all over South Carolina with him, wind whistling through the open space where a radio should have been and blowing *her* hair. The only thing she'd have liked better was being in one of those trucks alone, driving it herself.

I'm like that too. I've driven off alone any time they'd let me. By yourself is best. Wind blowing. Tires humming. Your own grip on the steering wheel, that column shifter in the bowl of your hand. That's control. Why a woman would want an automatic when somebody will sell her a straight shift, I've never known.

When I'm in the country, I hurt for all those people on their lonesome square plots of land, their little farms and sad frame houses with tacked-on porches. Not because they're poor.

But because way out there they always seem to have so little to do with government and Congress, with the passing of bills and lobbying for tax increases. All those things Dan Rather in his sweater vest dishes out to them every night as they eat their suppers in front of the TV. In Atlanta, in all big cities, people are somehow more responsible for knowing about those kinds of things. But in the country, what do they have to do with botched-up city planning and trillion dollar deficits? Country people ought to be let off the hook, is my opinion.

On the way to the blackberries we pass such farms and houses. Rural and kind Carolinians. It feels so good.

Daddy is a convert to four-wheel drive. He'd been needing a Jeep or a Bronco for years, but he had always shrugged off our suggestions, claiming those were rich men's toys and a second-hand pickup served him fine. But a couple of springs back, during a particularly bad rainy season, he was continually hav-ing to be pulled out of the mud and it was either get something with four-wheel or join the auto club.

Will cares about automobiles (he and Mama are the ones to talk to; she once took a course in Powder Puff Mechanics over at the technical school; I guess she thought she had to), and he began looking through the want ads and auto and truck traders for Henry. We drove out to check on a few, but most, Will could tell from the ads, weren't worth the trouble. He knew what to look for—when they had belonged to hard-drinking boys who had flipped them a time or two, and what it meant when the ad copy suggested a little engine work might be in order.

One night he tore out a page from the *Southern Truck Trader*, made a phone call, and said this might be it. The Ford belonged to a young dentist who had used it for duck hunting. The paint was scratched badly from too many hauls through backwoods and busting through tree limbs. But you could see the man loved the truck (many men *do love* machines, I've no-ticed), and he had taken good care of the engine. The inside was spotless, all shiny and slick from being sprayed and rubbed with Armor-All. Will called Henry that night, and even though I didn't get on the phone, I knew what Daddy would be saying on the other end of the line: Yeah, okay; yeah; yeah, okay. He's awful on the telephone. He and Mama can call, and you can be talking to her for three or four minutes before you hear a cough or a grunt and realize he's been on there the whole time. So I knew how the conversation would go and that he probably wouldn't ask a question except maybe, Well, how much is it? and then, Yeah, okay. I drove it up the next weekend (I wanted to be the one) and Will followed in our car. Several times then, and on every trip after, we went over the instructions with Henry about when you're supposed to shift the truck into four-wheel and how you get out and turn the handle on the lugs counterclockwise to lock in the front wheels. He forgets though, and sometimes he'll be flying down the road at fifty miles per hour in the four-wheel low position when he should be in regular drive. (Most people can *hear* the difference, but we're assuming he can't.) Sometimes he'll lock in the left wheel and forget all about the one on the passenger side. It's possible the man shouldn't be allowed on the road.

Our property is a flat piece of acreage, like a large man's wide-open hand. But all around us are hills, and in the distance you can see the beginnings of the Blue Ridge Mountains. The road we are on winds around a rocky knob and from up here our house is visible in the winter. The leaves are new and thick, though, this time of year, and you can't see more than a few feet through the woods. This road was a logging trail once, and now it is used only by hunters and forest rangers and occasional dirt bikers.

The blackberries are still that bright red, the way they are before they've had enough sun and start turning. They are small, way too small, but it is going to be a good year. The bushes are loaded.

It is too muddy to walk, so we just keep riding. We stop only once, at an abandoned hunter's shack, and poke around for a while. The place is covered with buckling linoleum and littered with a hundred or more empty Prince Albert tobacco cans—the thin, flat kind that fits in a man's shirt pocket—and a mice-gnawed mattress. It has that kind of smell once-lived-in places have and, hushed and still in there, I have the sensation of a cat jumping on my neck. (That happened once, when I was a kid; the cat's claws and whine scared me so I couldn't speak and a wave of my skin traveled all the way from my arched spine to my scalp.) Henry sticks his head in all the rooms, but I have to get out. On the porch I am sorry I didn't linger at least long enough to grab one of those red Prince Albert tins off the floor for Mama. They sell those things for a couple of dollars each at antique stores, and I know she would have been like a squirrel running up on a bag of peanuts if she'd been there and would have gathered up the whole lot. From out on the porch, I yell in to Henry to bring her a couple.

"She won't want those things," he says, coming out empty-handed.

"Yes she will, she'd love it." He knows it too. His wife saves everything. Old bottles, jugs, newspapers. The garage and basement and barn are filled with broken banisters, mantels, stained-glass windows, doorknobs—things she finds on the side of the road or at demolition sites and estate sales. She is hoarding it all for when they "rebuild," though the accumulation grows thicker and the chance of building grows slimmer every season. They have been in this same house since just after I was born. Still, she plans. She has a whole accordion-style folder full of color photographs she's cut from women's magazines—sun-filled kitchens, shiny new bathrooms, lacquered walls, stone fireplaces, stadium-sized living rooms, vaulted ceilings. All the things she sees and dreams about living with are in there. Henry's the opposite. He wants nothing. Not things, anyway. And he is constantly trying to throw out something she has just found. I know for a fact there's a box of ceramic tiles and some bricks hidden in the back of her clothes closet; she believes they're safest there. A time or two a year he makes an attempt to clean house, hauling out bed rails and newel-posts, boxes of brass hardware. It never works though. You can watch them out in the yard, standing over one of her boxes, and even without hearing what she says you know she's explaining to him the use she's got for every single item and what it would cost if he had to buy those things new. It all gets dragged back in, before it's had a chance to even get a good dusting.

She plants zinnias, he mows them down. It's not that he means to. His mind's just flown him off somewhere, and he doesn't even realize she's running after him, yelling and waving her hands.

"Get her just one," I say.

He looks at his watch. "What time did you say Will was coming?" He hasn't changed the subject; he simply isn't hearing.

"Around eleven. Did you want to get Mama one of those tobacco cans, Dad?"

"Well, we better get going, it's after ten-thirty."

I hold my breath, run back in, and pick up the first Prince Albert I come to, shaking it to make sure there is nothing living inside.

Henry's not deaf. There's just something screwy that happens between the ear and the brain with him. It's difficult for people who don't know him to understand: a man who lives in non sequiturs can seem an odd bird. Say hello to him, "How're you doing?," and he's liable to stare a hole in your head. But, ten minutes later, the same man is likely to slap you on the shoulder and ask how you've been. It's impossible to acquire that kind of peculiarity, not the kind that holds up day after day; it comes with birth, like being walleyed or double-jointed. You can overlook skewed comprehension in someone you love, especially if you're mature and have some confidence not just in yourself but in that love. But when you're a nine-year-old girl and you speak to your father and he doesn't speak back, it's difficult to understand that you haven't committed some unknown wrong but to know instead it is because your father's heart is a million miles away—on the moon maybe or in heaven, or in ancient China, or playing in some thirty-year-old baseball game.

Or maybe it's the future he goes to, I don't know. I have dozens of pictures of him I've drawn, or painted. But none of them has helped me a single bit in understanding Henry.

I follow him to the truck, the tobacco tin in my pocket. He is right about it being time to go; we have been out all morning and Will is driving up from Atlanta. I came in yesterday by bus, thinking it would be good to be with my parents before all the others arrived. I always think that, imagine that the three of us will have a nice visit and easy conversation. But I always get a closed-in feeling when CoraRuth starts following me around with her index cards, going over the weekend's menus. I am ready to get back and be there to welcome Will. He is bringing my former mother-in-law, Fitz, with him; and my brother Lucas and his family are supposed to arrive in the afternoon, in time for Henry's birthday dinner.

Some people, including my own mother, think it's odd that I'm best friends with my ex-husband's mother. Whenever Fitz is mentioned, Mama's voice ascends an octave and her neck goes hard. It's not that she doesn't like Fitz, she just doesn't think the relationship is proper, or that it has any future. She tried to explain it once: "It's like when you have a litter of pups. You take care of those little things, and you just love them to death and you feed them. But then after you give them away, you don't drive around to all their new homes every few months and expect those dogs to know you." She still calls Fitz "Mrs. Ballard" even though they're both practically the same age.

I've known Fitz since I was nineteen. And I've never felt more comfortable with anyone in my life except Will.

When I'm with my parents, though, I always lose sight of whoever it is I am when I'm back home in Atlanta. I'm not just talking about Mama, either. I'm sure not nine years old anymore, but self-confidence still isn't where I'm strongest.

"The way in about jarred my teeth loose," Henry says. "Why don't we follow the road on around instead of doubling back?"

This is fine with me. I'm not in any more of a hurry than he is to straddle again those washed-out stretches we drove over on our way in.

Normally, when we go on one of our rides, I take along a sketch pad and draw. I have notebooks that go all the way back to junior high school that I've filled with little pencil drawings of flora and fauna: arbutus, sweet shrub, laurel, rhododendron, Christmas fern, wild orange-blossomed azalea; Cooper's hawks, rose-breasted grosbeaks, flycatchers, wrens, owls, woodchuck, turkey, gray squirrel, whitetail deer, ten or fifteen species of warblers.

But I have forgotten pencil and paper this morning, and so I just hold on to the gray plastic strap by the window and look out. Water is still on leaves from the rain, and it smells the way it always does back in here—a mixture of clear air and decay.

As much as I love it, there's something unnerving about being deep in woods. A bird can be moving about on the ground in the leaves, and it will sound like a man walking. And galax, with its wide waxy leaves, as innocent as anything in a florist's refrigerator, sometimes smells like something wild. A red-tailed hawk floating overhead dips its wings, and it looks like a warning. That's why I like being here, because it's partly mixed with a hint of danger.

The creeks are muddy from the rain, and every time we drive through water, steam from the engine rises behind us and fogs the back window. We are still getting jostled, but it is an easier route than the way we came in. I have been out this way before and know it opens up on the dirt road a mile or two below our house, but I haven't been this way in years. Neither has anyone else, it looks like, and we have to roll our windows up from time to time to keep from getting smacked in the face with briars and tree limbs. The road is narrower than I remember and grown up in places with underbrush.

We go through a muddy spot, where Henry can't remember if we are in four-wheel low or high, and we spin for a few seconds; and then as we are digging out and coming up a hill, I see a pine is down in front of us. Henry stops when he sees it, and then he slowly moves us forward again until the front fender almost touches the tree. He pulls his mouth from side to side across his face, raises and lowers his eyeglasses, and lets out a long, loud exhale.

"We could back out," I say, ready to do whatever is easiest.

But he gets out and starts walking up and down alongside the tree. It is a tall one and stretches about ten feet beyond the road on either side. "We can't go around it—" he says.

Well, thank goodness; but he keeps pacing, moving his mouth from side to side, and drawing air through his teeth. The danger, I know, is that Henry is thinking.

"Dad, let's just back out and turn around in that spot past the creek."

"Well, we'll just have to go over it," and he climbs back in. "Get out, 'Nor," he says and starts the engine. "Stand back so nothing can hit you, and yell to me how I'm doing."

"Daddy, you can't go over that thing."

For the first time he looks over at me. "Honey, this is four-wheel."

"But that doesn't mean it climbs trees."

"What are we in here, high or low, you reckon?" His glasses are back up on the top of his head.

"Dad, no kidding. I think we just better go back the way we came in."

"Now don't worry," he says, leaning over to open my door for me. "This old Ford will make it easy over that pine."

From up on the bank I see him pushing and pulling the gears, trying to remember which is low and which is high. Then he backs the truck almost to where we've been in the mud. He lowers his glasses (a funny gesture, because he looks so determined, and it makes me laugh despite how worried I am), then he shifts into first, and guns it.

The truck hits the pine with a wallop. The left front tire goes up, hangs there for a moment, and then rolls down on the other side of the tree and stops. Henry gives it more gas, trying to get the right wheel to follow, but the truck just rocks in place, moving a little each way, forwards and backwards.

"Are you all right?" I yell. He is trying to back up. "Daddy, I think it's stuck!" Both front tires are off the ground, spinning.

He climbs out, goes around to the front of the truck, does the crazy movement with his mouth again, and finally looks over at me. "We're hung up, you know it?"

My life is so different in Atlanta, just Will and me. His job is bringing plays, musicians, jazz singers, all kinds of performers to Atlanta. Probably fifteen or twenty times a day he talks to famous or near-famous people; maybe Phoebe Snow's agent one minute and one of the stars from *Cats* the next. His office is downtown in a granite tower that has windows that can't be opened, and his view looks out over the lawyers and secretaries and street people in Mr. Woodruff's park. I don't know what to think about money. I always liked having my own, enough to buy what I needed—paints, stretcher boards, maybe a bottle of expensive shampoo I'd seen advertised with the promise to make me pretty—without having to go to somebody. That kind of money brings freedom with it. But the kind of money we're around in Atlanta worries me half to death. We spend a fortune just going out to dinner; my mother would die if she knew how much it is possible to spend on one meal alone.

We go too much. Know too many people. I try not to show

it, but I feel all used up so much of the time, like a flattened tube of dried-out oils. I think that's why my mind is here a lot, back in South Carolina. It's not that I always want to be here, it's more as if I feel there's something I ought to be doing— like I should be helping out. I have a hard time concentrating on party conversation when I know it's possible that brown rot and aphids are destroying Henry's peach crop.

I don't like being an anxious person. But I still worry. Sometimes in the middle of the day, I'll stop work on whatever I'm painting and I'll think: What if that piece of equipment falls on Henry? What if CoraRuth slips in the bathtub and there's no one there to hear her? I call every week, expecting the worst, but they're always fine. With me all those miles away down in Georgia, anything in the world could happen to them up here. But it isn't until this morning, with me right beside him, that Henry's luck turns on him again.

We work for more than an hour trying to get the truck off that damn tree. The axle is caught on it, and the tires have no way of getting traction. The first thing we try to do is force the tree down a few inches so the truck can fall free. We find rope under the seat and tie it to the end of the pine up on the hill. Henry pulls while I run around the truck and push the other end of the tree in the opposite direction. It barely budges. And even when it does, the axle is still wedged tight. I watch Henry straining and all I can think is: *Heart Attack.* I start to panic. "Dad, this isn't going to work. Look, let's leave it. Let's just start walking out of here."

His face is red from all the exertion, and the front of his shirt and his hands are already covered with mud from where he has slipped. He drops the rope and walks to the front of the truck and stares. He has returned to the mouth moving. Then his face goes still and he says, "Okay, what we're going to have to do is jack her up. Let's get some rocks, Eleanor." He crawls up the side of the hill and is throwing rocks back down to the middle of the road. I follow him, mostly to stay clear of what is being thrown.

"Dad, explain to me what you're going to do."

"Don't lift the big ones. I'll get those."

"Daddy!" It startles us both; my recollection is that I've

never, ever, raised my voice at Henry. I steady myself and speak more softly. "Please. Tell me the plan."

"We jack her up," he says patiently, "and we stack rocks under the front wheel, and then I back her up and she just rolls off."

I'm not sure. "Maybe we ought to come back with some help, when we've got Will and Lucas to help us."

"This'll work."

The ground is so soft that the jack keeps digging in, sinking down in the dirt every time Henry tries to raise the truck; and the truck was slung around so far to the left when it first went over the tree that its back tire hangs almost over the edge of the road on that side. Each time Henry gets in the truck and tries to back up, I am sure the thing is going to roll over with him in it. I am feeling sick, and every time he tries and fails, I feel sicker. I keep thinking: If I could just go lie down.

"Okay, one more time," he keeps saying, until finally we have pumped the jack up as far as it will go and there are enough rocks under the left wheel to position it almost as high as the pine.

"This is it," he says a last time. "This'll do it."

I nod and hold up a thumb for encouragement. But I feel as if we are digging deeper instead of getting closer. He gets in and fumbles with the gears again; he sometimes misplaces reverse altogether. "Watch your back wheel," I yell. He starts the truck, glares straight ahead, pushes down on the gas, and the left tire spins, then grabs, and as he gives it more gas, the truck bolts backwards, free. At the same time there is an enormous pop, then a *whock*! like a fired gun.

The truck dies, and Henry and I stare. The back left side is way below the road and he has flattened a flimsy pine and some laurel. He opens the door and sticks his head around. He turns back, with his hands still on the steering wheel, and just sits.

"What is it?" I ask.

He rubs his hands up and down his face as if he is scrubbing it. "Blowout," he says when he is through.

The truck had shot backwards with such force that a two-inch stump tore a gaping hole in the sidewall. Henry climbs out and drags the jack over the pine towards the truck. "We'll have to change the tire," he says, and then he looks over at me. "You think I've got a spare?"

My guess is that he doesn't, but we need hope. "Oh, yeah. I'm sure there's one in there."

It isn't much of one, about as much tread as on my palm, but if we can get it on the truck, it will probably get us home.

Down on our knees in front of the flat, it feels as if the whole weight of the truck is leaning on us. Even the piece of tin I've located doesn't keep the jack from sinking, and we carry one of the big rocks that was under the front wheel to give us something more solid. I put rocks behind each of the other three tires to keep the truck from rolling. "Now stay back," Henry says, and the Ford groans slowly upward as he pumps the jack handle.

"I don't know why those fellows put these dern lugs on here so tight," he says, carefully turning the wrench counter- clockwise. If he jerks, or applies too much pressure, the jack could slip. I try to think of things to promise God if he'll let us get out of here without getting hurt or Henry having a coronary.

When the lugs are off (I put each one in my pocket beside the Prince Albert), we try to position the spare. Henry wants to do it himself, but it takes both of us to hold it up and try to get it in place. We are trying to line up the holes and I have one hand up on the top of the tire, when Henry yells, "Get your hand out of there! This thing slips, it could take your fingers off."

I want to cry. Not just because of Henry yelling, but because I want us home and dry. I want to see Will. I sit back, and when I do, the jack moves enough for the truck to slam down, and Henry and the spare fall against me.

Every day I see accidents reported on TV where someone has been hit on the interstate and lost an arm or a leg, or where there's been an accidental shooting on a hunting trip. What do people do in those moments and hours between the time the awful thing happens and when they finally get the victim to a hospital and you see it on the news? How do people not die when they see someone they love cut in half or with a shotgun blast to the head? Thinking about what would have happened if the jack had slipped five seconds earlier, I feel as if I *have* lost my fingers or hands, as if the blood were now pouring from my body and I were seeing black. What if it had happened to Henry? Even if I could have lifted him on my back and carried him out, I'd never have been able to keep him from bleeding to death. And worse, what if the truck had come down on me? Henry would have died right there beside me. I know that for certain.

He looks sick; maybe he is thinking the same things. We get up together, helping each other, and leave the jack and the tire on the ground. I close the door to the truck, and we start walking.

Henry's glasses are down on his nose, and his muddy pants hang from his poor old buttless behind like a day-old diaper on a toddler. I wonder about soldiers. After they've seen blood and torn-apart bodies and they're cold and wet and filthy and have peed on themselves, there must come a point, right after battle, when for just a short time, they no longer care if they're alive.

The lug nuts clink against Prince Albert's face in my pocket. Daddy marches beside me. "It's cold, you know it?" he says.

Will loves old fancy cars. In the four years I've known him he's had seven. A 1965 Mercedes sedan, a Cadillac convertible, an old Jag, a red-hot Austin Healy, two bubble-bodied Volvos, and now this Saab. In my entire life I've owned two VWs and the Chevy LUV pickup I drive because the bed is big enough for hauling the large canvases I paint on. That Mercedes's windshield wipers cost more than I like to spend on tires.

It's not that I'm embarrassed (about Will's cars), it's just that when I get something, I tend to hold on to it for a while. I don't like trading anything—automobiles, phone numbers, in-laws. And every time we come home, it's, Now what did you say is the make of this one? Henry's called it a Squab and a Swaab and always asks if we don't think it looks like a snail. It's white, on top of everything else, and as pristine and sleek as the outside of the new High Museum in Atlanta. It has leather

upholstery, and heaters in both the front seats to warm your
fanny. Will is practically perfect, but riding around in that kind
of car can be difficult for certain sorts of people. You can recline
the passenger seat, and it's as if you're heading down the interstate in a brand-new La-Z-Boy lounger.

Will's car was parked in the yard when we got home. Everyone else was there too. It was nearly three in the afternoon,
and it looked as if my brother Lucas and his wife, Sally, and
their two children had just arrived, because the others were
standing around their station wagon, talking through the window to the baby.

Two kids in a Jeep had picked us up after Daddy and I
had hiked the three or four miles out of the woods and started
walking on one of the main roads. When we pulled in, everyone
looked up, and Will immediately started walking toward us, in
a hurry. He looked so good. All clean and crisp, that great furry
beard of his all combed and trimmed. I could see he had been
worried, scared, and I imagined the others had been driving
him loony. Will takes action. If something is wrong, he makes
a move on it. He *does* something. I knew in the hours we had
been missing, my mother and grandmother had probably been
wringing their hands, imagining the worst, in the back of their
heads planning what they'd wear to our funerals. When they
start up like that, Will thinks they're crazy. He has no patience
for moaning or irrationality, and though he probably didn't
know what to do himself, he would have done something.
Driven around, been on the phone.

I looked terrible. My face and hands were all crusty with
mud, I smelled bad, and my hair was tangled so badly from
the ride in the Jeep that I couldn't get my fingers through it.
It's thin anyway, and fine, and probably looked as if I had been
misting myself with engine oil. I didn't care. Will lifted me out
of the back of the Jeep and held me to him. He didn't have to
ask any questions; all it took was one look at us to know we'd
been in trouble.

The others came running up, CoraRuth in the lead.
"Where in the world have you been?" she started. "We've been
worried sick. Y'all, just look at the two of them."

Safety did something to Henry: he was picking up energy.

He jumped out of the Jeep and started explaining. I was glad he wanted to tell it; I was too tired.

Gram came over and put her sweet old bird hands on my head, tried to comb back the ratty hair. "Are you hurt, honey?" I shook my head.

Mama's head was covered in wire-brush hair curlers. It wasn't unusual; I could imagine why at three o'clock in the afternoon she was done up this way. She always scurries around like crazy when anyone is coming, even when it's just us, and she always tries to do too much in too little time: clean out the refrigerator, bake a German chocolate cake, Clorox the shower curtain. As if it all matters. It's the same whether you get there at seven in the morning or seven in the evening, she's still scrambling. So I guessed her day had gone like this: Will and Fitz got there right at eleven, or maybe a little early; Mama got caught in her curlers, but she started talking, walking Fitz around places, and, since her hair was probably still damp anyway and they'd already seen her, she decided why not just leave it. And amidst all the worry about us not getting home, she forgot all about those little metal brushes, and that was why now she was completely oblivious to the fact that she was curled up tighter than a roly-poly.

"You *walked* all that way?" I heard her saying.

Luke's little boy was riding up on his daddy's shoulders, listening. And Sally was strapping the baby across her stomach in one of those blue fabric infant carriers. I see women moving through the malls that way, and I know why they do it. People think it's for the baby, to make the child feel safe; but it isn't. Women like re-creating that full feeling of pregnancy. They want it back. So they walk around carrying their young strapped as closely as they can get them, marsupials in blue denim pouches.

I leaned against my husband. Fitz was swinging in a hammock chair up on the deck all alone and out of the way. But she was holding a newspaper over her eyes, to keep out the sun's glare, and was watching everything that was going on. I smiled and waved. Fitz is one of those women who is big and open, the kind you wouldn't mind going up to and crawling in her lap because you know she'd let you. "Let's go see Fitz," I said. She was the only other one besides Will that I really wanted to talk to right then. As I started to move, the back door opened onto the deck, and someone new walked out. I couldn't see at first, or thought I couldn't, and then I realized who it was. Marilyn, Will's younger sister.

"I would have helped you, Papaw," Luke's little boy was saying. But Henry kept talking and didn't acknowledge the child.

"That's Marilyn," I said to Will.

"Yes, I know; I brought her."

"Well, what's she doing here?" I whispered meanly and pushed away from him. I can be awful.

Too many people around makes me jittery, especially when I'm back home. I like for it to be just my own family. Fitz was family and even Sally and certainly the grandchildren. But Marilyn was his sister, not mine. The truth was, I didn't like her. I had tried, and I was always polite, but Marilyn was weak in my opinion, and a taker. She was twenty-six years old but she still mooched off her parents, and she came around grumbling to Will, taking advantage of his good nature and generosity every time there was some new trauma in her life. She had never been married, but she'd lived with a couple of guys, and in the last month or two had talked about moving in with some FM deejay Will had introduced her to.

"You know what, Papaw?" The child was kicking; I couldn't be sure whether he was trying to get Henry's attention or wanted down from his father's shoulders.

I wished all of a sudden we were back in Atlanta. I turned to Will, the person I loved most in the world, and demanded of him, "Why did you bring her?"

"Because," he emphasized the word, "she had no plans for the weekend, she and Chip broke up, and she was lonely. And because I didn't think it would matter."

"She won't fit in here, Will. And where's she going to sleep? It's Daddy's birthday." I was carrying on, and I was ashamed of myself, but I couldn't help it.

"It's just one night, Eleanor."

"Well, I just don't see why—"

But Henry broke in, asking if Will wanted to go with them after the Ford. "These two fellows have offered to help pull us out." He was all zip and go now, and I felt more tired than ever. But I didn't want to be left behind, especially if I was expected to entertain Marilyn. She was the kind who *needed* entertainment.

"I'm going too," I said; and everyone, almost in unison, said, *"No!"*

"Why not?" There was a slight whine to my voice, the kind you hear in thirteen-year-old girls, the kind I can't stand.

"You'll be sick as a dog." This was Mama.

"You're shivering now, babe. You're wet and tired." Will.

"We'll be back in two shakes." Henry.

"Daddy's wet and tired, and he's going."

"Eleanor, don't be ridiculous. Look at you, you're covered with mud." Will kissed me on the cheek and did something that always irritates me: patted my head. "Besides, there's not enough room in the Jeep."

Henry was already positioning himself on the backseat, waiting; and Luke was raising the little boy over his head, standing him next to Mama, giving her his hand. He and Will climbed in and sat on either side of Henry. The three of them waved as they drove off and yelled, "We'll be right back."

The little boy started crying. "I want to go with Papaw."

"How about a popsicle?"

"I want to go with Papaw!" He kicked dirt at his grandmother and then dropped down on the ground, squalling.

I knew how he felt; sometimes loved ones' protection has the cast of betrayal, and I could have kicked dirt too, if I had thought someone would let me.

From the kitchen come the sounds of my mother's birds. Parakeets, a pair of finches, one lone bobbing canary. Every couple of days, new sheets of newspaper are cut to fit the bottoms of the cages, and new gravel is poured in place. This used to be my job; but now the job is solely Mama's, and even though CoraRuth is vigilant, little empty husks continually blow from the cages out across the kitchen linoleum, scooting around corners and down the hall.

Cora has always kept birds. She used to take them out of

their cages in the summer, and let them fly around on the screened-in porch off the kitchen. They would fly up high and hold on to the screen with their wire toes, and Henry would have to bring in the ladder to get them down, the birds always pecking and biting, sometimes holding on so hard with those beaks that it would puncture his skin. Sometimes she taught them to talk: "Wipe your feet! Wipe your feet!" one of them used to call. But most of them just click and chirp and bob and hump on those sticks she puts in there.

Occasionally one would get outside when someone opened the door without paying attention. CoraRuth would follow it for a while with her eyes as it flew from tree to tree. But we never chased them down with nets or anything; she said it was no use. She'd just look out there after them and say, "Well, he's dead."

I like free birds the best. The kind in the wild. I've been standing here for the longest time, out on this deck Henry built off the back of the house, watching a hawk glide. It hardly ever moves its wings. It just floats, and soars, lifts itself up effortlessly on the slightest little breath of a breeze, making invisible patterns. Hawks move so smoothly they sometimes look like kites to me, instead of birds. Way out there on the horizon without any strings.

Henry told me it was the hawk they modeled the airplane after, because the wings are so efficient and move so little; you'd never model an aircraft after something dizzy like a humming-bird, who just to suck up a little nectar about has to flap itself into a stupor. No, if I were a bird, I've decided, I'd want it to be a hawk. A red-tailed: regal, a soarer, with dark streaks across my belly. Will is a hawk, or an eagle. Daddy is a barn owl: unmistakable, unique, "no close relations," the field guides say. Mother is a grouse, or a brown thrasher maybe; and Fitz is a flicker, large, bobbing, building her nest in the trunk of a dead tree. Those are all respectable birds, noble. Even little Sally is a phoebe or a chickadee: perhaps inconspicuous, but steady. But Marilyn is a starling: in everybody's way.

She's standing at the screen door behind me. She has said nothing, but I can smell the menthol cigarette smoke. I've ignored it, though, for the last couple of minutes. I can be a rude person. Mainly when I don't have anything to say.

I'm not that close to Will's family, partly, I guess, because I feel as if I used up that area of myself from having been married before. Will's really not that close to any of them, either. It's only his mother we call, the only one I really like to go see in that tiny, cramped house. Sometimes on Saturday afternoons we visit her at the restaurant. We stand in line with everyone else and she says, "What'll you have?" with this grin on her face, pretending she doesn't know us. And her weight and her hard life and that sweetness like Will's pull at my heart so that I can't even eat the chicken she has spent all day frying or those big thick rounds of tomatoes she has so carefully sliced. But the others—his father and Marilyn—I hardly know them. I don't think Will even knows them that well, and he only seems to feel responsible for Marilyn because she's so much younger than he is.

Will and I are both the oldest. "Most ambitious," "most hard working," all the books on siblings claim. Maybe. But I think *responsibility* is the main burden the books should say we carry. It's even worse for an only child, like Henry. I think responsibility has about loaded him down.

She's out on the deck beside me now, flicking her Salem into the garden.

"So, Marilyn, what have you been doing?" I try. She paints her nails: toes and fingers.

"Nothing much," she says. "I've been down."

"Will said you broke up with Chick."

"Chip. And he broke up with me."

I tell her I'm sorry, and she shrugs. She's a made-up kind of pretty, one of those women who learned to do things to their eyes. All the different shades of powder in the right places. She's nothing like Will. How is it people end up in the same family? is what I always wonder. Just look around: how many siblings do you know who are nothing alike, who seem to fit in the same family about as well as a cat and sow?

Lucas and I are almost nothing alike, either. I could never be a doctor. But, then, sometimes I think maybe being a doctor is the last thing in the world Luke should be. He's good apparently; his school files say brilliant. But the man cries when his own children get hurt; he had to wait out in the reception room when the pediatrician gave little Henry Lee his shots.

Whenever I came home from college, he'd be the one waiting out by the road at the end of our long dirt drive, sitting on a rock in the near dark, making sure I was all right. And usually, he wouldn't come around and get in the car, but would jump up on the running board of my blue VW and hold on to my arm as I jostled us down the drive. It's beyond me how that big-hearted boy ever gets through grafting skin or looking into someone's open skull. I think he's a doctor because of Henry. "You'll have respect, money, and you'll have the kinds of skills you can take with you anywhere," Henry used to say. "Now, it might be hard to pull up after you've been in one place a few years, after you've set up practice, but if you've got those kinds of skills you can always do it. Anywhere you want to go, anywhere in creation, they need a doctor. Even a place like Montana, where nobody else in the world can make a living, you could go out there if you wanted, if you're a doctor. You've got your sick people everywhere, your babies to deliver. Be a doctor." And that's what Luke has become. Henry's right; Luke could pick up any day of his life and move out to L.A., set up practice in Chicago. But my brother doesn't want to go anywhere; he doesn't even like to travel. All his time is spent with Sally and their kids, and when he has to, he gets in his car and drives to Egleston Hospital to attend to dying children. Sometimes I worry that every day of his life must be a trial. Lucas is a mourning dove: sweet, melancholy, quietly and unobtrusively doing his work down near the ground.

The men are inside cleaning up, taking their showers. CoraRuth and the others are in the kitchen getting supper. She calls to me to come set the table. And I leave Will's sister out on the deck, striking matches.

❧

It is said that a married couple begins to look alike over the years. This is true. My parents have many of the same lines. But it seems to me this comes not from having the same thoughts or disappointments at the same time but more the result of two faces put together, only upside down. My mother, always the sensible one—who knows to put water in car batteries and oil in the engine and when to reel in my father when he begins floating off too far—has become giggly, full of jokes, the one who wants to force fun. My father—the dreamer, the explorer, the believer in every vision that every man ever had —has become serious, laughless, so dry. Does compensation always lead to this end? Did my mother just get worn out from being the stabilizer, the reeler-in? My father get tired of justifying wild ideas?

We are all gathered in a circle around the huge cherry table. All the immediate family and all the others. We are eating T-bone steaks and baked potatoes, my father's favorite meal. The man did not submit to broccoli until he was forty. Still, he will not recognize: eggplant, yellow squash, asparagus, artichokes, carrots, cauliflower, zucchini. Beans of most kinds are accepted. So is tossed salad. We have that tonight with Russian dressing. CoraRuth has poured it from the Kraft bottle into a little cut-glass bowl, this in honor of her guests.

I have been watching my mother. She has brushed out her hair and dabbed black at her lashes. She's still a beauty, small, almost dainty if it weren't for her personality, which is large. None of us turned out as well. I look more like Henry. And they say Luke looks like our grandfather, Gram's husband— tall, quiet, Lincolnesque Charlie Lee Jensen. Maybe it would have been my sister, Diane, who carried on the fine delicate bones of our mother.

CoraRuth is nervous. As soon as we were all seated, she cut her T-bone in two and said, "Now one of you men will have to help me with this." She has been eating little rapid bites of the smaller of the two halves, but her eyes are on my husband's plate. "Will," she says, "are you ready?"

He waves her away. "I've got plenty."

She wants to give that steak to someone so badly. She helps herself to more salad, more bread, but she doesn't touch the charred piece of meat still hooked to its bone.

The conversation is on the White House, a risky subject. My parents, forever Democrats I believed, have gone Republican —ever since McGovern. But both Fitz and Gram are old yellow-dog Georgians and don't mind telling you so; Gram still has a picture of Governor Gene Talmadge thumbing his red suspenders. My grandmother would like to do harm to Ronald Reagan.

On the news tonight they showed Ronnie and Nancy striking out across the White House lawn to board the helicopter for Camp David. Ronnie was in his cowboy boots, his broad self cut in half by that big round belt buckle. Nancy was smiling, waving, following the stretched-out lead of her dog. "Look at that!" Gram said.

"Now, Mother, don't start," Cora told her.

"Well, just look at her! She's so skinny if she didn't have her little mutt to tie her down, she'd get sucked up into the updraft of that helicopter."

"Now Gram." Cora claims to be proud of the First Lady, which is a revelation to me: she doesn't give a hoot about china or clothes. And Henry: if he saw any other man but Ronald Reagan decked out that way, he'd think it was silly. I've decided their loyalty to this couple is in some way hooked up with abortion, but I haven't exactly figured out how.

Will starts in about the national deficit, and I wish I could get his attention so he would hush. Henry coughs and says, "Well, let's just not talk about it." But Fitz takes Will's lead and before I know it they're off on Nicaragua. This makes me nervous. She has already made Henry mad once tonight by telling him the spray he uses on his trees is full of human carcinogens and is poisoning the environment.

I look over to see how Mama's reacting, but she's nowhere near politics. Her eyes are darting around the table. That half a T-bone is driving her crazy.

"Well, what's for dessert, CoraRuth?" Henry says. He's finished his meal, and whether anyone else is or not, he's ready to get on with things.

"Wait a minute, Henry. Maybe not everybody else is through." Mama rises anyway to fetch the coconut cake he knows she's been hiding from him for three days in the basement refrigerator. But before she goes, she has to do it; she can stand it no longer. She forks the T-bone and plops it over onto Will's cleared plate.

Mama's cake looks like sputnik. The layers rose strangely high in the middle, and when she started assembling them, the cake became a white round ball. Since there is no real top, the candles radiate from everywhere, sixty little flames sunk deep in Cool Whip and coconut.

The grandboy gets to sit in Henry's lap and help blow out the candles. He starts before we're finished singing, then realizes his error and waits. He and Henry inflate their cheeks, ready to blow, but CoraRuth says, "Wait! Make a—" Maybe Henry doesn't hear her, or maybe he ignores her, because he and the grandson are already puffing like mad. And the last candle flickers, wavers, and then goes out, and smoke hangs in the air like burned-out wishes.

We all applaud and the child claps the longest, and when it's quiet he says, "Do it again, Papaw!"

We laugh, and for a moment the little boy is confused. He looks back and forth at the smiles of his parents, and he knows from Sally's face, small and smooth and as weightless and white as cuttlebone, that he has done nothing wrong.

CoraRuth starts to go for plates, then she turns around and snaps her fingers. "Well, darn. We forgot to get a picture."

Gram slaps Henry on the back and says, "So do it again, Papaw!"

We sleep in my old room every time we come home. This room hasn't changed at all since the first time I got married, except for the winter clothes CoraRuth keeps in the closet and the bolts of fabric she buys on sale and promises herself she'll sew something with sooner or later but instead keeps folded in my old bureau drawers. But everything else looks the same. The black-and-white fabric I hung over the windows one summer when I was home from college; the iron bed I painted black and the fireplace and mantel I painted white. Only the wobbly easel that used to be propped in a corner is missing. CoraRuth has replaced it with a dusty mother-in-law tongue plant she never remembers to water until we're coming home.

From up here I can hear the others. Sally is singing to the baby; Henry and Gram are parked in front of a Braves game on Channel 17, and Gram has already started listing her grievances with Bob Horner; CoraRuth says, "Scrabble or Rummy K?"; and Will and Fitz are reading to each other from the paper. Fitz is crazy for obituaries, particularly those in *The New York*

Times. And Will is equally taken with the classifieds. "Listen to this," he says. He reads to Fitz: "BRIDAL GOWN. Candlelight. Hat, dress, and shoes. Scarlett O'Hara look. Size sixteen." Fitz hoots and claps. "Oh, I love it!" she says. The baby screams.

Sometimes my family is too much for me. I have trouble taking them all in. So I get away like this, up in my old room or outside, until I feel I can breathe again. Sometimes I wish I could get out on the roof or stand on the rail of the deck, stretch out my arms, and just fly. Any day anything could happen to any of them. Gram, who is so old, in her eighties. CoraRuth with her small, brittle bones. Henry, scatterbrained as he is, likely to saw off his own hand. And those children. I do not allow myself to think about what can happen to children. Or Will. Fitz is the only one I never really worry about. Fitz, who is so big and strong, durable as stone.

There is clanking going on down there: someone putting up the dried dinner dishes. There is a crack and a roar; someone has hit a homer; and Gram says, "That's it, I'm going to bed." Chairs are being scraped on the floor in the dining room; they're setting up the Scrabble board and CoraRuth calls my name.

The handrail on the stairs is finally smooth, but it has never been refinished. When we were kids Mama used to keep a square of sandpaper on the newel-posts at the top and the bottom of the staircase, and anytime we went up or down, we were supposed to grab the paper and slide it along the rail. White paint flicked away under our hands. There has always been so much wrong with this old house—leaky roof, running toilets, bad wiring—that I always assumed we were poor. In fact, Henry took great pride in explaining just how poor we were. But the first time I brought Will home to visit, he looked around this place, at the land, the outbuildings, the house, and said, This is a far sight from poor, Eleanor.

In the kitchen Lucas is getting a bedtime snack for the little boy. A glass of milk and a graham cracker. As I pass my brother, I give him a quick rub on the shoulder. I'm forever amazed he got so tall.

CoraRuth has pulled out the *Unabridged* and put it defiantly on the dining room table and now is turning over wooden squares for the other three players: Will, Fitz, Marilyn. This is an odd quartet. Mama, her expression tight as a tick, thinking about nothing but the game. Fitz, her feet propped up on an empty dining room chair, comfortable anywhere. Marilyn, with her two packs of Salems and her fancy book of matches from Trader Vic's. And Will, with more intelligence than the whole lot, there to keep the women company. When my mother sees me she says, "Here, now you come take my place, Eleanor." But I reseat her. Scrabble is important to CoraRuth. She knows every two- and three-letter word you can play with Q, Z, and X, and when the letters get drawn, she's up for playing for money.

I go to the living room with my sketch pad and Pentel pencil. Henry is leaning back in his brown corduroy chair. I'm not sure, but I think he is sleeping. There is that *dunt-dunt dunt-dunt dunt-dunt* organ music from the TV, and the camera is panning the crowd at the Atlanta stadium. Kids wave, hold up their cups of beer, and someone raises a sign that says BRING BACK NIEKRO. I look at Henry and look away, recalling a drawing exercise I used to do in college. I study his face for a minute, then start sketching quickly without looking back again.

The game breaks for a commercial, and the audio all of a sudden gets louder. The noise startles my father, and a hand involuntarily goes up in the air. When he looks over at me, I turn the sketch pad up for him to see: a sixty-year-old man with a pair of glasses resting on his forehead. "Handsome," he says.

"Sure is. You tired, Daddy?"

"Just resting." But he closes his eyes again and in a moment I hear deep, faraway breathing.

In this family pretension is suspected everywhere, and simplicity and plainness are two of the virtues most prized. Hard work, that's a ticket. Hard heads. Hardened arteries. But there are no hard hearts here and not because it hasn't been tried. Silence: that's a cover I've noticed. So is coolness; also stiff arms. But underneath, soft hearts are constricted, squeezed like sculptor's clay. Hard hearts calcify. Soft hearts get their life squeezed out as though it were nothing more than excess moisture. You can almost hear it, the wet red bubbles and overused muscle flattened between two flat palms.

So: lie low, don't make a racket. Don't be showy. Cover

your head and between your fingers watch the sweet people
suffer. Cover your ears with your arms and you still hear the
noise.

I go back to my sketching. I am an artist by profession, a
painter. Sometimes people pay me for what I do, but not often.
If I did get paid more, I wonder, would it mean the work was
more important? *I* have trouble believing in its worth. It's nothing like what Luke does or Will or Henry or Sally with her
babies. And it's nothing compared to those people Fitz reads
about in the obits of the *Times*—researchers, scholars, judges,
choreographers. I just make pictures.

I feel something off to my side. It is Luke's little boy standing in the doorway. I hold out my hand, but he goes to Henry,
a soft yellow blanket bunched up in his arms. He wears Big
Bird pajamas. He climbs up on Henry's lap, and the man stirs,
then settles.

The tiny, hollow-boned fingers of Henry Lee (named for
my father and my mother's father) play on his grandfather's
hand. "You know what?" the child says.

"Come away, Papaw's sleeping."

"I can see up under his eyes."

"Shhh."

The child sits in my father's lap and whispers to me, "You
know what?" I go over to him and say, "What?" And his voice
is a long spill of words, words so tiny and brittle I'm afraid they
will break. Everyone says children are tough; it's a lie. I can't
stand to look at how fragile they are, their limbs like the handles
on delicate china cups. Their bare backs and necks as open to
assault as the underthroat of a newborn bird. How can parents
ever let them go? For one minute how do they ever let them
out of their sight?

The little boy whispers himself to sleep; his face is up
against Henry. Both the child's head and the man's chest rise
and fall together.

"What's the name of this one, Cora?" I hear someone asking
about one of Mama's birds.

"Doolittle," Mama says.

I try again to sketch Henry's face. My first task is to look.
Look hard. And then it is my job to trust that sight and accu-
rately re-create what I have seen. There are potholes, though,

on that stretch between trust and accuracy and sometimes my eyes aren't enough. Sometimes, in fact, I believe my eyes and hands are the least of it and that what affects my work the most is what happens when the lines and shapes I see and later draw are waylaid up high in my chest and wring my heart.

I have read that a giraffe's eyeball weighs more than its brain. Maybe that's the way I am. I see everything, it seems. But maybe my brain's not large enough to store, and comprehend, all that my eyes gather. Like my mother's garage and basement, what's the use of collecting if there's no more room to put anything and no sure plans that you can ever make use of something once you've lugged it home? But I still see. I can't help it. The whole world's there staring back at me. Mostly the faces of my family.

Southern families have become clichés, I know. You see it all the time, hear those awful fake drawls on TV, read those overwrought novels about self-deprecating women and emasculated men. But all clichés originate in accurate observation. It's just that from eye to hand, all the real information—history, wrinkles, nightmares—gets left out. What was it old Walt Whitman said about Tom Eakins? That he was the only artist who painted not what he wanted to see but what was?

Sometimes with families, and sometimes even with an entire generation, you see a kind of sadness that pervades. It's not the sort that keeps individuals from going on living or from creating and producing or even knowing joy. But there is that certain sadness at their core, the kind you see in an intelligent widow's face years after she's lost her husband. That's the way it has always seemed with my family, at least to me. Looking back at all the pictures there are of us—beach scenes of a wind-blown mother and children, thin young father without a shirt, Thanksgivings with all the in-laws and cousins chasing around the house, Easters out in the yard with all the pretty young aunts, children lined up by age in green and pink and yellow —I see it in my parents' eyes. Something is gone there that once was, something that no amount of money or accomplishment or physical pleasure or other children can ever replace.

I turn the pages of the Glass family album, and uncertain but undefeated eyes look out from the pages, first to the camera and then straight at me, as if the looking might show them what they are going to need to know. There's a picture of my parents together when she's probably no more than nineteen, my father a few years older, both of them sitting together on Gram's couch. Just *so* young, without a clue of what's coming their way. I can never bear to look at it, I always turn it to the wall when I'm in this house. How can anyone ever stand to look at such a picture, when they know what those thin people are going to have to face?

I look at Henry. So much is going on in there. But what is it he's thinking?

His face is a hard-knobbed one, whittled and nicked. It could be chiseled from some porous gritty stone, put in line with any number of Greek or Roman busts, and not seem out of place; his gaze is that constant, that ancient. His face that scarred. There's not a lot of hair left, but what there is, is thick around the sides, wavy and white. It's Mama who reminds him of it and who, each morning as he is walking out the back door, hands him the comb or takes the comb from his pocket and does it for him herself.

Sometimes I look at him and his head seems so full and tight with thoughts that I wonder if it doesn't feel to him as if he's developing fracture marks at his temples the way there are stress marks in the earth; maybe I shouldn't draw a face at all, but a boulder, split with hard breaks and spaces, pine seedlings poking out.

Once I heard someone say that all humans have been allotted only so much fuel to get them through their lives. Everyone is given pretty much the same amount at birth, the theory goes, all of us topped off with a full tank. No reserves, no overflows. When the supply is gone, the life is over. But some people go so much harder than others that they use up their supply more quickly. The body is left empty, that busy, anxious person that used to be inside having used everything up in what seems like an instant, with everyone else looking down the stretch after them, asking, "Where'd they go?"

I hate this theory; I can't *stand* to think about it. There's too much truth to it. I see too many people who can give it possible validity. *Slow it down, slow it down,* I want to beg every time I'm home; I want to pull at Henry's sleeves and hold him still.

There are those people with no blood pressure at all, of course, heartbeats like the tick of a clock that always gives slow time. Gram has outlived my grandfather by thirty-five years. She has been his widow now for the same number of years she was his bride. She has carried his name for almost seven decades, though he has not been alive since 1951, the year I was born.

I'm so curious about how people live their lives. How Gram's gone on alone all this time without her Charlie Lee Jensen. How we survive the death of children. How we keep dreaming dreams after dreams get shattered.

But maybe it doesn't matter about the dreams and heartbreaks. Maybe what we are goes back farther than we think, to our deepest history. Maybe we're all just the way we are, and events make no difference. Maybe Mama would always have been the kind of person who wants you close but holds you at a distance. Maybe she was that way as a girl, something Gram did to her. And maybe Henry was always removed, just him and his grandmother living in that little house in Chatsworth; maybe he never had it in him to show his secret places to a person.

Maybe.

Henry. Henry Glass, Henry Glass. *Henry?* Where is it you go? What is it you're thinking?

Henry: 1963

One time out at Ponce de Leon Park in 1951, I caught a pop fly running backwards, lining up the ball off the end of my nose. The second that ball smacked my mitt, the runner on third was off, and I looked out and the dern pitcher was about six days from home. So I'm back on my toes digging, my shin guards banging against me like fences. This fellow's got ninety feet to come, but it feels like I'm crawling my way out of a hole. So I just dig harder, I'm pumping, and then me and all my equipment we just dive. I'm on the plate and he's tagged on the shoulder, double play. Top of the ninth, and I've stopped 'em at four to four. I was catcher for the Crackers that year. I've got arthritis in my knees now from all that squatting. Lost all my front teeth—broke off at the gum —from getting both ball and bat in the face as a boy. But I don't guess I'll ever forget that one day in Atlanta, when we beat Birmingham, as long as I live.

When I slammed into home and that fellow was *Out!*, the people in the grandstands started stomping and shouting, the stands just a-rattling and shaking under their feet. Even from where I was you could feel the vibration. They carried on so I thought those wooden bleachers were coming down on top of us like a stack of stove matches. The Crackers, we were Double-A then, minor league, part of the Southern Association. Bob Montag was on the team. A lot of the fellows ran over to me and shook my hand. No, I'll never forget it. I'm spitting out sand where I ate it, grit in my eyes, and the noise they're making! It's thrilling. It's enough to last me forever. But wait.

Deep in center field, just in front of this big old magnolia tree out there, they've got this tall wooden fence with advertisements painted on it. You know, Merita bread, Lucky Strikes, Coca-Cola. Well, there was these two holes in both O's of the Coca-Cola sign, and if anybody hit it through one of them, they got paid extra. In this same game, after I made the double play, with two men on base I hit a homer right through that O in Cola. I'd never done anything like that before in my life; I wasn't even one of the best hitters. But it was just the excitement from those two outs, I think, and I've got all this energy going. The crowd's really crazy this time, see, throwing things out on the field, screaming and yelling. And I'm running around those bases so light I don't even know I'm touching, my heart's up beating in my neck.

But there's this railroad track up over the stands, and as I'm running I'm thinking: *Something's wrong.* At about the time you heard that hit of mine crack through the bat, you could hear the whistle from a freight train coming. Bums and coloreds used to sit up there and watch the games, and when they'd hear a train, they'd scramble. This one time though, some of them held back as long as they could, watching where my hit was going. And this kid, a colored boy, he waited too long, and when he tried to run right there at the last, he slipped and fell and some say the train drug him. There were all kinds of stories.

Everybody cheered me in while I guess that boy was on those tracks dying. All that noise ran together—the other players, the crowds, the train, the sirens, and yelling. Me and Montag and the others, we made the front page. That boy who got hit by that train, he was mentioned inside. About a paragraph. He was seventeen.

I thought about going to the fellow's funeral, but, I don't know, you just didn't do things like that. Jackie Robinson had already made the majors, but there weren't any colored boys on our team. Maybe if there had of been, we'd all have gone. All us players.

Well, I don't guess any of it matters now. But it's just something I think about sometimes at night when CoraRuth and the kids are asleep and I'm up by myself walking around the house, everything all quiet. I think, on the best day of my life, this fellow got hit by a train and died long before they could get him to the colored hospital. Well, what got me started on this was looking through this photograph album. It begins with me and Cora when we first started dating, her in high school, me in the Marines and then with the Crackers. There are the ones of us out in California and ones of all the children. Anyway, last weekend Cora's sister and her family were all down from North Carolina, and the women were in here giving each other permanents. I was looking out for the children. Eleanor, our oldest girl, brought this big old thing out and sat down beside me on the couch and we started going through it. She likes to point at the different pictures and say, Who's this? and she likes for us to tell her about how we got married, wants us to repeat every detail even though she's heard it all a hundred times or more.

I've got this BB up under the skin on my right hand from an accident when I was a kid (the doctor says leave it), and I was answering some question of Eleanor's and she was rolling that BB around instead of really looking at the pictures. And CoraRuth's sister Kathleen was standing up behind Cora setting her hair with these aqua-colored curlers. She'd take a piece of hair, and then take a piece of paper Cora would hand back to her and wrap it in that and then roll it around one of those green curlers. Anyway, I was watching the women and Eleanor was watching me and I was talking about China when all of a sudden Kathleen says, "You know, there are hardly any pictures in there of the other children. Nearly every one of them is of Eleanor." Well, it kind of ticked me off, but she was right. We sure didn't mean for it to happen. I guess it's just that with the oldest you're always so excited about recording every little thing, for history. You are for the others, too, I mean you're just as proud and all, but I guess it's just that you've seen it before and you don't think it's the first time in the world that walking and talking has ever happened. You know what I'm talking about. We've got naked-bottom pictures of Eleanor. First birthdays. Christmases.

There are some like that of the younger ones, too, but not near as many.

This one here is when she was two. CoraRuth made that dress for her for Easter, sat up all that Saturday night to finish the smocking. And, well, all the other stuff's in here. The piano recitals and report cards and training wheels off bicycles. She's smart as a whip and a real good little artist. Look at this, a drawing of a pine cone. That could have been done by some-body who was twenty. Her teachers say she's got a natural talent, say for us to encourage her about it. So for presents we get her colored pencils, pads of paper, those sorts of things.

She was born that year I was with the Crackers. CoraRuth was with her people up in Chatsworth, and I was down in Atlanta alone. Sometimes I wonder if I'd have stayed in baseball if I'd never got married, if we hadn't had the children. But we got married as soon as I got back from China. I was sent over there with the Marines. I was seventeen when I joined up, eighteen when I went over. I've got all these pictures here of me and the other fellows in my company. That one there was Wee Chun Leh, a Chinaman they assigned to us to help out with the language barrier. He and me, we became pretty good friends, he'd show me around. He had a degree in electrical engineering and he was my assistant. I'd been an electrician's helper one summer back in Georgia, and so they put me wiring, with this Chinaman as *my* helper. Think of that.

I've always wondered what happened to him. I tell you one thing, I still can't stand the smell of garlic. It was everywhere! They cooked it, wore it, ate it raw, I reckon. I've never seen anything like it.

Anyway, I got home and we got married. Just one Saturday night me and CoraRuth and two others—this guy I played ball with that we called Garbo and her sister, Kathleen—we went to this justice of the peace, and then we went to this restaurant and ordered a basket of chicken. There's a picture of us, all sitting around laughing. We've still got the basket; we snuck it out, and now CoraRuth uses it with a napkin stuck in it at meals for bread and biscuits. After supper we drove CoraRuth and Kathleen home and Garbo dropped me off at my grandmoth-er's (that's where I lived, she's the one that reared me), and we didn't tell anybody else about it for four or five days.

Somehow her mother got word though, and so we had to go ahead and let everybody in on it. I don't know what we thought we were going to do, just keep it a secret forever, I guess. Anyway, her mother about had a conniption. I never saw anyone carry on so in my life. Wringing hands, moaning and yelling. Her daddy just sat there, and finally he said, "Ruth, just let 'em alone. This ain't going to cause no harm to anybody."

We moved in there with them for a while, and then I got called back in when the Korea thing blew up. But we only got sent out to California for a time—Long Beach—and CoraRuth drove out there with her sister and we got this duplex on the beach. A flat-roofed thing made of cement blocks. That was a good time, I guess you could say. Here's a picture. That's CoraRuth in the shorts and turban. She's pretty, isn't she? She says her people's got Cherokee in their blood. That's why she's got those cheekbones and that kind of skin.

Then we came back and that's when I went with the Atlanta Crackers. Mr. Earl Mann sent a fellow up to Chatsworth to watch me play and ask me would I like to come work for him, how would I like to be a Cracker? But there wasn't any money in it hardly; I guess that was one thing. People didn't make much in baseball, and not that many got a chance to go on to the major leagues. Eddie Mathews did, but not that many others. And you had to be away from home, always on buses, staying in these hot hotels all over. It wasn't that CoraRuth ever looked at me and said, *Don't* or *Stop*. No, it's just like when I was over in China I used to do a little drinking, beer mostly, and some smoking. But as soon as I got up to Chatsworth and saw that baby girl right after she was born, I threw my pack of Chesterfields away and never lit up another. And of course now I don't drink, either; we're Methodists.

I bought a life insurance policy in her name when she was two days old. Don't say it! The salesman, he was glad to have the business and all, but he looked at me like I was crazy. But I said, "Here, write it down. Put her name on it. Eleanor Glass." No middle name; what could she do with it? And another time this fellow came along selling *American People's Encyclopedia*s door to door when she wasn't but about three months old (I think they must get your name from a list at the hospital), and I put down a deposit on the whole set, plus that yearly almanac. CoraRuth about had a fit. She said, "For goodness sake, Henry. Everything will be outdated by the time she's old enough to use it." But she does use those encyclopedias, all twenty-nine volumes (we stopped getting the almanacs some time back). We keep them lined up on this shelf in the living room, and she comes in here every once in a while at night and takes one down and smells it and copies things out of it for her assignments.

Sometimes she'll bring one over and sit down beside me on the couch, and we'll just look through it together. Stop at something that looks good and read about it. Easter Island, that was interesting. Did you ever hear about that, those statues, and those lost people? And Marco Polo, we both liked him, I guess because of the China stuff and the spaghetti and so on. Did you ever read Hemingway? I'm not all that much of a reader, but I do have two of his books up next to the *American People's*. I'd like to go to some of those places.

Well, I guess I've been to more spots than a lot of people. In the Marines I got to three foreign places: China, like I told you, and Guam and Hawaii. Well, that last one I know's not a foreign country, but I guess it seemed like it, and so did those Pacific Islands. I'd like to go back there someday. And if you could get in, maybe even to China. Look up old Wee Chun Leh. I guess none of us ever will though, go back over there now that the Communists have taken over. And Cuba. Who can go there with this Castro in charge? But I'd like to, if it was still like it was when Hemingway was over there, fishing.

My eyes aren't as good now, so who knows what kind of future I would have had if I'd stayed with the Crackers. None of us figured there was any security in baseball anyway really. Lots of fellows didn't last. That's why I came on up here to South Carolina. One of my daddy's cousins owned this land, but things went wrong for him and it was hard to make a go of it. He wrote and told me it was mine—the house, the orchards, everything—if I could pay the last two years' taxes. My grandmother let me borrow a little money and CoraRuth's people helped us with the rest. And we've been here ever since. It's not bad. I've built up the orchard, just about paid off the cost of building the canning house. When we're a little bit more ahead, we're probably going to add on to the house. I'm going to start taking off a little more too, you know, maybe drive down to Atlanta and take Cora and the children to see the Crackers. They're Triple-A now, International League. Some folks call them a farm team, but I still think they're good. Maybe we'll drive up to Washington sometime, too, and show the children all the monuments, the Lincoln Memorial. Go down to Daytona, or Panama City. Maybe even back out to Long Beach someday, California.

And the other thing I'm going to start doing again is taking pictures. I used to be pretty good, bought this camera at the PX and read up on how to use it. But I'm thinking about getting one of those Polaroids, so you don't have to wait so long, and I'm going to get more pictures of Diane and Lucas.

It's been a surprise to me how different children can be. Children from the exact same family, I mean. Look here at this picture of Eleanor and her little sister. See the way Eleanor's got her head cocked and how she's grinning, her dress held to the side, kind of prissy? That's the way she is. Friendly, talks to anybody. And affectionate, just all over you all the time (it can about drive you crazy). She gets to laughing so hard she can't control herself. When she gets like that, her grandmother will say, "If you don't stop that, you'll be crying before it's all over, young lady." And sometimes she *is* laughing one minute, crying the next. You just can't get on to her about anything, it goes right through her. Gets a look on her face like you broke her heart.

Now, look right there at Diane. See the way she's sitting so close to her mother in the picture, the way she looks so timid? Well, that's the way she is, shy and quiet most of the time. Things don't show across her face like on her sister's. Everything stays still there, like behind a closed window. And she's not as healthy as the others. Not a cutup, either. She laughs too though, when Eleanor gets to acting silly. And they both cry like you've beat them if the other one gets a spanking. And the boy, Lucas, I guess it's too early to tell how he's going to be, although you can already see he's different from both the girls.

Well, it's interesting how things turn and change, and sometimes it all ends up different than what you ever thought it would. It's funny how kids grow up so quick (Eleanor's almost twelve—before you know it she'll be a teenager!). And it's funny how you end up getting married and spend the rest of your life with this one same woman.

I think about things like that sometimes, about that colored boy and the train. About that kid that slugged Houdini. Now that was an accident, wasn't it? I mean you know he didn't think he'd end up busting the man's gut and causing poison to set in, did he? And what about during the war—if the same people hadn't been there? You know, Roosevelt, Churchill, the Russians. Did you ever think about that, if one of them had been missing? What it might have meant to all of us, to those French people? What if one of those Wright brothers hadn't been sick and thought he was dying—you think they'd ever gone down to Kill Devil Hills, just two bicycle shop owners, and tried to fly? And what about Kennedy? Nobody I knew thought a Catholic would be elected president. I think we all just figured a rich Catholic was better than a squirmy little Quaker.

Something else. What if I hadn't grown up in Chatsworth knowing CoraRuth? What if me and somebody else had got married, would I have ever thought about how there couldn't have been these children I have now? See what I'm talking about, how it all just seems like accidents somehow? And if everybody just moved one step this way, or that, things could be all different, forever?

CoraRuth says I spend too much energy worrying about answers to questions that don't have to get asked. She says all the time I spend thinking, wandering about the house in the dark, I ought to be sleeping. I guess that's right. I guess wondering doesn't dig trenches and it doesn't spray fruit trees and it doesn't pick peaches. And it doesn't get you to Cuba or put people back together after they're dead.

But there's something else I've been thinking lately. If you could get out of the way of things by taking a step to the left or right, then why don't folks do it more? I mean, if you're not all that tickled about being a peach grower, maybe you don't have to be one, right? Like it's this coincidence that somebody gives you a good price on some land at about the same time you're thinking you need to get into something steady. But then maybe it's no accident anymore if you keep on doing that right along; do you know what I'm saying?

It's like that one Wright brother, the one that was sick (Wilbur, wasn't it?). Now that part of it was a coincidence. But Orville and him could have just stayed up there wherever it was they were from and waited for him to die instead of saying what's to lose and going on down to North Carolina.

And that poor fellow that got killed the day I hit my homer. Part of that was accident, the train coming at the same time I got my hit, even his falling. But his staying to the last like that, now that was his doing, wasn't it?

So what about me, I've been thinking. What if there was something else I might be good at; maybe it's only me that's stopping it. There are plenty of places to live, aren't there, besides these few hundred acres off the road between Greenville and Spartanburg?

So what I've been thinking is that tomorrow after church, instead of going home like usual and eating that chicken she makes with the cornflakes cooked on it, maybe we'll ride into town and eat at the cafeteria. Have us some ice cream afterwards, or strawberry pie. And then maybe we'll just take a drive down to Greenville to those gardens Cora likes and look at those big banks of thrift blooming. Unless we're going someplace like back to Chatsworth, and we have to go over the mountains with all those curves (and the children spend half the time with their heads hanging out the window or stuck down into a paper bag), the girls like to ride. They go through the alphabet picking out letters on signs, and then they fall asleep, and me and CoraRuth talk. So I'm thinking we'll take this drive and when the children are sleeping I'll say, I've been thinking there's something else I want to do. And Cora will say, Like what?

She never acts against something, but she is always practical. And I'll say that I probably don't know what yet, but it just seems like at our age (dern! she's just thirty-four and I'm not but thirty-nine), there's nothing holding us back. That we can sell this place, make some money, head on out, try something different for a while.

There are thousands of places in this country to live, just look in the encyclopedias. What about Virginia? That's supposed to be pretty. And what about out west? Montana maybe, or Colorado. We've never been out there. We could try any of them, maybe buy a place in a city (I liked Atlanta fine), maybe open up a sporting goods store, do something with kids. Who knows?

Listen, it's not like we don't like it here, and not like I don't know how to have some fun. I play on the church softball team every summer. I guess it's the last thing in the world I ought to be doing, summer being our busiest time. But I like the feeling, sand in your hands, holding the bat, knowing you can run. This fellow, Ben, who works for me, he and some of the others think I'm a celebrity, because of the Crackers. Sure, I can step up and take a swing and make a piece of wood crack right down its middle. I can tag a man out. Skip around to home.

Yeah, and I coach the little fellows. There's a ball field out behind the church, and we meet out there, and I show 'em how to hold the bat up at ready, how to watch the ball, how to run. Some of 'em are pretty good, and others—well, CoraRuth won't go with me, says it kills her to see those little guys who are so scared. She just can't stand it when one strikes out.

Oh, and we're both active in church, and CoraRuth helps out over at the school when they need her. We both go real hard.

But I don't know, I guess I'm just ready for something different. I guess I just don't want to feel like I stayed my whole life in the middle of an accident. You know what I'm saying?

So I'm going to make some changes. Have my fellow Ben take on more of the responsibilities, turn things over more to him. Start looking in the papers, see what all's out there; I don't mind working. Take the children places, make sure they've been on an airplane ride.

Ben: 1963

$\mathcal{P}$acking up, leaving. I ain't staying here. Already stayed way too long.

That's what happened, stayed past the time I ought to. Should have left at the end of last summer, got on out of here. Walked out to the highway and stuck out my thumb. Rode down to Atlanta, or somewheres. I can get a job.

What did he mean anyway, saying I was his best hand? And what was she doing, bringing me my own little skillet of cornbread out here? Saying you ought to come to church with us sometimes, Mr. Bolt. They're nothing to me. Those children don't even know my full name, just call me Ben. Well, you look at them all dressed up like that—her so straight and pretty, both little girls each with a ribbon tied to their hair, the boy up in his arms dressed in yellow britches—and you think, now that's the picture of the American family. Well, this ain't no ballgame, buddy. I'm gone!

This was the first place I come to after Raleigh. Got off the bus at Greer. I was eating me some supper, wondering should I find a place to spend the night, and I heard these boys talking about how there was work down the road. They said this man named Glass that owned a peach orchard was hiring.

I guess I had figured I'd go on further than here, someplace on down the highway so Maxene wouldn't find me. But I don't know, this didn't look like a bad place, and I thought I'd stay a week or two, earn enough to get me back on the bus, heading south again.

But I stayed right on through the whole summer. I was picking at first, but Henry Glass, he comes over to me and says he's never seen such a worker, how would I like to be his foreman. I say I don't know, I guess I could do it temporary. I tell him right there that I don't plan on staying. And he says sure, he understands. So I'm foreman for a while out in the orchards. I drive the truck up and down, checking on how fast the coloreds and Indians are working. He says I'm doing good. And then he moves me up to the canning house, and I work there. I see that everything's running smooth, that the boys are backing the trucks up proper to the soaking vats, that the big wheel is turning in the water and the peaches are moving down that conveyor belt. But all the time I'm thinking, Got to get on going, can't let Maxene find me here. I'm thinking where I'll go next. I listen to what people say. What kind of jobs are where. But then this Henry Glass, he says they've got this old trailer out behind the canning house, don't I want to move in there. Nothing fancy, he says, but it's a free place to live, comes with the job, and I'll be right there if anything goes wrong.

And I think, Well no, she won't find me here, not in my own trailer. So I stay for a while. He keeps me on through the fall and winter, and now the spring too.

I'm the only worker, all the summer help is gone (migrant workers mostly), and I take care of the equipment, help him put out the smoke pots here in the spring in case it gets down too cold. We spray the trees together, and he says, Watch the wind!

Sometimes I ride into town with him, and I'll buy me a *Life* magazine. Sometimes I pick up a newspaper, thinking maybe I'll see my name and picture there, like I'm wanted or something. He tells me about when he used to play ball. I guess you could say they start treating me like family, sometimes asking me up for supper, him talking to me like he's known me forever. Every once in a while he says to me, Bolt, you ought to settle down, did you ever think about that? I don't say nothing. I just listen and maybe nod. He don't even guess.

And all this time I'm thinking about what's happened to Maxene and the girl. Maybe nothing. Maybe they're still right there, right where I left them in that green house in Raleigh, with Budd buried in the backyard and my *Life* magazines stacked out on the back porch between that old freezer and wringer washer where she had me keep them. Rubber bands on every doorknob. Her hair curlers rolling around in every drawer. Tubes of lipstick lined up on her dresser like a row of round metal soldiers.

Maybe they don't even know I'm gone. Or maybe she talks to the neighbors and says, "Good riddance. I always hoped he'd take off."

I didn't leave 'em helpless. I did it right. Maybe I even always had it in the back of my mind, the whole plan, every detail— like somebody drew it out for me with a pencil. Like somebody said to me, All right, Ben, this is what you do: you go to the tool shed and take out that money you been saving that she don't know about. Then you go over to the landlady and you pay the next three months' rent, tell her you came into some extra and don't like it around the house, that you'd just as soon get some things paid ahead. You get a receipt for it, and you put it in this yellow folder. And you put nearly all the rest of that money in there too (keep out enough to get you some- where, pay for some food) and then you close it up and put her name on the front in big letters so she can't miss it. And you write this note to Maxene and you tell her that this should keep them going for quite a while and then they can go on back home to her folks like she always wanted. Whatever she wants to do. And then you write on there: *Good luck, Benjamin Bolt.* You fold it, and you put that out on the kitchen table after she's gone to bed. And then you walk out of that house without a sound and you walk straight to the Greyhound station and you wait there for the next bus, and then you head out.

So that's what I done. And halfway down to here on the bus, I think, I don't even have a picture of the girl. I was always talking about buying a camera, and Maxene always said, Yeah, I guess you think you're going to send it off to *Life* magazine and they'll send you a million dollars. Just let her talk, I'd think, don't say a thing. But I always thought I'd buy one sometime, try to keep it a secret, just every once in a while snap a picture or two of Evelyn when she and her mama wasn't looking. Not even let them know. But I didn't ever do it, and the only picture we had was when she was just a baby. Some cousin of Maxene's came to visit, and she took a snapshot of Evelyn getting a bath at the kitchen sink in a turkey roaster. Holding her up, drying her off in one of those big slick towels.

I don't know much about babies, but I always thought she was a pretty little girl. I liked holding her, giving her the bottle. But Maxene always said, No, that's not right, you don't hold it like that, you're letting her drink air. I'd hand it over, go out on the back porch, and throw a stick to the dog. I'm sitting there throwing, the dog coming back every time just like clockwork, letting me take it from his mouth so easy. And she comes to the door, Hey, I could use some help in here, Mister. I throw the stick one more time and the dog comes back, standing at the bottom on the steps, his tail just wagging, waiting, the stick dropped at his feet. And I'm back inside and, Wash your hands, I'm told.

All along I keep thinking, sooner or later she'll get to know her daddy. But it just seems like everything goes so fast, one long slow day right after another. I come home and Evelyn's in her playpen, just in her diaper, and I go to her and pick her up, and Maxene snatches her so fast and Evelyn starts to cry, and Maxene says, See what you've done? And I go out to the kitchen, that baby smell still in my lungs.

Pretty soon she cries every time she sees me, and I'm thinking, She's that scared of me? Or is it the snatching she's scared of, what happens every time I pick her up? So I keep my distance, and little eyes watch me when I move around the room.

And she's getting bigger every day, older. And I'm thinking, She looks just like Maxene. Even sounds like her. And I begin to think too that maybe there's nothing left of me in her, everything that was ever there Maxene's got rid of like she had this big eraser and just rubbed me out.

Maybe it wasn't her fault. Maybe I misled her.

When I met her I told her I had this good job with the railroad. I thought it was. No Rockefeller or nothing, I knew that, but it paid something and I liked it. But I guess she thought it was going to be more. Right away she says, This is all? Her girlfriends had things, she said, stockings, hats, they rode around in automobiles, went to picture shows all the time, why wasn't there any of that? So I start saving, thinking: One day I'll get her something. I planned to spring it on her in one big lump instead of a little trickle here and there. But I think maybe it was the trickles that she wanted. Maybe every day a little surprise. Candy, stockings, tubes of lipstick.

So she gets them herself with the grocery money, and she shows them to me like she got them from another man. And all the time Evelyn's growing closer and closer to being her mother, and she stops looking at me like she don't know who I am and turns to looking at me like I'm this bum, like one of them guys who crawl up in the boxcars and freeze to death while they're sleeping it off. And every day I come home and her mama says, Goody, goody, the breadwinner's home, while Evelyn keeps her head down playing with paper dolls, not even looking up. And I go outside and free the dog from where she keeps him chained up and I toss to him, and he brings that stick back to me so faithful, slobber all over it, his jumps so light and easy.

She's watching me out the window all the time, I feel it, and every once in a while she'll call out, You better keep that dog out of my flowers, Mister. I just throw, watching that poplar stick turn and glide in the air. Later she'll come to the door, hold it open a crack and say, If you're hungry come get it, and I'll put the dog back on his chain and after supper I'll bring him out any scraps, give him a fresh pan of water.

Right before I left I was up for a promotion. Nothing much, just the next level and a little extra money. Every day she's waiting out on the porch on the glider and she says as I'm coming up the walk, Did you get it? They hadn't said yet, I tell her, but I have this bad feeling. I was working hard, it wasn't that, but there was this new guy in charge and he wasn't much for me, I could tell. I don't know why, just one of those things some people have, something against another and there's no real reason that you can put your finger on. So the day they announce it, I don't tell her. I keep it to myself for almost a week. But somehow it's almost like she knows. She's pacing, something strange on her face. She's there every day, getting farther off the porch, closer to me when I'm coming down that walk. Every day it's, Did you get it? Did you get it? Every day. And every day it's like that poor old dog's chain's getting shorter, and when I ask her about it, she says, He's digging and if he don't stop he's going down to one last notch, Mister.

He's just a yard dog, just a howling old brown yard dog, but none of this ain't his fault.

Finally I've got to tell her, I know that. But I think, I'll tell her about the savings too, tell her that promotion don't matter, that I've got money put away. We can buy some things, what is it she wants? So I move up that walk and she's there on the bottom step, her mouth stretched tight and crooked, and she says, "So did you get it?" And I say, "No, but wait, it don't matter."

But she's back in the house, the front door banging and I go in after her, and she's in my closet and she's pulling down the gun, and I say, "Whoa here. Hey now, what's going on?"

"I told you he was digging," she says. "Told you he was in my flowers." And she goes to the back porch and pumps the cock. And I say, "Hey now, wait a minute here." But she takes aim, and she shoots that yard dog right through the throat.

That's when the plan come to me, just like I'm looking at this picture somebody has drawn up. But I go out there and I bury Budd first. I dig a hole right in the spot where he's been digging, right where he's got it started for me. I dig it deep, following the lines of my plan as I'm shoveling. And when the hole's done, I put him down in there, the chain, the water pan, even the old pile of rags he slept on. All of it. And I cover it up. I stay out there past dark, and then I go on out to the tool shed and get that wad of money where I've had it hid, wrapped up in newspapers and string. When I see her light go out, that's when I go in. And I follow all the rest of the plan like I told you about.

I didn't take nothing, not even the *Life* magazines I had piled up on the back porch, the ones she kept saying needed burning. And that's when I come here.

Temporary, like I said, that's what I thought this place would be. I didn't mean to get stuck anywhere.

Right-hand man, that's what he told me. Yesterday I helped her carry in her bags of groceries. I brought 'em in and she unloaded 'em. After the last one, she says, "Oh, Mr. Bolt, there's some things from the drugstore in the floorboard of the back-seat." Some bottles of liquid vitamins for the children that she said she got at a Rexall one-cent sale, could I get them for her? But then she says, "How about a cup of coffee first?" And I say I don't reckon that would hurt.

One of the girls was at the table drawing, and every once in a while she'd turn it up for her mother to see and her mother would say, That is lovely, simply lovely. I wondered if Evelyn knew how to draw like that.

He came in too and we all had some coffee. I ended up staying for supper. We watched some singing on the television, and the oldest girl she sang along, pretended she was holding a microphone in her hand, her eyes closed tight and throwing out the words to "Blueberry Hill." When the song was over she opened her eyes and looked over at us and her mother said, "Silly," and all of us clapped. All three of the children fell asleep on the floor, and she dozed off too, stretched out on the sofa, her stocking feet crossed one over the other in his lap.

It was too warm in there. They still had the furnace going this late in the year, and you could smell the pork chops from supper all the way in the living room. I forgot all about those vitamin bottles.

It was about an hour ago somebody come to tell me. I was here in the trailer frying boloncy, listening at the radio. Somebody knocked and I went over and cracked the door. It was this woman, dressed up like she'd been to church. "Mr. Bolt?" she says, and I say, "Yes?" I'm thinking, *I'm found.*

She says, "Mr. Bolt, there's been this bad accident," and I think, *Evelyn.* But she says, "It's Henry and CoraRuth, Mr. Bolt. It's a car accident and they're hurt real bad, critical, one of the little girls is already dead."

Stop, I want to tell her. Don't tell me anymore. Don't tell me which one.

"Someone said you'd be the one that would know what to do here," she says, "that you could take care of things for Henry." I don't know what I say, *Okay,* or *Thank you* maybe. I close the trailer door, and for a time I think I can still hear her out there talking to a rusty wall. I smell the boloney burning, and then something spells out: GO.

I've cleaned this place up, leaving it just the way I found it. Every dish washed, everything swept out. I've got my jacket and my shirts, the new *Life* magazines down in a paper bag. There are all these cars parked over at the house, people coming in and out. Every light burning. I'm waiting until it's completely dark and then I'll head out to the road. Hitch or hike, wait for a bus, it doesn't matter.

No pictures, I think, not of anybody I ever knew. Just these ones in the magazines. But I look over at the lit house and I know that ain't true. I think about those children asleep last night on the floor, her with her feet in his lap, me and him sitting there with our shirts open watching until the television goes off.

We all got pictures, I think, up here in our heads, and everywhere we go we have to take them with us.

CoraRuth: 1974

Eleanor has lost her baby. The call came four nights ago. Henry and me were already in bed. He was asleep and I was reading the paper. When the phone rang, I knew. I know that sounds silly, like I'm pretending to foresee things, or prophesy or something. But the truth is I've always been able to feel it, when something bad's about to happen. I'm no fortune-teller or anything. *I just know.* I wish I didn't, because it comes over me like a sick headache, and I have to wait until the awful thing has hit, until the worst is over before I can breathe easy again.

Me and Henry had been waiting for the children's call, saying when the baby was here. And I had planned to drive down to Atlanta and help out. There was no hurry, really. Eleanor and Jay live with his mother, and Eleanor and Fitz (that's the mother-in-law) are real close. So I wasn't in a rush to get down there and be a third wheel, you know, get in the way and all that. I just figured I'd go a few days after the baby was born, if I could wait that long. It was my first grandchild, after all. But that night, as soon as the phone rang, I knew it wasn't good. I just knew—right away like that—that something had gone wrong.

It was Jay on the phone. His voice was shaky and tight, like something had a hold of his throat. He said, "CoraRuth. Something's happened."

"All right," I said. I sat up straight and nudged Henry. "What is it?"

"The baby's dead," he said.

I waited for him to say something else, but he didn't. So I asked—I know it was unimportant, but I didn't know what else to say—I asked, "Was it a boy or girl?"

I could hear him swallowing, all the way up here in South Carolina, over all those miles, I could hear him swallowing into the phone. He said, "We don't know." I didn't understand at first. Maybe I said something, maybe that I was confused. Anyway, Jay went on: "CoraRuth, Eleanor hasn't delivered. She's still in labor."

I said, "Oh sweet Lord in heaven." All I could think to do was get to my own baby, my firstborn, Eleanor. She was down in Atlanta somewhere, on some hospital table, trying to give birth to a dead child. I couldn't imagine.

"What?" Henry wanted to know. He was sitting up beside me, groping for his glasses. "What?" he said again. "What's happened?" He always wakes up in a panic. You can practically hear his heart beating from across the room. It scares you to death that just waking up is going to kill him.

Our son, Lucas, had come into the room, was standing at the foot of our bed in his pajama bottoms wanting to know what was it too. I hushed them both so that I could hear, and Jay told me how Eleanor had sensed something was wrong the day before, how she had called him at work and said she hadn't felt the baby moving. They'd called the doctor, and he'd said not to worry. But by midnight she was crying, saying she knew the baby was dead. So he and Fitz drove her to the emergency room and made them admit her. Some nurse put one of those things to Eleanor's stomach, treating them all like they were idiots, Jay said. She was slow and surly and acted like she couldn't have cared less if Eleanor had had a butcher knife sticking out of her belly. But then she looked up all of a sudden with this scared look on her face and rushed out of the room.

After that, Jay said everything was crazy, all these people running in and out. What they did was put a monitor in Eleanor, attached it to the baby's head, and when they did there was no heartbeat. I guess it was some kind of nightmare, them having to induce labor, Eleanor crying, poor old Jay just a nervous wreck. By the time he got us on the phone she'd been in labor six hours. It was the first chance he had had to leave her side, he said.

When Henry and me got there, the baby was already born, and Eleanor had been in labor a little over eleven hours, altogether. Eleven hours delivering a baby that was dead. We all saw the little thing; Eleanor wanted us to.

She was just perfect in every way. The sweetest hands, with those long fingers like babies have. Her fingernails needed trimming. And she had a headful of black hair, just like all my babies. Her head wasn't even messed up the way they are sometimes, right after they're born. All that looked wrong was this red mark right under her chin.

The umbilical cord had been wrapped around her neck, see, and when she began dropping in the birth canal, the doctor said the cord just strangled her. They've named her Angela Diane. All the letters of her name are typed right there on the birth certificate just like she was anybody else, with things ahead of her. Strange how the birth certificate and the death certificate both say the same date. Though if you think about it, the death certificate should really say the day before.

We had a service, just Fitz and us and Lucas (he and Eleanor are real close, even though she's so much older—he's just fifteen) and a couple of Jay and Eleanor's friends.

It can break your heart to see one of those children's coffins. That's been the worst part of it, I think. Seeing that little casket, watching them put it in the ground. Henry couldn't bear it. He walked out of the room when he saw it in the funeral home. Wept without a sound out on that cold cemetery, wouldn't take my handkerchief. I thought I'd die watching the wind blow his hair around like that, his old head bent down so nobody'd see. Right there I said, *Lord, I just don't think we can stand this.* I'm forty-three years old, but I don't understand any of it. Why must we suffer such things, do you think?

He's gone on home, Henry. Drove back yesterday with Luke. But I'm staying here in Atlanta for a few more days. I don't know why. Everything I say is wrong. I aim my words the right direction, I think, but the Lord only knows where they'll end up landing. You'd think I could help, be a comfort maybe. And not just because I'm Eleanor's mother, but because I lost a child myself. But I guess everybody's grief is different. I guess it's something you just can't share too easy, something you can't much help anybody with. I think back to what people said to me (I remember every syllable), how they acted, and I try not to say the things that hurt.

I've tried to touch Eleanor, but we both go rigid as a poker when I go to hug her. Why *is* that, I wonder? I *know* I'm not a hugger, never have been. But I'd like to put a hand on my girl, I want to be close to my daughter.

We're all so—I don't know—*sore* right now, it seems. Even our skin. It's like we've been in some bad accident, and all our bones are broken. That's the way I feel anyway, broken and sore. Cut to pieces.

I wish I was home with Henry. But I dread that too, really. Him and me sitting together after supper, after Lucas has gone on up to his room, asking what do we want to watch on the television. I'm lonesome here in Fitz's house, trying to be so careful, looking over every word I say. But sometimes I'm lonesome even at home, even with Henry. Sometimes at night we'll be sitting in the living room, the TV on, maybe one of us reading the paper, and I'll look over at him and think, Who is that man? I just hate it when that happens. Makes me feel so awful and lonely. Lost, kind of. I've known Henry *all my life*. Been married to him since I was seventeen. What's wrong with me when I get like that? Maybe I'm crazy, I think. But sometimes I see him looking at me kind of funny, or looking off to the side, not really out the window or at anything particular, and I can't help wondering if maybe he gets that same lonely feeling too. You know, from time to time.

This is such a big house. Eleanor and Jay say they're living here to save money, until Jay has a better job. But I think they're here to keep his mother company. She wants them here, you can tell. If I were Fitz and a widow woman, I'd sell this place, get me a little house where you didn't have to hire help to keep all the floors waxed and the furniture polished. Where the kids would have to get out and make a way of their own. But everybody's different.

Her husband's people had money. The house is full of good furniture. Antiques. Not the kind of oak pieces you see in shops with stickers on them calling them antiques, asking high prices: *stove wood*, stuff my family gave to the coloreds. No, this house is full of the real thing. Serpentine sideboards.

Cherry secretaries. High walnut beds. Big, nice things. Fancy and fine.

The room Eleanor and Jay sleep in used to have what I thought was a real pretty bedroom suite. Cherry wood. A petticoat mirror. Something you'd think Eleanor would have liked. They've moved it all out, though. Every stick. Don't ask me where. The basement maybe. Now they sleep on a mattress that's right down on the floor. No boxsprings, no bed frame on coasters; nothing. Just a mattress on the floor. Jay says it's a statement. Of what, I've wondered; stupidity? But I don't say a thing. They do what they want to.

Over their mattress is a big painting Eleanor did. There's no frame around it, and you can see where she's stapled the canvas to the stretcher boards. She does all that herself. The painting is a series of long columns of colors rounded at the ends, like heavy teardrops, I guess you could say. It's different from anything else she's ever done (mostly she paints people, though she's gone through her stages like everybody else—painted everything from Henry's work shoes to a pair of lacy underdrawers, real-life things though, not too much of this abstract mess). But there is something else different about this one painting, something about the canvas. "Oh, it's unprimed," she said. Eleanor's been drawing and painting since she was three years old, and I've learned all about this art stuff right along with her: how to cut mat paper; how to saw the stretcher boards to keep from paying the prices at the artists' supply store; how to stretch the canvas; all about priming the raw fabric before she paints on it. No telling how much money I've spent buying those big half-gallon containers of that white primer— gesso. We used to get it down at the lumber store. So I asked her, didn't she tell me one time that the turpentine eats right through after a while, if the canvas isn't primed? Isn't that why her and her daddy and me brushed that primer on all those canvases, had them lined up for her to use whenever she was ready, so she wouldn't have to wait for one to dry? "I'm not into that right now, Mom," she said. "Permanency. I think art can be temporary." I didn't ask any questions, but later, when I was back home, I got to wondering what she'd have thought if that Picasso nut had decided to be temporary. I never did ask her though. It's all a mystery to me, what my daughter's thinking.

But so are a lot of things these days. This whole Nixon mess. Drugs. Strange food. Crazy music. Girls in Little League. Ralph Nader everywhere. People living in trees and naming their children Rainbow and Moonbeam. It's ridiculous. All this worry about no gas. Every night on the TV more pictures of the war. When Jay was over there, Eleanor kept up with it all. One weekend, when she was home from college and we were watching the news, they gave this count of how many had died that week, you know—the way they do. I forget the number. Anyway, Eleanor sat there, not moving her eyes off the screen, and said, "I wish he had gone to Canada. I wish I'd talked him into it and gone with him." Me and Henry about fell out of our chairs.

"Why, he's not even fighting," I told her. "He's in supplies."

She turned to me and said, "What the fuck does that matter?" Well, I'm just glad she's married now and settled down. It's helped her language. Keeps you from worrying about a lot of things.

We were driving back from the hospital the day after we got here, Jay and his mother and Henry and me. And we drove past that part of Peachtree where all the hippies hang out. Up in that bad part of town around Tenth Street. They were just lying around in doorways, sprawled across the sidewalk. The windows all spray-painted, trash everywhere. Hair in their eyes. *Barefooted.* It may be April, but it's too cold for that kind of thing. Why, what in the world do you reckon their parents must be thinking? I can't understand any of it. What it all means. Why they'd want to run around like that when they've probably got good decent clothes in their closets. Even Jay won't wear anything but this one pair of blue jeans with a big hole in one knee. I've tried my best to get him to let me patch it, but he wants them that way. And him from this kind of home and all this money.

Anyway, I was watching from the backseat while we were stopped at a red light. I locked my door and motioned for Henry to do the same on his side of the car. "That's pot," someone said. "Where?" me and Henry both said at the same time. Fitz pointed (she knows all about these things), and I saw two boys passing this cigarette back and forth. Then they handed it over to this tall, skinny girl with a tattoo on her arm. Just awful. She inhaled and gave it back. I couldn't believe how young they were. But they moved like old people, like their motors were running down. Me and Henry looked at each other, and he shook his head. I started to roll my window down, to see if I could get a whiff of how it smelled (in PTA they tell us to learn the odor; it's one of the ways that you can tell if your children are on the stuff), but Henry snapped, "Roll that thing back up." He hardly ever yells. I guess I couldn't have smelled it anyway. The light had changed and we were moving on.

But I can't get those children's faces out of my mind. And that's what they were, you can believe it: children. I guess you never know how things are going to turn out. Eleanor and Lucas, they may not be perfect (they've both got their faults; I'm no fool about it) but they've been pretty good children. Caused their share of worry but no real heartaches. It could have been the other way. Of course what you always want to know when that happens is, What went wrong? The little girl we lost, our middle child, who knows what would have happened to her? And this little Angela Diane. I wonder what she would have been? It's hard to think about, you know it?

I didn't bring much down here with me, we were in such a hurry. For the funeral I had to wear the same dress I came in. I had forgotten all about the fact that there would even be a funeral; I don't know what I was thinking. I was afraid Eleanor might be mad or embarrassed, about the dress. But she didn't even notice. Usually she's real particular about everything. Wants everything just so. And *sensitive*. I've never seen a child that could get so riled up about almost nothing. All you have to do is look at her to hurt her feelings.

She's always been her daddy's girl. I'm not being critical. But I think it shows. Other children pick up on that kind of thing, in my opinion.

Always right there beside him. Never could stand to be indoors. She'd work with him out there in the peaches, ride with him in the truck. Couldn't stand to come in and help me with the house or the other children. It was like pulling eyeteeth just to get her to set the table. In the summer after supper,

when Henry'd put on his cap and say he was going back over
to the canning house to check on things, she'd jump up right
along with him and say, "I'll go help," and the back-door screen
would be slamming before I could even say, "Well, what about
these dishes?" Of course he never said anything to her, let her
go right on. Never said, "All right, young lady, how about helping your mother some." He's never mentioned this, but I think
it about killed him when she got married. Not that he thinks
Jay's a bad boy. He has nothing against him. But her daddy
just had his heart set on her being a great artist or something.
I didn't care; she was already three years older than I was when
I got married.

When they came up to South Carolina that spring after Jay
got home from Vietnam and said they were going to get married, was it all right with us? I said sure. Eleanor was going to
quit college, work till Jay could finish school, they said, then
she'd go back. "Daddy," she said, when they had finished giving
out all their plans, "Daddy, did you hear what I said?" He said
nothing, just got up from where he was sitting, and turned off
the TV. I think if he'd said anything to her, anything at all, she
wouldn't have done it. But he didn't say a word.

She worked with him all that summer at the canning house,
earning money, planning the wedding. She paid for the whole
thing. Flowers, caterer, everything. I thought it was real smart
of her, but it seemed to hurt Henry's feelings.

They got married out in our backyard. She had this trellis
made that they walked under. It's just like I said, she can't stand
to be inside.

Our one that we lost was just the opposite. It was like the
outside scared her. She stayed right with me, her thumb in her
mouth, with that old blue blanket. Talked to this friend she
made up, called her Amy. Who knows where she got it, not
from me. Her name was Diane. I think it's sweet that Eleanor
named her little girl that (funny how children do things you
never even know they're thinking).

She was sick a lot. Allergic to anything she touched. Cow's
milk, pineapple, yeast bread, dog's hair, even the peaches. Just
everything. We had to feed her goat's milk when she was a baby.
The smell was terrible. They gave her some kind of medicine,
and it turned all her baby teeth brown. Made it look like they

were rotten. I was looking forward to when she'd lose all those little teeth and could get a fresh start. We used to save the children's teeth when they lost them. Slip them out from under their pillows in the middle of the night and replace them with new silver dollars. Pretend we didn't know a thing about it. I've still got one of Eleanor's, a molar. I've kept it all these years in a compartment of my jewelry box. Still has the string around it where I pulled it. I tied one end to a doorknob and slammed the door after counting to three. Henry didn't speak to me for a day, said I tricked her. I didn't think it was such a mean thing. Happened so fast she didn't even cry about it. Just let out a little gasp. What did he want me to do, go after her with a set of pliers? I said, "Okay, from now on you do it." I guess he did; I can't remember. Seems like by the time Luke came along we took them to the dentist more. Of course Diane never got that far. Never lost a single one of those ruined teeth. All the enamel was eaten away, up to the gum. It looked like it would have hurt, but she never said anything.

Lord, it's cold for April. Well, if it doesn't get down to freezing, it'll be good for the peaches because this is the first cold snap we've had. All spring we've been running around in shirt-sleeves like it was June. Not many people know it but if you don't have enough cold days, the crop won't be much good. Of course if it gets too cold, you can lose everything. It'll wipe you out. A couple of years before Eleanor graduated, we had an awful time. We were trying to save for her college, putting every little extra aside. But that spring was so cold, we had freezing temperatures almost clear up to May. We lost so much of the crop that all that summer we had our workers canning green beans, limas, tomatoes, anything we could get our hands on to make up for it. I wanted to get a job in Greenville to help out, to make ends meet. But Henry said no, wouldn't hear of it. I don't know why. If it didn't hurt my pride, what was it to him? Eleanor was supporting Jay there for a while, before Fitz had them move in here. Henry didn't seem to think anything about that, at least he didn't say so. Times are changing though, anybody can see that. I'm not just talking about what the kids are doing.

Look at politics. My people were always Democrat. We voted for men that helped the farmer. The little fellow. But everybody's gone crazy. Ten years ago who would have ever believed Henry Glass would vote for Richard Nixon? But what are you going to do? Vote for this McGovern crackpot? I don't know what's going to happen.

Kennedy was shot on my mother's birthday, the same year Diane died. Isn't that weird, the way some things stick in your mind? *What date was it that Kennedy got killed?*, Henry asks me. Mama's birthday, November twenty-second. *What year was it Diane died?*, an insurance form wants to know. The year Kennedy was killed, 1963.

It was spring then too. But a little later. May. We were coming back from church. The baby had been sick, so I left him home with this colored girl that worked for us: Carrie. Diane had fallen asleep during the service, so I carried her out to the car and just let her stay in my lap. She always liked to ride up front with me. She wasn't quite six, so it was okay for her to do that kind of thing. Eleanor was in the back, sulking. She had wanted to go home with a friend, but I had said no, she needed to have Sunday dinner with her family. We had planned to eat out. She was almost twelve, just at that age when they start arguing about things. Henry was driving.

The other car just came out of nowhere, they said. I don't remember a thing about it and neither does Henry. We've always been thankful for that, not to have that to play back through our minds. It was some kid in his uncle's car, drinking beer. Eleanor hardly had a scratch, just a little cut on one of her knees. Since it was nearly the end of the school year, they went ahead and took her out of school, and she lived the summer with my sister. Mama took care of Lucas. Me and Henry were in separate hospitals because we had such different kinds of injuries. They sent him up to Duke and me over to Charlotte. I didn't see him for two months, or maybe a little longer. Maybe it was good. I don't guess either one of us had the strength to help the other. It took everything we had to get over our own injuries, is what I'm saying. And it's what I said before too, about one person not really being able to help another person with grief, if you know what I mean.

It's like I've been watching Jay and Eleanor. They're real polite to each other, but they seem to get out of each other's way as quick as they can. He goes out to the den and closes the door and turns on that rock music. Stays there all day, his long legs sprawled out on the sofa. I wouldn't have it if I was his mother. In about two shakes I'd have him snatched up from there.

Well, Eleanor's not much better. She sits outside with a sweater on, pulls a chair out into the sun. This morning I was down with her and his mother at the kitchen table, eating cereal. Eleanor was just staring. Not saying a thing. Fitz spoke to her, asked her how she was feeling or something like that, and she didn't answer. She just kept staring. It was rude. Finally I said, "Someone has asked you a question, young lady." Well, she burst out crying. I should be more patient. I know she's still sore from the delivery, still so upset about the baby, but that's no excuse for losing your manners. "Do you think you're the only girl in the world that ever lost a baby?" I said. "You're young. You'll have others." I don't know what came over me, what made me say it. Henry says I've always had a terrible temper. Well, maybe I was mad. Maybe I felt like she should be pulling herself together. But I felt so bad about it afterward. No one said anything. Eleanor ran upstairs, and Jay's mother walked out of the room. Picked up some mail, acted like she was busy with things. I went upstairs, tiptoed around. When you're the visitor, you're afraid to touch a thing, make too much noise. But you know what? It feels like everybody is a visitor in this house. Nobody walks freely. Nobody yells out and slams a door. Maybe it's because of what has happened, but it feels to me like it was going on before.

I've been up here in the guest room until just a few minutes ago, when Eleanor knocked on the door. I said to come in. I was sitting over here in this chair, trying to work on my Sunday school lesson (I'm going home Saturday) but mostly looking out the window. She stuck her head around the door and said, "I was wondering if you'd like to go for a walk, Mama." I said sure, that sounded good. She hardly ever asks me to do anything with her, to go anywhere.

She's down the hall, changing into her tennis shoes. Atlanta's so hilly (much more than it is up where we are in South Carolina), and I wonder if it's smart for her to be hiking around yet. But she says she wants to, says she's got to get out.

I can hear Jay's music from downstairs. He's played the same record I bet a hundred times. I never listen to that stuff, don't know who any of those musician people are. But he's played that record so much even I can remember the words to those songs. Listen. *Tin soldiers and Nixon's coming, we're finally on our own. This summer I hear the drumming, four dead in O-Hi-O.* Why would he play such a thing? It all sounds so sad, makes you crazy. Well, he's going to have to snap to, I say. Buck up. Act like a man. Go on out and get himself a good job.

The room they were going to use for the nursery is across the hall. There's a crib in there, with a mobile hanging from it that Eleanor made. She's a smart girl, very creative. All the gifts from the shower her friends gave her are in there too. But they've been stacked in a corner and put back in the tissue and boxes. Soft little gowns. Padded bumpers. Music boxes. I guess maybe she'll take everything back. I'd tell her no hurry. When I got home from the hospital after the accident, some of the people from the church had cleaned out Diane's room. Packed up all her clothes and toys and put them in storage. They thought it would help, not to see those things. But I could have killed them. Sometimes murder seems so easy, doesn't it? Where *did* they put that blue blanket? I've always wanted to know. Why didn't anybody ever say her name?

Eleanor's door just opened. I guess she's ready. She'd better pull on a sweater. The sun's shining, but it's blowing hard out there. I know she won't wear anything on her head.

Well, I'm ready too. I could use some fresh air myself. Stretch my legs.

I wonder which way we're going, what we're going to say?

Fitz: 1974

$\mathcal{I}$ am traveling to farthest points, collecting miles. I stay in small, family-owned inns I read about in travel guides and leave only when the owners get too friendly and begin inviting me in for dinner or asking if I'd like to play gin or watch a little TV. A couple of times I've said okay, but I'm always sorry. That's not to say I don't get lonely. I guess we all do, don't we?

When I was in Portland, Eleanor's postcards started coming. (I call home every few days and let them know where I am.) This first one was addressed to me in care of the Oregon Inn. There wasn't a word on it from Eleanor, just a scribbled note from my son (*work, weather*) but on the front, painted by my daughter-in-law, was a view of my Atlanta house. Heavy front door, red, rounded window shutters, stone steps. In Monterey another one came. More *work*, more *weather*, and a sketch of the garden that my late mother-in-law tore her cuticles on: dwarf boxwoods, English ivy, leggy quince, dog-eating rosebushes, all seen through the open door at the end of the back hall.

There've been plenty more cities—Tucson, Albuquerque, Pueblo, Rapid City, Minneapolis, Chicago. All along the way I collect things for my store: dung-fired pottery, arrowheads, old magazines, erotic-looking lamps. I send home truckloads of chairs, paintings, sides of barns, and ask my son to see that they are placed in storage. (He balks, but he'll do it I know.) I find an Apache basket that is over a hundred years old and a woven bowl that is priceless. In a secondhand store I find a pair of silk-screen evening pajamas that once sold for a thousand dollars. (I buy them for fifty and wear them—no one knows me here—before adding them to the inventory.) Objects, treasures, junk. I collect them with the miles.

And in the mail I get these three-by five-inch hand-painted postcards. On one side there's *Dear Mother;* on the other, scenes from home by Eleanor.

Here is a view of the chair in my bedroom, the tall, lacy windows, the firescreen, the carved, pink-Georgia-marble mantel. Here is my old neighbor, a retired psychiatrist, weary, wiry, missing one eye. Here is Jay's orange-colored cat, who once peed on the dining room carpet, which, because of the smell, had to be thrown out; I always thought that cat did it with pleasure, just to show his spite; I am a friend to dogs.

Here is the view out my upstairs window—curving city street following the dry creekbed, the hill with golfers, the club. Here is the iron gate with those deadly roses. Here is my son.

Here is my mail from Atlanta. I know what she's saying: *Come Home.*

What Eleanor doesn't know is that I stay away because the sight of her makes me sick with sadness. They're in bad shape, my son and Eleanor. Anyone can see it. So I stay away because I'm afraid that if I'm around, my fear will spread, maybe contaminate any chance they still have.

I've got this rented car, paying a fortune for gas, and I'm driving around outside Chicago. Around these little towns on the river (flat land, wide, not like at home), where they've got arts and crafts from the locals. A few antiques here and there. I don't care about any of it, really. What I like doing is parking the car and walking down the sidewalks, listening to people at lunch counters, looking in the frosty windows. It's October; I'm not used to this kind of weather. Yet every place I go I think, *I could live here.* I like to imagine it. Myself becoming friends with the lady who runs the laundry. Getting in shape and jogging every morning down that path on both banks of the river. I could do it. I could live someplace besides Atlanta. And if I lived in this little town or one of the others, I wouldn't have to see Eleanor's face. I wouldn't have to watch my son come home every day, plop down on the sofa, and turn on the record player and close his eyes. They don't ever talk anymore.

I've never thought he was easy to get close to. I'm not sure why. He was always such a sweet, good boy, but one that stuck to himself. Sullen, you could say. He'd come home from school and I'd say, How was it? And he'd say, Fine. What did you do? Nothing. Who did you see? Nobody. Did you want something to eat? I guess. That kind of talk can leave you out in the cold, make you want to wring a child's neck, stick a smoking firecracker up his you-know-what. Anything to get him going.

It may have been his father. Of course I'm not blaming. I'm the first to admit I've made a lifetime of mistakes myself. But there was always something between them. Dan was such a perfectionist, and it was just so hard for him to let anybody alone. He tried. I could see him trying. But something in him just wouldn't let things go. He'd show Jay how to do something, something simple like raking the yard. Not just: here's the rake, here's the basket, let's get going. He'd show him step by step. And then when Jay would do it, Dan would always be sure to praise him, to tell him he did it well. He was good about that. But after he'd done all that patting on the back, he'd go and do everything again himself. Rerake a whole section of the yard. He'd tell the boy to put up the tools, and Jay would do it. He'd go out to the gardener's shed and say, That's good, son. And then he'd go in there and rearrange everything. Move the rake to a different hook, knock dirt out of the shovel. What did it matter? Jay never stopped doing what was asked of him, but he went no further than where he was told to go. Lost all his enthusiasm, it seemed like, just stopped trying.

A doctor told me it would happen. He said, Your son's the type that will give up if he thinks he's not the best; as long as he's at the top of the class, he's fine—as soon as he thinks there's someone smarter, he'll slip all the way to the bottom. That's pretty much the way it happened. It was even worse though after Dan died.

Jay was just sixteen. He'd come home after school every day and slump down in the den. That boy could flat wear out a camelback sofa. And he watched so much television I just knew it was going to ruin his eyes.

You'd think his father's death would have made us closer, but it didn't. It got to where I didn't even know what questions to ask. He'd get mad about almost anything. I'd try to talk to him about college, had he sent off his applications, things like that. But he'd storm over, didn't want to listen to any of it. It's not that he was bad, that he was off drinking or stealing hubcaps or anything like that. He hardly ever left the house. But for all the talking we did, it was like there wasn't a soul at home.

Strange how I'm actually closer to my daughter-in-law than I am to Jay. It started before they got married, I guess, when they were still just dating.

We live near Emory University, in this area of town called Lullwater, in a house that my husband's father built. Eleanor was going to Emory, just a freshman, when she and Jay met. He was a couple of years older, but he was like some young people are, you know, unsure of what they want to be. He had been in college, and then he quit. It's not like he got thrown out or anything. His grades weren't even that bad. He just didn't know what he wanted to do with himself. He got jobs here and there, with former associates of his father, something to give him a little spending money. Anyway, he met Eleanor down in the bookstore at Emory Village. I think he would have gone back to school after meeting her, maybe gone to Emory too if he could have gotten in. But he got his draft number: seven. We laughed about it, you know, because that's always considered such a lucky number. He talked more to me then than he ever has, was kinder in a sense.

I've thought a lot about this—and now, I may be wrong—but I have the feeling he was relieved somehow. Not that he wanted to get drafted, to get put on some huge airplane and be sent halfway around the world to fight in some war none of us knew anything about (he didn't even *play* with guns when he was a child). But I think he felt that it made up for things. You know, for his floundering; his not knowing what he wanted to make of himself.

By the time he left for basic training, he and Eleanor had gotten serious. Right after he left, she started walking over from the school to see me. We'd talk about what he said in his letters: it was snowing up in Knoxville; everybody called him Reb, because of the Georgia accent; he was hungry. We'd bake things and send them to him (he said that even a Snickers bar and a Coke tasted good). When he left for Vietnam, we both took him to the airport. It was so hard. I walked way up the long corridor to a coffee shop and sat at a table looking out at the runway, to let them have some time alone. I thought, But he's so young; why don't they get old men for this job?

When we were driving back from Hartsfield, I asked Eleanor if she'd like to spend the night at the house. It was a cloudy, rainy Sunday afternoon, and Sundays always seem so lonesome, I said. She said they were for her too, even in a crowded dormitory. So she spent the night, and we ate a bowl of soup together in front of the fire, played a few hands of gin rummy. Every once in a while she'd look at her watch, and one time she said, I guess he's in California by now.

All that year he was over there, she'd spend one or two weekends a month with me. (Actually he was there less than a year—eleven months; they let some of them out a little early, though of course it didn't seem like it.) Eleanor and I talked a lot, and not just about Jay. We went to plays. To movies. I'd treat us to a nice dinner out, maybe have a little glass of wine or two (though don't tell her mother about it). One time we caught the train at Brookwood Station and went down to New Orleans to see an art exhibit. While we were there, we went to one of those girly shows, sat in the back in the dark so nobody would see us (though who would have recognized us, of course, way down there?) and stared and giggled and elbowed one another. I bought a pair of blue jeans, and we put our feet up on the back of the train seat in front of us and talked like teenagers all the way back home. She *was* one of course—a teenager—but I wasn't. I felt like one though.

A couple of times I had gone by her dorm to pick her up, and when I'd walk down the hall to her room, looking in at what all the girls were doing—jam-packed rooms, posters all over the walls, music, them sitting around on the floor—I'd think, I could fit in here. I'm forty-seven. But I don't feel it. But then, who does?

Somehow I didn't miss Jay so much that year with Eleanor around. I guess she felt the same. But she should have dated some, that's what I told her. She was too young to be waiting around like that. How could it help Jay anyway, her sitting at home, him over there? But she said no, what she was doing was what she wanted.

He got back in January, and they got married that summer;

first of August. They rented a little apartment in Decatur (didn't own a thing but boxes), and she quit school. He was going to go back to the junior college and then try to get into Emory. When he finished, she'd go back too, they both said. Everybody went right along with it, her getting that drafting job, perking coffee for architects. Her parents didn't say a thing. I thought it was ridiculous. *Stupid!* She only had a little over a year left of college, and she was such a good student.

It wasn't until she got pregnant that they moved in with me. She came by the house right after seeing the doctor. She hadn't even told Jay about it yet. I've always worried about how I reacted. I was happy later, of course, and I'd give anything in the world if that little girl had been all right. But when Eleanor told me I thought, *They're too young.* I'm not sure what I said, you know, the first thing that popped out of my mouth. But oh, it hurt her feelings—she looked so shocked, so surprised that I wouldn't be delighted—and I had to explain that I was just thinking about her, how hard it was going to be, that was all. I smoothed things over as quick as I could and even talked about how much fun I'd have with the baby if they'd come live with me. From that point on, I acted like it was the greatest thing in the world. Still, I've always been sorry about my first reaction that day.

These postcards are the only things she paints now, my son tells me, these little watercolored cards he writes me on, the only thing she has done since the baby died. It's such a shame. Every bit of it.

Just two days before the baby came, she was still upstairs drawing. She's trying to teach herself everything about color and line, composition. She reads things in art books, looks at other people's pictures. I've tried to get her to go back to school. I've told her I would pay for it—I want to. But she won't let me. (Stubborn as a mule about taking anything from anyone.) She read me this quote by Mary Cassatt about how you could learn as much from museums as you could from art classes. I tell her, Look, we don't have that many museums in Atlanta, do we? She just laughs. (We have one.) So I buy her art books for presents, anything they've got at Emory or over at Ansley Bookstore. They order things for me, things I read about and think she might like. Jay's proud of her, that she can pick up things like that from books. But at the same time, I think it makes him kind of mad.

Before the baby came she worked every night up in her studio. There's a third floor to my house, a big, open vaulted room with windows at each end that you can open up, and they let in the best breeze. She asked me right after they moved in could she fix it up for her studio. I was so excited. I had the man who helps me out in the yard carry up this old cat-scratched sofa that used to be in one of the bedrooms, and her easel and all her things. I love the smell of turpentine, the sight of all those tubes of paint. I used to go up there sometimes in the middle of the day when she wasn't home and just lie down, maybe take a nap.

I asked did it bother her to have me up there when she was working (she doesn't like any noise, can't stand it when Jay's playing his music—I don't know how they worked it out in that little apartment they had). But she seemed to like having me around, liked to use me for a model.

She used to have me strike a pose, and she'd stare at me for a couple of minutes, then turn to her big pad of newsprint and say, "Okay, relax." Without looking at me again, she'd start sketching with one of those stubby pieces of charcoal. *Intent*: she wouldn't look up once. She called it "memory drawing," read about it in one of her books, how it's supposed to strengthen an artist's eye. "You actually get it down better," she'd say, "when you try to draw it from memory than when you're looking at the real thing."

I'd try this myself. She had a coffee can full of paint brushes next to her easel. The label had been torn off the can. I'd stare at it and the brushes, then close my eyes and try to remember the number of ridges on the can, the colors of the brushes: eight, I think; yellow, green, red. I'd look at Eleanor. Close my eyes. Twenty-three-year-old face, puffy and blotched from pregnancy. When I was her age, women called those brown splotches the lovely mask of pregnancy. It was a honor, that mask, something everyone was proud of.

When she was painting me, I'd remember all kinds of things like that. I'd remember playing Rook when Dan and I were first married. This couple down the street would come over, and we'd put Jay in his playpen and we'd play till ten or eleven o'clock. The men would mix themselves drinks. The other woman and I—her name was Peggy—we didn't drink anything at first. Women didn't much then. But slowly, bit by bit, the fellows would have us take a sip of theirs: bourbon and Cokes, whiskey sours, Tom Collinses. Just a swallow. It was sort of thrilling, like we were doing something wrong. I guess that sounds ridiculous, but that's the way it was. After a while, Peggy and I were the ones who mixed the drinks and we'd bring them in to the guys, red maraschino cherries bobbing in the sours. I remember that we giggled out in the kitchen like foolish girls. I guess it made us feel sexy, who knows?

Sometimes I'd lie back on that old sofa upstairs (we threw a fringed shawl over it and an assortment of odd pillows) and close my eyes, and Eleanor would paint me like that. We didn't say a thing to one another; I'd just listen to her brush rubbing back and forth across the canvas. Maybe she thought I was sleeping. But I was awake, remembering. About when Jay was a baby, about how scared I was before he was born. And I'd go back even further, remembering living with my mother and Nannie. I'd think about those family reunions up in Tate when I was a child.

Before Eleanor started drawing me, I hardly ever thought a thing about the past. I didn't even think I had any early childhood memories (we must block things like that out, and it's only when we're really quiet and peaceful that we let ourselves remember). Listening to that scratching on the canvas, to Eleanor letting out a little sigh every once in a while—I knew without opening my eyes that she was standing there staring, her brush held in the air, trying to figure out a problem maybe, or which color to use—I began to remember all kinds of things. Things that happened when I was just a baby. Things I didn't have the slightest notion I knew. Maybe they're only things my mother told me and I think I remember, I don't know. I know there are not a lot of three-dimensional pictures I can slide into view, the way you would look at something in a stereoscope. But I remember my grandfather's face (he died when I wasn't but about two). It's long and angular, caved in near the mouth from illness and a life of bad luck. His few teeth have long, brown vertical stains, like the porcelain cracks in the bottom of a coffee cup.

But these are probably things I know from looking at those old fading photographs I have in the attic, not from personal recall. The memories that I believe *are* truly mine—not from family albums, not from listening to my mother and Nannie talk—are centered around motion and touch. Sometimes sound and smell.

What I'm certain is *my* memory of my grandfather is the vibration of a rocking chair, its runners sawing across the slatted boards of his sagging back porch. The chair slows, stops, and he pulls himself upward a section at a time, and the back steps give—even under his light weight—as he waits for me on each rotting two-by-four. I am two years old, and when we are in Tate visiting, I am with him every step. I know only from since seeing similar hands that his must have been rusty and yellowed at the bottom of each bony finger. I know from holding those hands that they were rough and moved in little jerks and held far tighter than he must have realized—holding to the point of discomfort, against danger. At the bottom of the steps, I follow him (it isn't hard to keep up—his breathing is so labored and his movements are so slow) over his rutted yard. His arm makes a long, lingering arc above my head, and there is a noisy fluttering at his feet, all around me. I run from his chickens, and he stops laughing only because he can't breathe. His cure is pulled from his pocket and set fire to. Smoke and burning phosphorus make their way to my nose, and I breathe in hard. It won't be long before my family learns that my lungs are vulnerable too, and all my life since I've tried to stay away from the men's Marlboros even though their smell is so intoxicating.

Less than a year later, Gandy will be dead from the emphysema that sits in his chest and inflates it like a water-soaked barrel—the accumulation of too much nicotine and marble dust. But for now he smokes with difficult pleasure, and I follow him step for step, breath for breath. All around my feet are dusty little sticks left over from a dead hardwood that's been sawed down and chopped for winter. I pick up these rough twigs, rub them on my clothes, slide them in my pockets. One by one I pull them out for a smoke, but mine, unlike Gandy's, are reusable—never tossed aside—and my mother dumps scores of them out of my pockets each night and saves them for me, even though her firmest belief is that imitation is harmful.

I don't remember Gandy's dying—they must not have told me—but the hands and the shuffle I see, I know they're real. Today, I can pick up some twig, run it over my fingers, stick it between my lips, and immediately remember his sweet, sick, tobacco-scented breath. I tell you, it's the truth: I never remembered a bit of this until Eleanor moved into my house and started painting.

We never went back up to Tate much after Gandy died, and even when we did, on Sunday afternoons to visit Nannie, Mother always paced around the house, across that yard, like something was about to grab her. And when we'd leave, her Plymouth flying back down Highway 5 to Atlanta, she'd demand, "Roll down your windows! We need some air!" She had screens put on all our doors at home, and had some handyman who was hunting work unstick all the windows that had been sealed with years of paint and caulking. Even in the middle of December, she'd still have the kitchen door propped open with a little iron frying pan, and the furnace blowing. After Nannie moved to Atlanta to live with us, we returned even more rarely, just to take Nannie back to visit her husband's grave in that weedy cemetery near the railroad tracks, or to visit a cousin or one of her old neighbors.

My mother hated the place. She feared, I think, similar suffocation. Not the kind that had killed Gandy (breathing in quarry dust and unfiltered cigarettes), but the kind of smothering that goes on in poor, isolated little places, from the kind of oppressive air she thought she breathed in Tate. From mountains closing in, maybe. She always used to say, when she'd get back to Atlanta, that she was amazed to see how high the sky rode overhead in other places. In the foothills of Appalachia on a wet foggy morning, the sky can come down and sit on your lap. And with that sky weighing on you, you feel like you can't dare move or breathe.

I think she was afraid too of marrying some boy who'd work at Georgia Marble and perhaps have his hand or his skull crushed before he was forty. Of having a pack of skinny, black-headed kids and watching them grow up in Gandy's chicken-pecked dirt yard, pinworms in their guts, and ringworms making red circles above their ankles. These things happen.

My mother wanted prosperity. She wanted Atlanta, with sidewalks and brick houses. She wanted nothing to do with the Tate she had known as a girl—milky plastic flapping over the windows in winter; rusted old cars sitting dead out by the road or bumping over mud puddles in the yard; chicken shit on the sole of every shoe; Gandy's rattlesnake skins flat and shiny, stretched out and nailed to boards on the inside walls of his barn, the rattlers collected in a Mason jar like some kind of treasure. She wanted no part of it. She had seen men flattened by falling boulders, seen women pressed into old age as they tried to make their life in the crack of a hill. Mother wanted flatter land and blowing air: a city.

There is a mountain road up above Tate where you can pull over in your car and on some nights see all the way to Atlanta, sixty miles away. When my mother was growing up, looking out over the ridges to Atlanta was like looking at something as far away as the face of the moon. But she believed in flight, and believed that reaching either place was possible.

She married the first person who could get her there, a flat-topped, overweight Life of Georgia salesman from Statesboro named Louis Fitzgibbon, who ate a whole package of chocolate ice cream Hunkies every day and who promised a lifetime of luxuries he could never deliver. Well. He was fifteen years older than my mother and died when I was four. I remember him less than I remember Gandy. He traveled most of the time. When he came home, I do remember he brought packages that my mother ripped open, throwing wrapping paper around the living room like confetti. He smelled of chocolate and shaving lotion, I remember that too. And he habitually jiggled the coins in his deep pockets with thick, wide fingers, making it sound like sad, lonesome, faraway music. I was named Louise (for him), but no one but my mother and Nannie has ever called me anything but *Fitz* or *Mother*. I like both those fine. I've always thought I was too large for a soft, musical name like Louise, too untidy. Even my *husband* never called me anything but Fitz, and he was about as much a stickler for things being proper as you could get.

I married a wealthy boy, trying to make it up to my mother,

I guess. But I never felt anything but embarrassment and shame when she came to visit me in my big house. Not embarrassment of her, of course, but of all our *things*, the money. I nearly died the first time she saw the Ballards' uniformed maid. Funny how you can so misread your parents' wishes, like holding up to the light a strip of dark negatives and everything having the opposite values of what they have in real life.

Dan and I were only nineteen and twenty when we moved into the Ballards' cool, gray stone house on Lullwater Road. I got pregnant right away (much quicker than Eleanor), and everyone said that we should stay. I didn't mind, really. The place was so big and weighted and seemed as perfect and clean to me as a piece of fine lead crystal. I was pampered; the Ballards liked me. And in those early weeks of morning sickness, when it was a burden to keep my head above mattress level, and when I was half listening to Dan and half wanting to die, when he spoke steadily and patiently of *opportunities* and *dreams*, I didn't care what we did. I just wanted to be well. And since the house was so comfortable, so roomy, it simply worked out that we stayed.

Sometimes now I try to move through the patterns of that early period of my married life, to see how it happened, to imagine how it would have been if we hadn't lived with the Ballards, if I had married a poor man instead of Dan, if I had gone on working at that photographer's studio around the corner from my mother. But nearly everyone stayed home in those days if they could afford it. No one imagined working unless there was a financial reason. And they were right about my staying home, I believed, every time I looked at the sweet damp head of little Jay. I just loved smelling him. "No," I said, "compared to this, nothing else in the world is important."

It was during that first year we were at the Ballards', with Jay just an infant, that someone started fixing up the old Carson place next door.

The Carsons, I had been told, were a wealthy, childless couple who had built their house the same year as the Ballards and had lived there for nearly thirty years. I had heard the story several times about how Mr. Carson had died of a stroke when he was in his early sixties, and how the week after his funeral Mrs. Carson and her maid had begun unloading the china cabinets and had packed up every piece of dinnerware and sterling and crystal in the house and stored them in boxes at the far end of her kitchen. "You could go over there," Dan's mother told me, "and there wouldn't be anything out on any of the tables, anything that showed someone lived there. Not a picture on the wall, not any little whatnot on a shelf. Not even a loaf of bread on the kitchen counter. Nothing. It was like she had everything packed and ready and was waiting to die." But Mrs. Carson had lived on for eleven more years, her tiny French tea cups sitting in damp cardboard boxes at the back of the house. She finally died, of malnutrition it was guessed, and her property had been tied up in an estate for the nearly two years since.

On several occasions, Dan's father had his own yardman mow the lawn and try to trim some of the overgrown privet hedges over there. But the place still had a black, dead look. And there was a musty, animal smell that came as freely through its dark broken windows and rotting screens as the cats who let us know they made their home there in the middle of every night.

Sometimes on those nights, when I'd wake up suddenly to what I thought was the baby crying, I'd go over to the window and look out at that old house and wonder what had gone on there when the Carsons were alive, what they could have said to one another in all those high empty rooms. I listened as though I thought I was going to hear ghosts in conversation. But all I ever heard from that house was the sad sound the cats made, and sometimes the imagined voice of an eighty-pound, diamond-studded old lady crying for her husband, or the baby she never had.

A work crew suddenly appeared at the old house and woke us one morning with sawing and hammering. The bank that had been trying to settle the estate decided finally to get the place cleaned up enough to sell. Most of the Carsons' furniture had been removed long before, but all those things that hide in the bottoms of closets and the backs of cabinets and shelves were now being swept and shoveled out of the house. All one afternoon, while upstairs with the baby, I watched them haul off truckloads of old papers and books, broken light bulbs, a man's flattened straw boater, black-bottomed pots and skillets, the worn-down bristles and metal ring of a Fuller commode brush, twisted curtain rods, unmatched and mildewed shoes, a yellowed piece of woman's underclothing. All those intimate, insignificant articles that had been of use when the Carsons were alive. But like the Carsons themselves, the house had died too, and its corpse was being attended to at last: undressed, disemboweled.

It was the university that bought the house, and the young couple that moved in temporarily were two poorly dressed anthropologists who were guest professors at Emory for two quarters. They ate strange foods, attended the Unitarian church in the basement of a nearby elementary school, and they had five children—two from previous marriages, though we never knew from hers or his. In Lullwater, they did not fit in; of course they didn't bother. They kept to themselves—their lives, their work, their children, and each other.

They played some kind of African music over there, and when no one was looking, I'd move my shoulders to it. I was dying to know what was in that house—probably nothing, but I imagined all sorts of fascinating things: skeletons, shrunken heads, tribal masks, poison darts, phallic symbols. More than once I was told: Now keep away from over there.

But I used to watch them out the window, secretly follow the children around the backyard, hoping I'd see them carry something terrible like a bone. One time on a Sunday, after they'd come back from church, I saw the husband playing out there with the little boys. He called in to her, and a few minutes later she came out carrying a tray of red drinks. I had no idea what was in those two tall glasses, but I believed I could taste it. It smelled of ground dark herbs and something animal-like, I imagined. Apparently she had been changing clothes when she decided to make the drinks, because she was wearing nothing but a slip and a pair of stockings with a run. The afternoon light was passing through her red hair, making it look like that pink angel's hair Mother and Nannie and I had decorated the tree with every year at Christmas. With her glasses off, and in that slip, I believed she was the prettiest girl I had ever seen. Her face was heart-shaped and small, the kind you might see in some magazine advertisement, resting in the model's own perfect hands. And that cream-colored slip stuck to her so, you could see this little indentation in her chest, just below the breastbone, and her tight little set of ribs. It made me feel so big and awkward. I wished that I could make an appointment with someone and say, Listen, I want to start myself all over. I always felt I moved like a steamer trunk and this little red-headed scientist moved as easy as a cat.

She stood so close to her husband that I thought for a minute or two she was going to forget that even her children were there. She was rubbing her fingers over his chin, brushing off something that was caught in his bushy brown beard. Something ran through me. Something rose and dropped inside me as I watched them touch that way. It reached something in me that had never been reached before, not even in the darkest hours of any night with Dan.

I had been missing something lately, but I thought it was me, and the baby. I thought too that maybe people just had to let up after a while on how they feel, that it would be impossible to spend your whole life dwelling on someone the way you do in the beginning, when every waking second you've got them on your mind. The summer I met Dan, I'd walk along the streets and think I'd see him—even though I knew he was someplace else. Or I'd pretend to see him and imagine running up to him or imagine that he'd seen me and I hadn't known, that he'd stood staring at me, and then I'd look up and find him there. And when I'd be at home, sitting in the kitchen with Mother and Nannie, waiting for him to phone, something would catch in my throat and I'd think, This will kill me if he doesn't call soon. And I had married him by Christmas, even though I felt like maybe after all it wasn't what Mother wanted me to do. But I couldn't wait to have Dan, couldn't wait to be able to hold on to him all the way through the length of one full night. He acted like he felt the same way, but it seemed that as soon as he had that, it was enough for him. He wasn't fond of touching. He'd do his business and then be through with me until the next time. He didn't like me coming over to him, draping my arms around him, putting my breath up near his ear. "Come on, Fitz," he'd say, rolling his shoulder at me, pushing away, "stop fooling around. You know I've got work to do." When I was pregnant, although I was hot and swollen and scared about what was happening inside me, I still wanted his touch, for comfort. But what we had done to one another in those earliest nights before the baby came wasn't half what this redheaded girl was doing up next to her husband, right in front of me and their string of children.

Thinking about them later has made me guess that maybe what my mother disapproved of was never the money, the big house, the expensive clothes, the different accents of the Ballards. I think she had looked at us—Dan and me—and had known some things. In those few years she had with my father, what she enjoyed was not the gifts, not the showering of wrapping paper. What she had had was this: what that scientist and her short, bearded husband appeared to have. Something that went beyond simply being faithful and polite to another person. Dan Ballard was a good man. And so is my son. But what my mother knew, and what I know now, is that there are ways of feeling that most of us never even try for. Never even imagine.

The scientist and her husband moved on. To someplace in California.

I'm no fool; I know about the mind's ability to make lots out of small, seemingly romantic visions—to turn visions into the sentiments that suit you. Maybe those two penniless anthropologists had nothing more than the average married couple. But I had seen them long enough to know there was something out there *I* wanted—love, touch, adventure, *something*. I guess it must have showed. I heard my mother-in-law whispering to Mr. Ballard and Dan about my nerves. In those days women were never unhappy, they just had spells with their nerves. People didn't take it lightly: a nervous woman was believed to be in more danger than if she were suffering from typhoid or cancer.

We stayed on. Dan's parents died, one by one, without a lot of pain or bad years. And except for Dan's illness and death, we had no great tragedies in our married life. We had a child, an inherited house, a great deal of money. We padded along.

If it had been different, if there had been some awful thing—the death of a child, an infidelity, a lost fortune—maybe we would have looked closer at what it all meant, where we were going. Maybe I would have let the beat of my heart race on instead of holding it so in check. If it had been now instead of then, if I had been a woman of Eleanor's generation, who knows what might have happened?

When Dan died, I lost a companion. A mate. My husband. We had been married seventeen years. I can hold my head high about the way I cared for him when he was ill. I stayed with him every day, went with him to every doctor's appointment, watched them put the needle into the veins in his hand and fill his body full of the chemotherapy treatment. I pulled handfuls of hair from his comb and from his pillow and threw them away. I held his forehead with a cool washcloth when he vomited into the trash can at the side of the bed. The whole thing confused him so, totally baffled was the way he looked, like *how could this have happened to me, Dan Ballard, who was always so in charge?* Sometimes I see a large man with silver-specked hair, and a cigar in his mouth, and for a second or two I think, *Dan.* I would like to see him. I'd like to have a conversation. But when I am alone now and yearn for the dips and swells and the warmth of a man's body, it is not him I think about. Maybe that's wrong.

I was crazy to have the kids move in with me. What was I thinking?

I'm going to sell the house if I ever get back. I'll give them most of the money if they want it, and I'll find myself a shop where I can sell this junk I'm collecting—something with maybe a little apartment in back. None of us has all that much time, really, is what I've been thinking, and what I've got left I sure don't need to spend wandering around in a three-story mansion. Eleanor and Jay don't need it, either; they need to get out. Other than that, I have no idea what's going to happen.

Maybe nothing.

But I watch Eleanor and I watch my son. I see the way he tightens up when she speaks to him, when she walks across the room to the sofa, stands between him and the TV, and tries to touch him. She turns away and looks as if she's bracing herself for disaster.

One is not right and the other wrong. Two hearts are

breaking. There has been one death already in their small family. And now I think there is another kind of dying going on. Something else is getting strangled.

So I stay away. I can't bear it.

Yesterday I checked into a bed and breakfast here in northern Illinois, in an old Victorian house by the side of the river. The owner is a sharp, quiet woman, just friendly enough to be polite but someone you know is plenty busy with her own life, doesn't have time to fool around with chatter. But she did ask where I was from and what I was doing. I told her the places I'd been, how long I'd been gone. And she said, "Don't you miss your family, your friends?" And I thought, *Who are my family? Who is my friend?*

Maybe I'll stay a few days here, just drive around this flat, broad countryside, pick up a piece of furniture or two, a piece of old lace. Maybe I'll accept a dinner invitation from this woman, if she asks me. Maybe I'll pick up a stray dog, hold out my hand and let him lick my fingers, buy him a nice leather collar, and at night sneak him into my room.

I'll call home now, give the children this new address. Wait here long enough for another postcard to come.

It's their loss that I worry about. *Their* pain that pains me. I can't think about what it means after that. Can't think about losing the woman that has become my daughter, or watching the drifting of my lost son.

Eleanor: 1981

⟨⟨⟨∼⟩⟩⟩

They knew at work, almost immediately, that I was hooked on Will. I'd be bent over my drawing board just staring, and Carroll or Carter would come over and snap their fingers and say, "Earth to Eleanor." They knew what was happening.

I work at the Atlanta newspapers in the art department. My cousin Mason, who is a reporter there, helped me get the job. My job description says "illustrator," but usually I work on charts and bar graphs, little boxes of lines and columns and numbers showing the state's economic forecast or the annual rainfall of drought-stricken Southern counties or the SAT scores of Georgia's high school students. Yesterday I finished a map of the Atlanta interstate highway system to go with a story that predicts how many more years the roads here will be under construction and how when they're finally finished they'll already be outdated by a good ten years. Every once in a while I get to draw an illustration for the op-ed page or for the Perspective section of the Sunday paper. But not usually. Usually it is graphs and charts and maps.

I don't mind so much. In fact, in the beginning, when I first got this job, it was almost a relief. The work was monotonous but simple; I didn't have to think; and for those first years after I left Jay in that big house and found myself the basement apartment behind Garden Hills Cinema, I didn't want to think. Not about anything.

The people who worked with me then always covered for me; they told people I was spacey, but they walked around me as gently as if I were a burn patient down at Grady Hospital. I'd well up with tears so much in those days that they thought Jay had left *me*, instead of the other way around.

I've been in this office longer than anyone. The others have come and gone, gotten better jobs at ad agencies or as free-lancers, or they finally go do what they wanted to do in the beginning: paint and draw. But I've just stayed on here, waiting for something, but not ever guessing it would be Will.

The two who've worked with me for the last couple of years are young and good, and they'll go on too. But for now we work side by side every day and know each other's quirks and sounds almost like family.

Carter has one eye that looks off at an angle, the kind where you don't know which eye to follow. It makes me nervous, but it's probably even worse for Carter. You can see him trying to be patient and act natural when people keep looking back and forth during a conversation. But I bet he wants to hold up a finger and say, "This one!" so they will stop. He was hit in the face with a rock when he was a child, and that same eye (I never really know if it's the left or the right one) has been blind ever since. It has affected him, you can tell. Most of the time he acts scared to death of women. (Not me; *other* women.) And when one of the editors talks over a story with him, he hardly ever says anything; just nods and mumbles behind his hand, "Yeah." "Yeah." "Yeah."

Carroll is the tough one, or at least he pretends to be. (I can't imagine parents giving a boy such a name.) He is always bringing in things such as fake shrunken heads and cut-off hands and hanging them from mine or Carter's Luxo lamps or hiding them in one of the supply drawers. One time he let a chicken loose in the newsroom. A memo went around offering a reward to anyone who knew anything about it. No one could prove a thing, but it felt as if a hundred pairs of eyes were on our glass walls all of that week. Carroll likes the attention, I think. Likes to feel that no one thinks he's a sissy.

Whenever someone comes in to give us an assignment, he will crack all his knuckles and bend his fingers backward or curl up in his chair and moan as if he is dying. He closes the door to our office and cranks up the radio, and at least twice a day someone from the newsroom comes in yelling for him to turn the thing off. Sometimes he will even carry the radio with him to lunch, up on his shoulder, and he'll stop black kids on the street who are doing the same thing, hold up his hand for them to slap at, his and their music blaring at each other, and he will yell to them, "Hey, man, how's it going?"

Carter and I, if we go with him, stay about ten feet behind.

The day I told them I was getting married, Carroll rolled on the floor holding his sides and yelling, "No, darlin', no. Don't do it." He spent an entire week listing every reason why a person should never get married. Of course you just can't argue with a lot of those reasons.

He's come around now though. If he had to admit it, he would tell you he's crazy about Will; that week of ranting was mostly for show. I am older than Carroll and Carter (they're twenty-three and twenty-four), but they're both very protective.

We are the odd birds around the paper. We wear our jeans to work and our sweat shirts. (The first time CoraRuth came to visit and saw me getting ready to go downtown that way, she sighed and said, "You don't really have a job, do you?") There's some kind of dress code for the newsroom folks, but they don't say a thing about the way we come in; they think we are different.

I believe they have us in that glass office at the side of the newsroom just so they can keep track of us. The truth is, none of them hardly says a thing to us except the three or four newsdesk people we work for. And even then, it's as if they aren't really talking to us, they're just standing over a printout arguing with each other about the art. The younger reporters are dressed so smart, rushing in and out with those little tan notebooks in their hands. I sit back and watch them moving around the newsroom and they look to me like those figures on computer games. It's funny how people can act so tough and big, when if you really look closely (or really know them, like I know Mason), you can tell they feel about as tiny as all the rest of us.

At the newspaper was where I met Will. Carroll had been doing projects for him on the side (he's always doing free-lance work), and I had seen him several times. Once we rode up to the eighth floor together on the elevator; there were three other people in there, including a couple of young feature writers. They kept talking about their skis, how they had to get them waxed because they had gotten so banged up the winter before. When the two got off on six, Will turned to me and the other passenger, a copyboy, and said, "Y'all's skis all right?" He didn't even know who I was. But it was probably then I knew I liked him.

He didn't speak to me again until several months later when he came to pick up a poster and an ad he needed designed for a black dance troupe that was coming to town. I heard Carroll saying, "I couldn't get to it, Will. I thought I'd have time, but I'm swamped, man."

"Somebody's going to have their butt in a sling, Hardin." (That's Carroll's last name, what he tries to get everyone to call him.) "I *need* this thing."

I didn't like seeing Carroll in trouble, so I said, "I can do it." Both of them looked over at me as if neither one of them had any confidence that I could. Will said, "I need it quick and I need it to be good."

I just nodded. In the beginning he was so brusque and all-business that I never dreamed there would be anything more. He talked so fast you would have thought he was a Yankee, and sometimes when I'd take a layout to him he'd never even speak. He'd be on the phone, barking orders to someone at the Omni or at a limousine service, and he'd motion for me to open up my portfolio and let him see what I'd done. He'd inspect it closely, without missing a beat on the phone, and then he'd look up at me and nod and mouth, "Perfect," and then not look up again even to see if I was gone.

Something was strange. I was actually beginning to look forward to him calling and saying how he needed something yesterday. It felt slightly dangerous, dealing with someone so demanding, someone whose reaction I was rarely able to guess.

This one time, when I'd stayed up nearly all night designing a flyer on a series of summer concerts at Piedmont Park, he looked it over and said, "This isn't what I wanted. I can't afford three-color on this, and you didn't leave enough room for copy up here. This isn't what we talked about at all."

I stood there for a minute chewing my lip, then I said that if he gave me more than a twelve-hour notice on something every once in a while he might get back what he wanted. "Everything you want is a rush, and I'm sick of it." I turned to leave, and then I turned back and said, "And you know what else? I don't need it." What I was looking for was an argument; but he just rocked back in his chair and smiled. "You're right," he said. "Let's go get some lunch."

I was floored. Everybody I knew sulked if you got angry, or else they liked to keep the argument going. Will was the first person I'd met who if he was wrong, said so; and if you were, he expected you to do something about it. I'd seen this with his secretary, Josie. She was about six inches taller than Will, a large-faced black woman built like a coat hanger. All day long he yelled from his office to hers and she yelled back. I'd been there several times at the end of a day when she'd come into his office and give him a whole handful of things he had to take care of, reminders of appointments the next day. She'd stand there shaking her finger at him and say, "Now don't forget this." Over and over she would appear to be leaving, but she kept coming back to tell him one more thing, and then she'd say, "And go home. I better not call here at nine o'clock and find you still working."

"I hear you," he'd say, and keep on with what he was doing. What most people don't hear from Will is thank you; but what they do hear sometimes is that silent, "Perfect." Will lets people know things, if they're good at paying attention.

I was beginning to catch some of what Josie had, I could feel. It wasn't love exactly, but like her, I was getting to where I'd climb mountains. I could be bone-tired from the job at the newspaper, but if it was something Will needed, I seemed to get my energy back; once I even stayed home from work—said I had a sore throat—to finish a job for him. But I couldn't quite figure him out. He was predictable (I learned from Josie that he ate the same thing for lunch from the counter of Wool-worth's every day: fried chicken, sweet potatoes, turnip greens, and a Diet Coca-Cola), and then he wasn't predictable at all. As busy as he always was, he'd take time for the strangest things. On that first day we went to lunch, we were walking down alongside Central City Park, and he picked up fourteen cents' worth of change. He'd crisscross in front of other pedestrians when he spotted a coin on the sidewalk, and each time he'd bring it over, hold it up for me to see, and say, "Lucky penny." (I have seen the man crawl under a parked truck to retrieve a quarter, and yet spend a thousand dollars without thinking twice about it.) And that same day at lunch, as big a hurry as

I thought he was in to get back to the office, when we passed an ice cream shop, he took me by the elbow and steered me in and said, "We need one of these."

I told him, "But I'm not hungry."

He looked at me hard, like there was something wrong with me at the core. "What does hunger have to do with it?" he said, and he ordered us three scoops each of pistachio almond fudge.

I'm pale compared to Will. And I'm not talking about skin coloring. I'm talking about what CoraRuth would call gumption. I'm just sort of pink and light. Pastel. And Will is red. Will Turner is crimson.

No one lies to Jay. I mean Fitz doesn't say to him, No, I haven't seen her. She just doesn't say anything. He travels a lot (drives this big blue Buick that makes him look so straight-backed and proper), works for an insurance company that his father used to own a part of, and never guesses how much Fitz and I see of one another. Whenever he's in town, he'll stop by to see her, dressed like a lawyer or a stockbroker (he's taller than Fitz but not as large), and she'll try to get him to stay for dinner or walk around the corner to the Thai restaurant she likes. But he is always in a hurry, as though Fitz or her shop or the dogs make him uncomfortable, and he never stays long. And of course I never run into him; we move in different circles.

But I was here in her shop talking with her earlier this morning, waiting for Will, when the bell over the door jingled, and I saw him come in. "Oh Lord," I said. "There's Jay."

I'd been sitting back in a broken Morris chair scratching between the ears of one of Fitz's dogs. "Get down, Gus," I said, and ran behind one of the display racks that holds used sheet music and piles of old *New Yorkers* and *Life* magazines. Fitz tried to get to the front of the store, but Jay met her halfway, making his way past all the furniture and lamps and books as if he were moving through cobwebs. He kept inching back toward the rack where I was crouching. It was the dog that was getting his attention.

Gus was sprawled out on his fat belly, his nose in my direction, thumping his tail and whining. He wanted more of what I had been giving, and he was trying to get me to come out of there. Jay squatted and snapped his fingers; but dogs know who likes them. It was me Gus had the point on.

"What's wrong with that dog?" said Jay.

Right away, of course, I realized my mistake. If Jay found me hiding, it would be far worse than if he had simply seen me sitting in the chair. And if Will arrived as soon as he was supposed to, to have lunch with me and Fitz, what would I do? I couldn't just keep crouching there with the dog sniffing at me and leave all of them to figure things out and introduce themselves to each other. There was no doubt Jay would think someone was trying to put something over on him, and it would all end up seeming like a lot more than it was.

Good old Fitz was trying to get Jay's attention, showing him a desk set she'd just bought at auction. But the dachshund was crawling toward me, bit by bit, and Jay couldn't stop watching him.

If I had any guts, I knew, I would stand up, go over and shake Jay's hand and say, Good to see you. I'd tell him I stop by from time to time (not several times a week as I really do), and Fitz and I just visit. But I have no guts when it comes to Jay, not even now. So I stayed hidden, praying that for once Will would be late.

"Have you got mice, Mother?" Jay asked her.

"I wouldn't doubt it," she said and then asked if he was hungry and tried to get him upstairs for one of her bacon, cheese, and pineapple sandwiches. He might have gone too, but the bell over the door jingled again, and we all looked toward the front of the store.

Instead of Will it was Lawrence, the man who helps Fitz out in the shop. You can always tell it's him by his rapid little toy soldier steps on the hardwood and then the *bangbangbang* of his voice as he greets a customer. He is a tight wire of efficiency and chatter, and he makes more sales than Fitz does and knows antiques better. Jay seemed to have forgotten the dog temporarily, and I could tell it was now little bald Lawrence who was making him nervous. When the man was out of earshot, I heard Jay whisper, "Why don't you get out of this neighborhood? There's bad element everywhere."

"Oh, don't be silly. I've never even been robbed."

"You know what I'm talking about, Mother. These guys are everywhere. You're living in a neighborhood of them. It makes me uneasy just to go shopping at the Kroger."

He looked uneasy, too, when Lawrence came back from the little office he and Fitz share, and in a moment or so Jay was saying how he'd better be going. Normally, Fitz would have tried to get him to stay, but she hadn't forgotten who was hiding behind those *New Yorkers*. As he walked toward the front of the store, he turned and looked back my way one more time and said, "That dog's not right."

My pulse was pounding like wild. Not from seeing Jay after so long, but from fear of getting caught. As I watched him leave, I had the same sad feeling I used to have during those last weeks before I moved out, when I'd wake up in the middle of the night and see him lying on his back on the far side of our king-sized mattress and for a second or two not be able to think who he was. A couple of times, and this is the truth, I couldn't even think of his name.

Fitz and I didn't say anything, but you could tell we both thought the same thing. Not that we had done anything wrong, but that somehow we hadn't done something right.

I never dreamed I'd be getting married again. I'm not exactly sure what I had pictured for myself; maybe my dog, Harley, and me going on as we have been, and then moving someplace where it's inexpensive to live, one of those little fishing towns on the Gulf maybe, or someplace up in the mountains, someplace where I could afford to do nothing but paint. Sometimes on the weekends, we get in the VW and drive, Harley's head stuck out the window, his ears blowing and him biting at air, and we go places where that's possible. I drive us up to the mountains, to Dahlonega, the old gold-mining town, and we walk around the courthouse on the square (Harley running around with his nose to the ground, sniffing and hiking at every signpost and building corner), and I look up at the second-floor windows above insurance offices and hardware stores, and I wonder if maybe someone would let me live and work up there. I've dreamed about that, about being the local artist and how I'd sell my paintings at the crafts fairs when people from Atlanta drive up there in the fall to look at the leaves. I'd set up a stand and sell four- by five-foot canvases next to someone selling jars of sorghum syrup and pear preserves. That's one of the lives I've imagined. But I never thought about being married again. Until I met Will, I didn't even want to think about dating.

I've told him every bad thing I've ever done, thinking that might make him go ahead and give up on me now. In one afternoon, I spilled it all—every lie I could remember telling; every mean thing I had ever done to CoraRuth; every sin I had committed; even what I didn't think I'd ever admit to anyone —that when things were so bad between me and Jay I'd sometimes, just for a second, wish he were dead. I know that's awful, I know it's the most awful thing in the world, but his being dead sometimes seemed easier than trying to figure out what we were going to do about one another. That's a terrible thing to put in words—that death seemed preferable to divorce. That somebody's death did, his or mine.

The loneliest I've ever been was sitting in the same room with Jay, on the other end of the very same sofa, with the beam from the TV the only thing coming between us. How strange: to be sitting next to someone you're supposed to know and feeling as if you're the only person left in the world. Maybe the brave thing would have been to stay. If he had been an alcoholic I don't think I would have run out, or if he had had some illness. But there wasn't anything wrong with Jay except he couldn't, or wouldn't, pull himself up off that sofa long enough to love anyone enough to matter.

On some of those lonely nights with Jay, I'd think there must be people like Will out there, people who swallow life instead of it swallowing them. But I guessed I'd never meet one of them, not one who would love me back; I guessed I'd only know nibblers, people who taste just a few things, one little bite at a time.

Will's waistline is the same as Jay's trouser length, and the other way around. That doesn't bother him a bit, not that or his sweet woolly beard or that little monk's cap of no hair on the back of his head. I've never once seen him walk into a crowded room and appear to be concerned about what people were thinking of him, or that he even cared how he looked.

But as great as Will is, he can wear you out with all his

energy. Sometimes I try to keep up, but I just can't. What happens is that Will seems to take up all the air in a room. And when he's gone, I'm left feeling like this deflated, stretched out balloon.

So much living goes on in other people's lives that my life always feels small in comparison. And I'm not just talking about Will. Sometimes it's people I see in the grocery store, or walking down the street. Once I followed this woman home from the farmer's market because it seemed like there was more going on inside her beat-up old station wagon than there was in my whole existence. There were faded and peeling bumper stickers on that Chrysler that said: BAN THE BOMB, and DON'T EAT LETTUCE. Sayings like that; you've seen them, I guess. There were four or five children of all ages in that car, bouncing around like Nerf balls. And the woman just kept throwing an arm back and resting her hand on one of the heads now and then to stop someone's vaulting. The car pulled into the drive of a Victorian house near Grant Park, one of those transitional neighborhoods where the prices were still low and a fifteen-room house could be bought for a song. There were Big Wheels in the front yard and a lawnmower, left where it was stopped, with half the grass cut and the other half ankle high. A tray of limp impatiens was near the front door, left there apparently by someone with good intentions and not enough time. I sat out in the VW with my windows down, hearing some of those kids calling to one another, listening to doors slamming. I pictured books and magazines strewn everywhere inside, bicycles propped against walls in the foyer, shoes and shirts and caps cast off here and there, sand scattered outside the cat box, a jar of peanut butter left on top of the piano. Big pots on the stove full of good things cooking.

It seems I am unable to live that way—I don't know how to do it—but I love to look in other people's windows. If I were a braver person, I would have gone up to the front door of that house and knocked and asked if I could stay for supper.

Maybe that's why I stay here so much, why I let Fitz cook me chowders and bubbling fruit pies, why I lie on the sofa and eat her pickled green beans with my fingers. Why I fall asleep listening to her make her Conservancy telephone calls and why, before I met Will, I would sometimes sleep over.

I love Fitz's room. That's all it is, really, just one large room that was built for warehouse storage above her shop. It's a strange place to call a home, I guess, with sale stickers on half the furniture and fat, round bolts of upholstery fabric propped everywhere. But it's where she wanted to live. She had a little kitchen installed in one of the back corners and there's a bathroom in the other. And she has three big crates back there where she throws recyclable things—aluminum cans and newspapers, certain kinds of glass bottles; once a month she hauls them off to one of the places that buys those sorts of things.

But the main area where she lives is up front, next to the tall, wavy windows that overlook Piedmont Avenue. That big space is always packed full of things: odd chairs, a gateleg table, books, paintings, Belgian lace curtains, antique clothing hanging from a Victorian hall tree, statues, maybe a four-poster bed with big throw pillows on it made from old oriental rugs. All that color and texture. It's almost too much for the eyes.

If a customer comes in looking for a special item and Fitz doesn't have it in the shop, it's just like her to decide that a piece of furniture she's got upstairs, maybe even what she's been sleeping on, is the very thing they want. There's nothing she has that isn't for sale. She doesn't do it for the money; she just likes helping people find what they think will make them happy. It's all just stuff to her, not much more important than some old ketchup bottle. I'm the one who occasionally gets attached to something. I loved this oak stack bookcase she used to have that was filled with all kinds of objects she couldn't find another place for. I had in the back of my mind I'd put it in a painting someday, it and all that Depression glass and those oriental fans. But Fitz sold it for nearly nothing to a young couple who just needed some storage. She didn't even unload it. Sold them the whole shebang, even the fans.

It used to be that I practically lived here, I came around so often. Up until last year, before I met Will, I'd come over almost every evening after work, and Fitz would cook us something in the back, and then we'd sit around and talk or listen to her music. Sometimes I'd just lie down on one of the sofas and stare while she bumped around doing things—ripping articles from environmental magazines, writing letters to the governor, making phone calls. Every once in a while, if it was on a Friday or a Saturday night, we'd turn out all the lights and watch the men going into the club next door. Fitz loves to look at the gays, study what they're wearing. Once she ran down and tried to trade something in the shop for a black fringed shawl this one guy had on. He took an earring (she's still got the mate) and an ebony bracelet. He's become one of her most frequent customers. They all love her, the homosexuals; and she's great friends with the club's owners and their regulars.

I didn't see Fitz for nearly two years after Jay and I were divorced.

She moved out of the Lullwater house before we did, thinking, I guess, that it might give us a chance to work things out. But with Fitz gone, it was just the opposite. The house got smaller instead of larger. We were knocking into each other everywhere. It seemed that no matter where I went in the house, I'd hear that sad soundtrack from him watching reruns of M*A*S*H.

Everyone knows it, but it's still true: divorce is awful. Those months right before and right after I moved out, I had trouble functioning; I felt as if I'd lost my arms, or as if they were wired behind me, and every step I took I knew I was going to fall hard on my face. Every morning when I'd wake up and wonder how I was going to get through a day of work, I'd think: I've lost all my blood. That's what it felt like, as if I were walking around with all my life-giving forces sucked out of me. Fitz called several times to see how I was doing, if she could help with anything, but I always told her I was fine, and then I never phoned back. I didn't go to the shop, either. I guess I believed I had let her down for one thing (though in a different way than I felt it with Henry and Mama). But the main reason was that it didn't seem fair to Jay. I didn't know how I would feel if every weekend he got in the car and drove to South Carolina to be with his former in-laws, although I couldn't imagine such a thing. And, as bad shape as I was in, Jay didn't have anybody. I wanted to be around Fitz, but I believed he needed to be with her more; and the last thing in the world I wanted was for her to spend time worrying about the both of us. That's one of the ways people can be so stupid: I thought that if Fitz didn't see me, she wouldn't think about me. But of course she was thinking about me all the time, just as I was about her. It was similar to grieving in a way, that black hole of a feeling you have when you know you're never again going to be with someone you've loved. That's what all three of us were doing, grieving, and it lasted for years, it seemed.

Fitz read in an article somewhere that pets help reduce loneliness and depression. So, on one of her regular runs to the Fulton County Humane Society, she got me Harley. (She goes once a month and adopts the dog that's been there the longest and the one next in line to get put to sleep; she usually finds a home for it, but sometimes she doesn't and she has to keep it herself; she's got five at present: Gus, Winfred, Estelle, Gilbert, and Herbert. She's good with names; she's the one who named Harley.) She brought him over to my apartment, brought with him this basket bed and red and green plaid pillow, and a bag of Ken-L-Ration and heartworm pills, and let him run around sniffing all the empty corners of my basement apartment. She said I needed company; said this same article told about how animals are good for the human psyche. I think that's right. Unless maybe you and the animal are too much alike.

Harley's nervous, and so eager for affection it's kind of humorous. A manufacturer's reject is what Will calls him. He's a mixed breed, of course (the best kind of dog, if you ask Fitz's opinion), about the height of a coyote, with a little narrow mouth and flyaway hair. I don't believe I've ever heard the dog bark, but he does wail; he cries to come up on the bed every night. He's also a great pretender. But the thing about Harley that's different from humans is that he's got a tail that tells the truth: he can be lying down, his eyes closed, appearing to be asleep and unaware of a conversation that might mention his name, but while his face and body don't give away a clue, that tail will be flopping, flying, sending fur balls down the hall.

Before Will started coming over, it was always just Harley and me in that damp apartment. Every night at eleven, we'd move from our position in the living room to our position in bed. He'd always start off as a tight ball down at the footboard, usually already sleeping while I watched the evening news. At eleven-thirty I'd start reading something to make me drowsy. But generally, even if the book worked, by two A.M. I'd be fully awake again because Harley had wormed himself up toward the middle of the bed. Sometimes he got as far as the pillow, and I'd wake up with him next to me, on his back, paws held up limp in the air, and snoring.

While the dog slept, I'd fret. I'd worry about whether or not Henry had enough money put away for his retirement, if CoraRuth knew a woman her age ought to be taking those calcium tablets. Things that never seemed so urgent in the mornings.

I know I spend too much time worrying, but how can you not worry when there's so much out there that can hurt the people you love—car accidents, heart attacks, carcinomas, tax audits, loan officers, brittle bones: the possibilities are endless.

But nothing ever seems to worry Will. Not these things, not the kinds of things he has no control over. And if he does have some control over them, he fixes them. Snap, just like that. Action. I've never seen so much action. I mean this man starts his day with both feet moving, without a dab of anxiety, with him saying, "Okay, ready!" He can fall asleep in midsentence, in *his* midsentence, and then go without a toss or a tumble or a single concern for the next seven hours.

When he stayed the night those first few times, I'd sometimes pretend that I'd slept just as guiltlessly as he had, that I hadn't stared at the glowing green numbers on the alarm clock at three and four and five in the morning. It worked for a while, but the more comfortable we became with one another, the more my own awful normal countenance took over (I can't help it), and he learned the truth.

Sometimes now, when he sees me struggling in the mornings, he'll come over and help me out of bed and say, "Don't hurt yourself." Then he'll whistle and I'll hear him and Harley clicking down the hall, going after my coffee. You wouldn't believe all the activity. All that whisking of eggs and omelet making and music playing. I used to wonder if there was something wrong with *him*. I'd think, What if this man's hidden the fact that he's not all there and I've just slept with someone who's a little moronic? But no, Will's a wonder. My love. Even now I can't believe my good fortune at simply knowing such a man. And to have him for a husband? It's scary.

We're only inviting Fitz to the wedding and our closest friends and my cousin Mason and his wife. But no other family. CoraRuth's been mother-of-the-bride before; and I don't know what Henry's thinking, me a divorced woman. And Will's family—he says it doesn't matter, that they won't care one way or the other. I'm not so sure about that. But one thing I do know, I don't want anyone sad being there. I just want those around us who are happy. And that's why Fitz is coming. She's all for this wedding.

We're having lunch here with her today, she's cooking something special and she's got a bottle of Brut iced down back there in the kitchen. Then tomorrow we're going over to the stone house they let you rent at Emory for special occasions, and we're getting married. Just us and Fitz and Carter and Carroll and these few others. Then we're going on a honeymoon to Europe. (I'm not so gung ho as Will is about that; I mean Mother and Henry are twice my age, and they've never been to Europe. I haven't got the nerve up yet to tell them that we're going.)

Will keeps saying that after we're married, I should quit my job and start painting. He looks at some of my old work, the big canvases that are stored up at CoraRuth's, my notebooks full of sketches, and he says I don't need to be bent over some drafting table pasting up charts about the Department of Transportation. He says I need to be back at my easel. Says that if I don't want to work at home, we can find me a studio.

I don't know.

I've worked as long as I can remember, since I was a child. And I've always liked making my own money.

Painting would be working, too, of course. In fact, in many ways it would be a lot harder, with no one but me to say stop and go. But I don't know how I'd feel if I couldn't sell anything and it was only Will paying the bills and me having to ask him for every dime. Not that he'd make me feel that way, that I had to ask. No, he says that everything he's got is mine, and the other way around. The thing is, I don't have anything, not even any money saved to help with a down payment if we buy a house. So right now, it's something we're sort of arguing about.

All the rest of it though, it's everything I could want. Just perfect.

Then why am I shaking?

What I've been worrying about is that maybe it wasn't Jay at all. Maybe it wasn't even the baby. Maybe it's me. Maybe I'm a jinxed person, and everything I touch turns to tragedy. Maybe I had something to do with the wreck and Diane. Maybe I'm the reason Henry's peaches can go wormy in your hand, why he can lose a whole crop in a season. Why there is never any money.

I love these old windows of Fitz's. Love the way the glass waves and ripples. Sometimes I think I could lie right here my whole life and just look *out* at Atlanta. I could be satisfied to hear about the world through Fitz, have Will come up every couple of days and tell me what's going on out there. Repeat to me all his conversations with clients. Tell me what's happening in the news. I could do it.

But instead, I'm going to get up from here and we're going to have this lunch—there's the jingle from the door downstairs (it's Will)—and tomorrow we're going to stand up in front of that Methodist minister, and nothing, not now, is going to stop us. Not even worry.

Ben: 1985

I'll leave was the first thing I thought when I realized whose house I was living behind. I was already packing up my things, stuffing my razor and shaving cream into my bag, when it suddenly hit me: Why? I was living here first, wasn't I? It was them that bought the house from the woman I already rented from. This is where I've lived longer than anyplace in my life.

That day I watched 'em moving in, I knew right away who she was. It was like something taking a hold of my chest when I saw that face. That's the same face she had when she was twelve years old. Now that was the darnedest thing: this little bit of a girl with skinny legs and scratched-up knees, but with this grown-looking face. So serious, like her daddy. That's Henry's girl, I said when I saw her.

So I'm packing up my things as fast as a squirrel. But then she and him comes back here knocking on my door. They say they just want to meet me, just want to let me know they'll go on with the same rent as the other folks, that they was glad to have me. I look at her real hard, waiting for her to say it. But she don't say nothing. There's not a thing there on that face that says she knows. So I say my name. I hold out my hand and say, Benjamin Bolt. And she takes the hand and says, "Well, we're glad you're here, Mr. Bolt." I'm watching her eyes though, checking. *Nothing.* She don't know me from Adam.

Okay. But what about Henry? What about if he comes down here, visiting? But then I think, hold on here, Bolt. What's Henry Glass going to do to you? There wasn't none of that your fault, was there?

So I start unpacking. Restacking the magazines. I'm staying.

But it was seeing her just out of the blue like that that got me to thinking. How many people do I know anyway in this world? Not that many, right? So how in the Sam Hill is it that I've run into one of them down here in Atlanta? What are the chances of something like that happening, one of them moving in right slap in front of me?

Well, maybe that's the way it's going to happen, I start thinking. Maybe that's the way I'm going to run into Evelyn. I'll just be over to my shoe stand, my head down, working hard on some customer. And I'll feel somebody behind me and I'll look around, and there she'll be holding on to the arm of some fellow that wants a shine. What then? Maybe she won't even know me, like Henry's girl. But maybe she will. Maybe she's been thinking about me too all these years, maybe she's even been looking for me and that's how come she's standing behind me like that. She and her fellow will take me somewheres for coffee and we'll sit down and she'll say, "So tell me about you. What have you been doing with yourself?" That's when something grabbed me again. I can't think of nothing. Evelyn finds me after all these years and I can't think of nothing I've been doing. Twenty-some years and I don't know what to tell her I've done.

So that's when I started writing it all down. That same day after Henry's girl knocked on my door, I start making my notes. I take this Day At A Glance appointment calendar one of my customers left behind on the seat of the chair, and I start writing it all down. Like this:

MONDAY
1 piece bacon 1 toast breakfast
7:04 bus to Five Points
customers waiting
1st / lawyer from upstairs, black wing
tips, dollar 50 tip, sore throat &
hangover
2nd / not a regular, busted-out penny
loafers, "Give me a spit shine Pop,"
talk talk talk, no tip
3rd / old Judge Dodd, same brown
lace-ups, old turtle face behind
newspaper, 25 cents tip

I get it all down. What I have for breakfast, for lunch, who my customers are, what kind of change they put in my hand, what they say. A man'll tell you lots of things when he's sitting up above you and you're down there slapping a rag over his shoe. It kind of relaxes 'em, you down there with the top of your head nodding, that rag going back and forth, back and forth. They just start talking, telling you things about their family, problems with the children, what the wife says, everything. There's a fellow over at the Trust Company that I know how much taxes he's paid over the last seven years. There's another one. A certified public accountant, nose like a worm farm, who goes to A.A. every day of his life and not a soul but me knows it. A man, if he don't know you, will tell you anything.

I let 'em. It's free. I just twist up my rag, rub a circle of color on their leather, and I shine and shine and shine. They just think they're talking into the top of an old head and not at anybody.

He don't talk. Not the one that married Henry's girl and moved in here. I'd been selling him a shine every month or so for a couple of years before he ever becomes my landlord. He just says, "How's it going?" and then goes to writing things on one of those yellow pads of paper. That pencil is tap-dancing. He's a man in a hurry. I know it's him by the way his heels click across the marble floor of the lobby where I've got my stand. He's polite, but he's thinking. He always takes out a extra dollar, folds it in half, and presses it in my hand. And then he'll say, "We'll see you," without really looking.

Since they've moved in here, he sees me on the street downtown, or when he races across that lobby, and he throws up his hand and says, "How's it going, Ben?" *Ben*. Yes, sir, he's got plenty on his mind, but he won't tell it. Not now. Not now he thinks he knows me.

Them others, they tell though. And I'm writing it down, every little thing. And when Evelyn says, "Tell me about you," I'll read it all out. I might even take her down to my stand and point at a face here and there, and she might say, "That's the judge, I'd know him anywhere." She'll see all these people who step up on my chair and tell me all their secret things and she'll think, He's an important man. She'll call up her mother and say, "Come see!"

* * *

She's somewheres. Maybe making up things about her daddy. Maybe she thinks I'm still with the railroad. Maybe she thinks I'm dead. I used to write letters, say I was making good. I'd write down her name with the old address, lick a stamp and put it in the corner and then wait. Some fellow would come in with a hang-up bag slung over his shoulder, heading out, to the airport or the train station, and I'd think of saying, "Hey, how about mailing this when you get where you're going." Let her think I was the one traveling to all those places, Atlantic City, Pittsburgh, Milwaukee. But I never did.

She might not have got them anyway. Her mama could have hauled her anywhere from Raleigh; maybe Maxene remarried, is what I'm figuring. She could have told some court I ran out, and got a divorce without me knowing. And this new man, he might have adopted Evelyn, given her his name. Might be him she's been calling Daddy. There might not even be an *Evelyn Bolt* anywheres around, no matter where I sent a letter, not one that would want to answer.

But still, it could be her that's wanting to find me. You read about these things in the newspapers. Children hunting down their real parents, even though they say they've had a good life with the ones that adopted them. I can understand it. We all want to know where we're from, want to look right in the eye of someone that's got our same blood.

When I come down here, I didn't know what I was going to find. Getting out was all I was thinking, getting away from Henry and all his hard luck. I didn't want nothing to do with broken-up folks, watching them try to glue their lives back together like some smashed-up mirror. No, Henry Glass wasn't paying me to take on sorrow. One old rusted trailer to live in ain't enough payment to take on that.

So I come down here, rode the bus down to Atlanta. I wasn't ever in a city before excepting Raleigh, didn't know where to go first, where to start looking. I just camped out at the Greyhound station for a couple of days, slept on one of the benches, ate flattened-out cheese sandwiches in the coffee shop. I didn't even walk out on the sidewalk, scared to take a step out of the place, I reckon. Then I started watching this guy shining shoes. He was a colored fellow, and he knew everybody in the place, or seemed to; called out to anybody. I watched him close. Started counting how many people he'd give a shine to during the day, and I started thinking: I could do that. I liked the feeling of it. Liked the way he seemed to know folks, but they didn't stay long, just got their shine, tossed him some change, and then walked on. He didn't have to *be* with any one person all that long, is what I'm saying. I watched him for such a spell that he finally come over to me and said, "Who is it that's paying you to look so hard?" I looked at him like I was dumb or something, because I was so shocked to have him ask it. Then he says to me, "I'll tell you one thing I'm not looking for, and that's competition."

I got up off my bag I'd been sitting on, and walked with it out those glass doors, walked up this narrow street to Peachtree. Picked up a few things here and there, odd jobs, washing windows, busing tables. Cooked eggs for a while at this pancake place. But it was that shoeshine stand I had my mind on. At night I'd go back to this room I rented and I'd draw it out, my stand, designed it myself, one with some storage under the chair. Drawed up a stool for me to sit on to match it. That's what I wanted about as bad as I ever wanted anything, that one shoeshine stand that was set up somewheres like it was my own business. Just a one-man operation. Hardly any equipment. I started collecting old pieces of clothing and towels I'd find, cutting them up and washing them at the laundromat, smoothing them out and folding them, stacking them nice and neat in my top drawer, saving them for shining rags.

One thing I learned: if you're going to shine shoes, you've got to be where there's folks going places or where there's folks that's got money. A poor man, and one with no place to go, he don't care whether he can see his face in his shoe or not. It's the man with the extra dollar that is going to climb up and be bothered to put a shine on his toe.

I started watching around: where is it that a rich man's going to have him a office? Where is it that he's going to stop in and have a cup of coffee or buy his lunch? I'd get on a bus sometimes and watch the ones with leather briefcases and nice shoes. Other folks would get off here and there, but them with the best suits and shines, I noticed, they went all the way downtown.

They're everywhere down there, men who are making money. They come around those revolving doors quick as rocks down a gutter, smooth as silver. The more successful they are, the straighter their eyes are looking ahead. A man with appointments to make don't give hisself any time for looking around. I can spot 'em.

Something else I soon figured out: it's them lawyers and bankers that care most about a good shine. Newspapermen and doctors, they don't give a hoot about what they're wearing. But a lawyer or a banker or a broker, and sometimes a preacher, they take care of their shoe leather on a regular basis. Some of 'em even got heads that shine.

So that's how I settled on where I'd set up, down in one of those buildings that's got lawyers' offices all around. There's a whole row of stands in a couple of them buildings, colored fellows slapping rags across rich men's shoes like tails wagging on a pack of dogs' behinds. That's not what I wanted, having to turn up a grinning face to the rest of that row, listen to their joking. I wanted my own operation, just mine, like I've been saying.

I got to following some of them slick business fellows from time to time, watching where they was going. This one, he comes out of a tobacco shop downtown, wearing one of them raincoats that I'm guessing cost him as much as a hundred dollars, and fancy Italian loafers. I've got my eye on him, and he's got his eye on hisself—caught his reflection in that store's window. He puts a hand up to his neck and then runs those long fingers through his hair. He looks down at his watch and then back at hisself, and then he's off walking fast, me right behind him. Four blocks I'm keeping time with him, and then he rounds a corner and that's it, gone! I've lost him, I'm thinking, and then I look through the lobby of this one building, and I see him standing there, standing at the door of a barber shop. This fellow's needing a trimming. He's also needing a shine, I'm betting, and that's how I ended up where I did, putting my stand right in front of that barber in that wide marble lobby. Where I set up, it's the kind of place you catch them fellows coming and going.

They're always leaving things behind. Newspapers, hats, briefcases, writing pens, packs of cigarettes. They leave 'em right there in my chair. Well, their minds is off on money matters, I reckon. One thing I've seen is that the more a fellow makes, the more worries he has. A poor man, he's got his mind pulled in to think about one or two big things: food, and sometimes sleeping places. But these ones that's making top money, they've got their minds stretched out in forty-'leven different directions.

I keep all the things they forget to take with them. I put them under the chair in that storage compartment I designed, just in case they remember where it is they've left something. They come back, some of them, after a little time. But most of 'em, what do they care about a pack of Viceroys or a day-old newspaper?

It was after I got my stand that I moved in here. Sometimes on Saturdays when my stand is closed (no businessman's going downtown excepting those first five days of the week), I get on a MARTA bus and just ride, trying to see all the neighborhoods. This one Saturday I was riding on the one that winds through Lullwater, just me and a couple of kids and a old colored lady, and we're riding down this nice street with big houses and stretched-out yards. I'm just sitting back thinking about who's inside one of those places anyway—somebody who's got in his closet a pair of shoes I've shined, maybe. Rich folks, you can tell, 'cause on a Saturday like that, warm and not cloudy, there ain't nobody outside cutting his own grass. Yeah, rich folks has got more worries, but they've also got people working for them on everything: washing their underwear, cutting their grass, rearing their children.

Well, I was sitting back, like I said, just taking it all in, when we pass this one house, smaller than most the others, and there's this woman pounding a sign into the yard with the wide side of a brick. I'm thinking, That's funny, and then I read the sign: GARAGE APARTMENT FOR RENT, with little letters after it that say, *apply within.*

I'm off that bus in two shakes, hiking back up that street, waving down that woman before she's back in the house. She don't like it I can tell, having to rent out. There's some money problems though, she's hinting, and we all do what we have to, I guess. She looks me up and down, and then I think pretty quick and say, "I'll be glad to help out here in the yard." *That's* the clincher. Nothing off the rent and free help with the zoysia. I've flat got that sign pulled out of the dirt before her brick's cooled down.

Every Saturday since, every Saturday till Henry's girl moves in, I'd been cutting grass, raking leaves, cleaning out the gutters. That woman's husband had been gone forever, just her and her two boys, and both them lazy as house cats. She let me do it, never said a thing. That's all right. What have I got to do anyway with a Saturday and a Sunday coming at me every week? I like it. Like keeping things up, and long as she don't start coming back and thanking me, I'm happy. But it's a different story with Henry's girl. She's the thanking type, like her mother. (CoraRuth could about worry you to death with her good manners.) Nope, cutting this grass is up to that hurried fellow. He can hose out his own gutters. I ain't going to start getting friendly with the landlord now.

Still collecting magazines. Only *Life* though. I tried a couple of others for a while, but none of them, not them newsmagazines anyway, have the stay power. But a *Life* magazine, you can pick one up from any week in any year and it'll tell you something you don't know. When they stopped making them there for a while, I started collecting the old ones, all those I left on Maxene's back porch next to that rust-marked freezer and wringer washer.

I've got my favorites: some from during the war, some from when Evelyn was a baby. This one here's a good one, July 16, 1951. It's got TV's DAGMAR featured on the cover and the announcement

IN THIS ISSUE
IKE'S PROGRESS
A REPORT ON EUROPEAN DEFENSE

I remember it good because Maxene thought she looked like that blonde on the cover. "Don't you think, Ben?" she kept saying. "That we look just like one another? We could pass for sisters. *Ben.* Did you hear me? Don't you think Dagmar and I look alike?" Maybe I said yes, I don't know. I just kept wanting to take that *Life* and add it to my stack out on that back stoop before she could toss it in the garbage like she sometimes did, where I'd find it later with corn silks and wet tea bags all over it. But I never did get that one back. Maxene kept it, carried it with her to the bathroom and to bed, got it wet and wrinkled and lost it over time, or else she hid it, I reckon, to see if I'd ask about it.

I found this copy though, a week or so back, at one of these places I go that's got old records and books and things. Traded it for a later issue I had a extra one of.

Old Gold!, Vaseline Hair Tonic, '51 Ford Victorias, Borden's Buttermilk, Fatima Cigarettes. I like just looking at them ads, how things have changed, disappeared. The clothes, too, what people was wearing, how they did up their hair.

But there was something particular in one issue that I remembered soon as I turned the page to it. It's a two-page spread of pictures taken of workmen in New York City, all of them in their uniforms, by this photographer fellow named Irving Penn. This Penn fellow, he's got pictures of your PLASTERER, your HOTEL DOORMAN, your CHEF, a DEEP-SEA DIVER, a PNEUMATIC DRILLER, a short, smiling PLUMBER who thought the assignment was silly, it says. A TREE PRUNER. Some others. I remember it because a couple of these fellows was my own age at the time, and I thought, Wonder why they don't have 'em a railroad man?

Think about it. On July 16, 1951, me, Benjamin Bolt, was twenty-five years old with a wife that thought she looked like Dagmar and a four-day-old daughter named Evelyn who was named for Evelyn Keyes because her mother had seen the actress in *Smuggler's Island* the week before.

Yep, that tree pruner, he was about my age then. Well, where's he now? I wonder. At home in New York City still, with the same wife, same misnamed children? Or maybe he made hisself a bad calculation once, put his foot on a dead limb, and fell from some old sycamore in Central Park and cracked his skull.

Most of the others, they were mostly middle-aged. *Middle-aged in 1951*. You figure that means at least a few of 'em are underground now, or in some nursing home, maybe in some daughter's apartment, ailing and complaining, saying every day that they wished they were dead when everybody knows it ain't so. That fat plumber, that one with a smile on his face, he could be dead. Maybe from a stroke or heart attack.

Anything is possible. Anything could have happened to any of them; but no matter what, if they've all lived till now, they've read the same headlines over the past thirty-five years as Ben. And if any one of them comes by my shoeshine stand in Atlanta on any day in 1985, we all know we've seen at least a couple of the same things: Eisenhower, Kennedy, NAACP, Nixon, Jane Fonda.

I wonder if any of them would say that one shot in *Life* magazine was the most important event of their lives? I would, if they'd had a railroad man there, if I'd been chosen. I could have been standing in my railroad uniform, holding up a red flare. I'd have put down that lunch box Maxene would have packed me, with maybe a tomato in it and a shaker of salt and a jar of tea and a glass container of lima beans from last night's supper. I'd have put it down out of sight, and stood up tall, holding my flare, and know that that picture was going to make Maxene clap her hands and holler. Make Evelyn take a dog-eared copy of the magazine to school years later to show her friends and come home at night and say, "No, I want to sit next to Daddy."

RAILROAD WORKER, the line under Benjamin Bolt's photograph would have said. Well.

That old plumber. You reckon where he is?

Some folks wonder what it is that happens to people's lives. I know. You get divided up by days, clicked off—one, two, three, four thousand ninety-seven. Click; you eat supper in front of the TV. Click; children fall through your fingers. Click; you get yourself a view of a brick wall. Click; twenty-two thousand days. *You're* dead.

Here's what I hope: I hope that old plumber's still around.

I remember exactly the fellow that left the camera.

He was loaded down with things. Briefcase, suitcase, plastic shopping bag with a teddy bear sticking out of it that's wearing a T-shirt that's got *Hotlanta* written on it. That was for his son, he says. There was something else in the suitcase for the wife.

Heading home. Here on business, a seminar. I don't ask from where, and he don't say. But this man's ready, you can tell. It's home he's wanting, that boy and the wife, because he's nervous as a cornered dog with a bone in its mouth. His eyes are darting everywhere; keeps pulling a airline ticket out of his pocket and checking the time. "How long will it take me to get to the airport?" he asks me five, six times. I tell him he could leave next July and still catch that flight he's got. But he keeps tapping one toe the whole time I'm shining the other. He wants *on* that plane, you can tell.

When I'm through, he gives me a ten, and I start opening up my cigar box, looking in there for his change. But he's already down off that chair, telling me to keep it. He's got that bear up under one arm, the suitcase and briefcase banging against him. He's *scooting*, for a airplane that ain't leaving for another four hours.

I don't even notice that Minolta till the next customer steps up, and he hands it to me and says, "This is going to walk, if you aren't careful." I tell him to hold on, and I grab the camera and run out the side of the building that traveler has left on. I'm looking everywhere, up and down that street, walking between the traffic. Nowhere.

I call Delta and they just laugh. "You don't know the passenger's name, or destination, or flight number?" No, just the time it's leaving: 7:42. They ain't going to help me.

Every night I carry that camera home, where it's safe in case somebody jimmies the lock on my chair, and every day I carry it back downtown, thinking he might come looking. Two, three months I do this. Nothing. Maybe he don't even remember where he left it. Maybe he's thinking *airport*, or *airplane*, or *restaurant*. Maybe he's forgot all about that ten-dollar shine. But still, I keep thinking he might come back. Every night I look at that camera, and I see that fellow, and I think, *Where are you?*

Every night I sit it on the table, and it's like it's something alive there. I can't stand it.

Finally, I do it. I figure how to open it up, and I take out the film and I take it downtown and take it to the photo place that's on my same block and say, "Here. Develop it."

I can't look at them pictures for several days though. I put that envelope they come in next to the camera, and it's worse than ever. There's something inside there. But I just don't want no part of it, not other people's personal business.

Thing is, when I do look, there's nothing there. A couple of shots of some fellows that must have been at the seminar with him. Some more of Atlanta: the museum, a hotel, different buildings. And there's one of a backyard, a boy and one of them scooter things. It could be any backyard in the world; it and that two-year-old don't tell me nothing.

I put it all in my sock drawer, the camera and them pictures. They just sit there, making me feel like I've done something wrong. I think about throwing them away—the pictures—but that don't seem right, either. I don't know what to do. Then one week goes by and I don't even think about any of it till I need a sock in the mornings. Another week goes by and I'm touching that envelope when I pull out a sock, and it don't even matter. Well, he knows how to get back on a plane and fly to Atlanta, don't he? It ain't my fault he let something slip off his shoulder and don't know how to find it.

I don't know what made me buy that Kodak film. Just saw it on sale in the window of that camera store and thought, *Why not?*

I never worked a camera. Had to read how to do it. Threading the film through there with these old cordovan-stained hands. Learned about focusing and that light meter. Read all about it. And then I'm set, but who in the Sam Hill am I going to take a picture of? Me, a man who don't really know nobody.

What I'm saying is, this whole thing with Henry's girl, it happened by pure accident.

That woman I rented from before, she had material heavy as a pea coat hanging over all her windows. Then Henry's girl moves in, and she yanks all that stuff down. Put up a shade or two here and there. But that glassed-in room off the back that she works in, there's nothing on the windows there. No curtains or shades. Day or nighttime, from my place, you can see straight in.

Now, it's not like I've got my eye glued to that plate-glass window all the time, trying to see something. I haven't wanted nothing to do with it. But sometimes, when you steal a glance out that way, you can't help but see her standing there. That's what she does nearly all day, stands there looking back and forth from something she's painting to what she's painting it on. Then sometimes she don't move for the longest time, just froze there like she's what's been painted. Other times she paces back and forth, keeps moving back and then up close. Chews on the end of one of them long brushes. Patience is what she's got, I reckon, to stand there like that all day; that or not good sense.

It was a couple of days after I bought that film that I was standing there at my window adjusting the light meter. Looking down every once in a while, reading what my book says about backlighting and so forth. There's lots to know, really, about a good camera. So I'm reading up on everything one more time. And then I aim out my window, testing something I've been reading. And then I just snap.

I don't even think about it for a second or two, then I lower the camera and I realize what I've done. I've got Henry's girl locked up inside my Minolta. I move behind my brown curtain, thinking she's going to look up at where I am, thinking she's heard that loud click. But she don't stir.

I move back in front of my window. I'm not even sure I got her, to tell the truth. So I look through the camera good this time. There she is, too, plain as life. Wearing a blue T-shirt and blue jeans, with paint smeared all over them, and this bandana kind of thing rolled up around her head like she's a Indian or something.

She's not as pretty as CoraRuth, I'm thinking. Nose too big. Looks like Henry.

I keep looking, and then my finger does it again. Another click. It's so easy. I've got part of a person locked right there in that black box I'm holding, and there ain't nothing to it. She don't even blink. Don't look my way. It's not hurting her one bit. She don't even know it!

I take the whole roll. Thirty-six pictures. It's like before though. I'm not sure what to do. They sit there on my table in that white envelope, them pictures just screaming out. I do it. I look.

They're too dark, most of them, and you can just make her out. I read up about light again, and about not taking a picture of somebody next to something like a telephone pole so it don't look like that pole is coming out of their head. That makes sense. I buy more film. I do it again. Again.

Before I know it, I've got piles of pictures around this place, all of Henry's girl. I'm thinking, Is this here thing I'm doing wrong? But it's not like I'm causing harm to anybody, trying to take something away from Henry's girl. It's just that I don't know what else to do with this camera or know who else's picture to take.

I keep 'em hidden in drawers though, just in case anybody comes in. What would they think? Two hundred pictures of her and that dog, and sometimes that hurried fellow she's married to.

On a Saturday one time, I thought I'd do something else, take some pictures on one of my rides. But people look away if they think you're going to point a camera their way. Maybe children's different, I got to thinking. So I get off when I see this playground up ahead. For a long time I just sit in one of them low swings, watching, my shoes digging trenches in the sand. Then I open the case, take off the lens cover, and I go over to where there's this boy coming down a slide. *Click.* I'm winding the film, thinking I'll take another. But this boy's mother comes over and grabs him up and runs with him to the car. She slings one hard word at me from over her shoulder. I don't say nothing.

So I just take pictures of Henry's girl. They aren't dark anymore. Or too blurry. Every day I practice.

That fellow I pay my money to over at the camera shop, he figures I must have a string of grandchildren, the amount of film I buy. Nobody knows nothing. Nobody knows there's not a soul in the world but Henry Glass's girl that I'm taking pictures of.

I'm ready though, in case this one person I know ever comes along. They come tapping a finger on my shoulder, I'll be ready. I'll say, Now stand right there. Smile.

And I'll pull that smile, so quick, up into my camera, and I'll never let it out.

Eleanor: 1986

I t's as if someone has flared out all the bristles on my brushes and sawed several inches off one of the legs of my easel. Everything is out of whack, mostly me, and I can't work at home anymore. I stand there and try to paint, but nothing happens. So I leave the house every morning after Will goes to work, I take the phone off the hook so he'll think I'm still there working, and I set up shop at the Waffle Hut.

The first time I ever ate at a Waffle Hut was with Henry. He says it's got the best plan of any restaurant in the world: breakfast food (the best kind), a menu that never changes, profit-sharing for the employees, and waitresses that yell *Mornin'* to you as soon as you walk in the door. I agree with Henry about breakfast, and so on these cool mornings I get in the truck and drive over for eggs and coffee.

I like listening to the way people talk. The way the waitresses throw out their orders to the cook all at the same time like a handful of bouncing balls. I'm impressed with talent, and it sure takes a certain kind to remember an order such as *Scrambled cheese plate easy, bacon, wheat, browns on the side, waffle dark,* when three other people are tossing you similar combinations.

I sit at the counter (tables are reserved for parties of two or more) and watch and listen. And after I've finished eating, I pull out my sketch pad and draw the cook, or some of the customers. I go so often I know the regulars: there's this man who has a scar that runs from his ear to his chin that I've drawn at least a dozen times. That's a challenge, that scar, and I think about how I'd get the colors right if I were painting it, all that purple and brown, a little yellow.

I draw the construction workers who come in for early

125

lunches slapping the Sheetrock dust off their clothes and throwing their legs over the stools at the counter, hitting up on the waitresses and lighting one cigarette off another; the smoke never settles, even while they're eating. Cops and cab drivers come in with their hands on their beepers, saying, "Hey, girls," to the women behind the counter. And there is usually a family or two with a baby or small child who always leaves toast on the floor and water or milk spilled across the table.

When there is a child, one of the waitress's expression will soften and she'll say, "How old is it?" and then tell how she has one about that same age at home. This always shocks me. Not because they shouldn't have children, but because of how hard it has to be, leaving their babies with *who*? while they're out trying to make a living sloshing coffee.

It's the waitresses I like best. Those women with faces hard as pellets, scrappy tongues and broken teeth, fingernails jagged as kindling wood. You can tell they aren't that old by looking at their bodies; but you'd never be able to guess their ages by looking at the faces. Those faces have lived. Some of them have died a little, too, you can see. Die a little every day. I cannot take my eyes off the eyes, eyes like the eyes on those sad old animals they keep in cages down at our zoo. I look at what I've drawn sometimes and I think, This could be an illustration for Chaucer. All you'd have to do is change the clothing and they'd look as if they were hiking along with all the other ailing pilgrims towards Canterbury. Because faces don't change. Look at the portraits Sargent did, or Thomas Eakins, or those artists from Colonial times. Just change the clothes, put them in a pair of sneakers and a warm-up suit, comb the hair, and you've got somebody who looks just like somebody today.

The waitresses know me, bring me my decaf without even asking. Ask to see what I'm drawing. They look at themselves as if what they see is news to them. Sometimes I tear a sketch out of the notebook and give it to one of the women. Sometimes they say, Here, put your name on it, and I scrawl in a corner my thin vertical *Eleanor Glass*. A couple of their faces are taped up on the stainless-steel hood over the stacks of plates and the big wire basket of eggs.

Nearly every day I think about getting a job at the Waffle Hut. Wearing one of those cheap orange uniforms and pulling my hair back with a rubber band, talking to the men as if they were sailors. That's what it always reminds me of, that talk between the waitresses and the regulars; it's like men on leave from a warship, teasing the females who serve and flirt but always keep their virtue. You never see one of them going home with someone after all, or making plans, just playing along and then, when the guy leaves, telling him to be careful. Something maternal kicks in when a woman slides a plate of food in front of a man, I've noticed. That's what they do—Brenda and Deb and Kitty and the others—treat the policemen and construction workers like teenage sons.

The thing I miss the most about not having a real job is people. The kind you know like family from working beside them every day. I miss Carter and Carroll, those times feeling I was being protected by two younger brothers. Carter and I have lunch every few months, but it's not the same. He's grown quiet with me, just like I'm any other woman. And Carroll's off in New York, living with a Frenchwoman and illustrating short stories for slick magazines and painting book covers.

This is the thing that always gets me, how people live. And not just me. I want to know everyone's story, all the people I see come and go at the Waffle Hut. Those waitresses, like Kitty, who tattooed her own hand by puncturing the skin with a Bic pen until she got LARRY with a heart around it to stay permanently on her. I always wonder where it is they go when they get off work at seven in the morning or ten o'clock at night. Sometimes I just want to say, Go ahead and talk, you can tell me. But I've noticed that no one ever really thinks their life is particularly strange. It's just what they're living. Living it every day. They might want it different, want it better, want it like someone else's they've seen, but they don't ever think it's strange.

I do, think my own life is strange. I'm always wondering, How is it I got here? What is the reason? How in the world did I find Will Turner?

And why is this strange man living behind us?

I know, of course, who he is. When we were first looking at the house early last spring, I saw him pushing a lawnmower down the driveway, and I thought, *I know that man.* I never forget a face, but sometimes it takes me a while to remember exactly where I've seen the face or how it is I know someone. Then in the middle of the night it's liable to come to me. But we had had the real estate closing and were already moved in, and I still couldn't figure out who he was. It was driving me crazy because I knew I knew that face from somewhere, but I couldn't remember where. Well, ask him, Will kept saying. But I never ask, because the face could belong to someone who only waited on us at a restaurant once or sold me a tube of paint at the artist supply store and not to someone I really know.

It wasn't until we went out there to meet him that I finally figured it out. It was something he did, this gesture of his I remembered from when I was a child. When he spoke, he took this long, deep breath and held it in a minute before he said anything. And that's what he always did before, took in this long line of air before speaking, as if he thought talking to someone was going to wear him out. Then I remembered the name, Ben, and I knew exactly who he was.

I started to call Henry and say, Hey, do you remember that guy who worked for us for a while and lived out in the trailer? But Henry was hurt, I remembered, when he found out Ben had gone. And for years afterward, whenever he was trying to hire somebody, he'd say, I wonder what happened to that fellow?

It's a sure thing he doesn't know who I am. I doubt he remembers anything much about us. So there's no point saying anything to him, or to Henry. But it's strange, that he'd end up here, after all these years.

There's also other strangeness going on. All around me. And not just me or the fact that this man, Mr. Bolt, is living behind my house. It's everybody.

Will is off in some world of his own lately, working so hard. He has always worked hard, always, but now it's different. Now he is *driven*. And he is driving so hard and fast I don't know where he's going.

Even CoraRuth is doing some outside work these days, and sometimes Henry will call at 5:30, and say, "Where is your mother?" as if I live around the corner and should know these things. "She isn't here," he'll say. "What does she expect me to eat for supper?" She's got little round microwave-proof dishes stacked in the cabinet from all his TV dinners.

And Fitz doesn't ask me to go to auctions so much anymore or even to come over; she's always at some demonstration, attending a waste management seminar, going to one of her environmental group's meetings. Once a month or so I pick her up and take her and her newspapers and cans to the recycling center, and then she gives me a quick peck on the cheek and jumps out of the truck and is gone before I've had a chance to really tell her anything.

Everybody is just spinning, faster and faster. Everyone seems to have purpose. Everyone but me. It feels like my only real purpose is worry. And if I ever let up on that, all of us, Mama, Will, Fitz, Henry, all of us would be in big trouble.

This house wasn't my idea. We were looking for a place to buy, but not for anything like this. Not in this neighborhood. It wasn't until I drove Will by the house where Fitz and Jay and I used to live that he started looking around here.

"We can't afford this, can we?" I whispered when the real estate woman strolled off to another room, discreetly giving us time to talk. "Do you like it?" Will asked. Of course I liked it, I loved it, all the windows in particular, all that light. "Then we can afford it," he said. Just like that.

He says that what I collect from the renter offsets how much more we're paying here than we would have on one of the other places we looked at. This isn't really true. But Mr. Bolt's rent is something, and since I'm the one who accepts his cash-filled envelope (never a check) on the first of every month and keeps his payments written down in my red book, it does make me feel as if I'm helping out.

It was that garage apartment out back that drew us to the house in the first place. We had planned to convert it into a studio, a place I could go (especially if later there were children) and work without distractions. But at the time, Mr. Bolt had been living there with five months left on his lease. We had planned to ask him to leave when the lease was up, give him a month's notice or two, and return his deposit. But I couldn't do it after I found out who he was.

He's a strange man, with no friends that I ever see, no family that ever visits, and I have never been able to get him involved in a conversation. He answers with nods or grunts, with yes or no, like a child responding to the questions of an overeager stranger. It is so irritating and yet at the same time I pity him—I can't imagine, if he doesn't live here, where he would go. How he would even set about looking for another apartment.

Will and I have lived in two houses since we've been married. The first we rented while we decided where we wanted to live, until we found a place that suited us.

That first house—the one we rented—was lower, colder, and newer. It was temporary, we knew, so we never painted or decorated or even hung many of my pictures on the walls. Books and boxes stayed stacked on the floors. In the back bedroom the same sheet stayed nailed over the window from the day we moved in. And in the basement we piled sports equipment, old clothes, our own separate cardboard boxes, and envelopes full of history.

When we bought this house on Lullwater Road, we decided to clean out the basement before we moved, get rid of all that junk we never used instead of hauling it across town. One Saturday afternoon we started, dressed in sweat clothes and old tennis shoes. I took down a cooler of Cokes and beer, and we could hear a ball game from the TV upstairs. At first we called back and forth to one another, from our separate corners of the gritty basement, and every once in a while we'd say, Come take a look at this, and we'd show each other some photograph or memento from when we were in high school or college. And then we'd toss unwanted articles (ticket stubs, dried flowers, notecards) onto our shared pile of discards in the middle of that cement floor. But after a while we both stopped talking, sifting through all those things of our past.

I found letters of Jay's I didn't even know I still had, letters he had written from basic training and when he was in Vietnam. I guess Will found the same kinds of things on his side of the basement.

It's not easy to sort days and say this one meant something and this one did not. Since we had both been married before, at the start of our marriage we said those things about former spouses that divorced people say. We spoke them because we each knew the other wanted to hear such things, because there was some selfish comfort in learning faults and grievances. But there was little of that really, because we both knew that neither of us had the kind of heart that could ever have been drawn to monsters. We simply had married too young, unwisely, all those hateful boring details that turn couples and individuals into statistics. (There was something about Jay and his reserve that had attracted me, his aloofness and quiet ways. I didn't know what it was at the time. Now I do; now I know I was marrying someone as hard to reach as Henry. I guess I've been afraid to ask enough about Kate to know what drew Will to her, but I know that neither he nor I married mean human beings, only the wrong ones.) So all that long afternoon we sat on a cold, hard floor, working in silence, getting rid of parts of our lives.

Will plugged in a radio (maybe so we wouldn't think about how quiet it had gotten), but the music of the sixties and seventies being played only made it worse, only struck more chords of separate hurtful history. Linda Ronstadt sang "Love Has No Pride," and I thought I'd die.

He turned it off. We worked till suppertime, and after we ate we went to bed and at first rubbed against each other self-consciously. Sometime during the night we each woke to the other one's touch, and in the dark we made slow, tender, tearful love. We wept not out of fear of losing one another's love or even out of any kind of jealousy; we wept for what we had now and had not had before; we wept because of the unhappiness all around us. It seemed it was everywhere, with all our married and unmarried friends and not just in that common pile of discarded articles on the basement floor.

·I am astounded at the depth of what I feel for my husband—by how many times of the day I think about phoning him at work and telling him this in case the unthinkable should happen. Constantly I fear his death; I fear I would not be able to live through it. And yet I know I would; people always do except those women Henry read to me about from the encyclopedias, those women who were thrown in the graves and buried alongside the corpses of their husbands. I guess most of them went screaming, but I can't help thinking that some, at least one or two, maybe weren't thrown at all; maybe a couple of them just swung their arms and jumped.

I am astounded at the strength of the human heart, my heart, that after injury it just keeps pumping. When someone coined the term "broken heart," there was a reason for it; hearts do get broken, you can feel them breaking, breaking apart.

The next morning we went back to that basement. With a shovel we scraped everything off the floor and into plastic bags. We tied them up with metal twists and heaped them in the back of my truck and took it all to the DeKalb County dump to be incinerated.

We know so much about each other, and yet there are all those things that never get shared. What would be the point? There are pieces of him all over this city—I know that—and history doesn't fade because things get burned.

I do love this house. It's not big like the others on this street, but it is wide-feeling, with windows like Fitz's that let in so much light. We both like the stone, the grayness of it, the fact that it feels solid and weighted, its age (built in the early thirties), its angles and gables, the sloping green yard that we have let turn brown. I liked it, too, because of the neighborhood, the rolling streets I walked when I was in college and when I lived with Fitz.

When things first started getting bad between me and Jay, and he became less affectionate, I guess I thought that all my hugging and loving would rub off on him and he would love me back. Maybe in the beginning I expected too much, maybe like with Henry I wanted to know his secret places. But not later. Later I just wanted talk, conversation, the kind friends have when they meet for lunch and then sit for hours over coffee and cigarettes and desserts gone limp. Talk was what I wanted, any kind of talk. But talk dried up between us as quickly as August rainwater.

And now I've married my talker. Will goes nonstop; he's like a human helicopter sometimes, flying into the quiet of my world on weekday afternoons, his engines running, hands signaling, telling me about all the people he has met with during only the nine or ten hours of his day, his problems. It can be exhausting, and of course all I'm doing is listening.

Our lives are so hectic, and it makes me feel pushed and panicky, unpeaceful. Shaky with anticipation of the next social function, the next obligation, the endless waves of responsibilities: paying the bills, purchasing food, calling friends, cleaning clothes. Simple chores, and yet I am lousy at all of them. (We're forever getting late notices from the power company. Every morning I listen to the sound of hangers being slid across the metal bar in the closet where Will hunts for one last clean shirt. And he asks, Don't we have any toilet paper? Are we out of soap? It's not even that Will expects me to take care of these things. He says he'll do them himself—stop by the store, drop off the laundry, take over the bills. But I always say, No, I can do it. But I rarely do, at least not well.)

Other people manage. People who have children and car pools and nine-to-five jobs. *They* find time to get to the grocery store and the cleaners. Somehow they get meals on the tables and bills paid and in the mail.

I'm not a lazy person. Usually (until the last couple of months) I work hard all day, stand at my easel for hours. But I don't know what happens to the time. Will comes home at night and I'm sure he must be searching for what I've added to a picture, trying to figure out what has changed.

I used to be more resilient. When I was in college and Henry would come to visit, and he'd look at one of my pictures and ask, What is it?, it only made me more determined. Obstinate, really. Instead of explaining the picture, I'd make it more abstract. But if that happened now, if someone questioned or kiddingly criticized my work, I guess I'd just go straight back to bed.

Of course if I made money, that might help. Increase my self-worth a bit. But since I've given up portrait painting, and am trying to start a new series, I've had no real income for months.

Will and I aren't in financial trouble or anything, and I don't care about money like some people do. I mean, I don't *need* anything. And I hardly ever think about clothes or cars or furniture. But, well, wouldn't it prove that what I do is worth something, holds some value, if I did get paid what Henry calls *cash dollars* for it every once in a while?

* * *

My last major show was a series of domestic scenes I called
"Urban Dwelling." See three young children, two in car seats,
staring at their father as he shouts at an unseen bank teller
behind the tinted glass of a drive-in window. See a man in his
twenties helping his elderly father into bed, a bloody shin ex-
posed beneath a dirty nightshirt, a jar of teeth on the table. See
an aproned child standing on a kitchen chair, helping her father
cook supper. See four members of a family seen from the rear,
sitting apart from one another, watching *Cagney and Lacey*. See
two grown sisters, dressed in black, sitting across from one
another at an empty kitchen table, grieving separately, differently, for their dead mother. See a black woman hunched over
a stack of bills, a baby asleep in a playpen behind her, a wedding
band absent from the ring finger on her left hand.

What I had wanted to show with this series was how members of a family are tied to one another, and that what passes
among them is fundamental, unavoidable. I had worked on the
project eleven months, and when I was through, my friend
Carroll's agent negotiated a one-woman show at a high-class
gallery.

I never know about clothes. All year long I live in a pair
of Keds and blue jeans, and when it comes to dressing I feel
like I've put on a costume; it sure never feels the way other
people look. Every time I go shopping I'm overwhelmed at the
expense of all the things I see people wearing and what it would
cost to buy one complete outfit starting from scratch, and I
come home empty-handed or with something I know will go
with the one pair of black heels I bought a couple of years back.
That's why for the party the gallery hosted for my show, Will
bought me a beaded necklace he found at a shop of African
art in Little Five Points (and paid more for it than I would ever
have dreamed of spending), and Fitz put up my hair so that
for once I wouldn't look so flat-headed and sloppy. But an hour
before the party I was nearly drunk from nerves and a bottle
of champagne Carroll brought over to the rented house.

The gallery's patrons were sleek and gray and polite, and
they constantly nodded and said, "Ah." That night I learned
what power a word (an utter) can have, what a shift in timing
it causes. Whenever I'm asked a question, I always feel com-
pelled to give an answer, a long one with every detail; whenever

there's a lag in the conversation or a space after a comment, I feel obligated to fill it. But that night I learned a sentence could be spoken, and one of those patrons felt no compulsion to give more than an "Ah." I also learned that just because you watch someone else master a tool, it doesn't necessarily mean that you can pick it up too and know how to use it.

I woke the next morning with a hangover and a review in the Atlanta paper that called my work "hollow" and "conventional." "Do we doubt for a moment," the reviewer wrote, "that we have been dropped down in urban America? Not I. Eleanor Glass carefully layers her details until we are in the bedrooms, kitchens, and living rooms of the middle class. The images are richly resonant; her show is not. In Ms. Glass's world sons take care of ailing, elderly fathers. Children cower at the shouts of an adult. Abandoned husband and child cook a meal together. Ms. Glass has all the nuances right: the claustrophobia of domestic life, the miscast roles in broken homes, the isolation and loneliness so visible among the members of a family. But it all leads the viewer to no surprises. Ms. Glass has talent, but we must wait for this artist finally to open up and give us more than these banal scenes to merit much attention." The show sold poorly. Two paintings. Carroll's agent said he thought it was because the pictures might be depressing to some people. "You know, maybe a tad too realistic, Eleanor. People like to escape in their art."

Everyone said it didn't matter. Who gives a damn? You'll show 'em next time. And besides, they said you had talent. "Ah," I tried, and nodded my head.

After the gallery got its take and the agent got his commission, I figured (subtracting the cost of the African necklace and my paints and supplies and the hours of work spent not just in the painting, but also in Will helping me frame pictures to get ready for the show), I made thirty-four dollars and twenty-six cents.

All right, so what're you going to do, fold up and die? Just because someone doesn't pat you on the back and tell you you're Picasso, you can't throw out your brushes and say, I quit! But I couldn't get the taste of "hollow" off my tongue. And whenever I picked up a brush and tried to work on some new project, I saw streaked across the canvas the line, "banal scenes."

For two years I painted nothing but portraits. Somber and assertive CEOs for Atlanta's major corporations. Round-faced three-year-olds commissioned by wealthy grandmothers. New-moneyed lawyers' wives who wanted their likenesses staring out over mantels. It bought me my truck and helped with the down payment on the house, but I hated it.

It was Will who got me to quit.

It was Will who got me to painting in the first place, talked me into leaving the job at the paper. (He's no critic at all, of course; he likes everything I do, even the doodles on the telephone pad.) Mostly because of him I set up a studio in the spare bedroom of the rented house. I brought out of storage (it had been too large for my apartment) the big wooden easel Henry had someone make for me when I was eighteen; it was a surprise for my birthday, and he had given the carpenter a photograph of John Singer Sargent's studio that I had torn from a magazine and for a while had taped for inspiration to my wobbly little metal easel that had come from Sears. The carpenter had copied Sargent's easel exactly, down to the number of ridges in the brush tray, and he had stood back with Henry, grinning, nodding, when they brought it home. When I saw it, so big and heavy, love pricked my nose, but I drove my fingernails into my palms and said to myself, I will not cry. I didn't cry either, but went over and grazed Henry's old rough chin with my lips. He tilted back, away, and said, "Okay, 'Nor. What're you going to paint first?" One sharp clap of his hands, to set things in action. "How 'bout Pete here," and he had pushed the carpenter forward and everyone laughed. But through that summer, when I painted every afternoon (and sometimes into the night) until I left for college, he knew how much the easel meant.

With that solid, paint-marked easel back in my life—in mine and Will's home—I felt somehow safely on the ground, in touch. In those single-woman years before Will, I had floated, lighting here and there, but never really landing anywhere. People who knew me then said I appeared like a dark soul, sad and serious. But with Will I felt for the first time since I was twelve years old that I had a sense of humor: he said I was funny, laughed at my corny jokes and imitations. He made me feel smart, too, and talented and even pretty. All that time I had thought life was something to get through; but now with

Will, I found it was something to cherish. And I found it made me want to paint.

The thing was, I wasn't sure I still knew how. For the first few weeks I was home after leaving my job at the paper, I stood at the easel just staring, not sure what to do, and particularly not sure what I wanted to paint. I did still lifes, made lots of sketches of Will, did a small portrait of Fitz. I propped up a coffee-table book full of Mary Cassatt paintings and copied them, trying to match the soft colors and feelings in those mothers and children. But no ideas of my own welled up inside me and demanded to be painted. There was no real rhythm to what I was doing, no consistency or what anyone would label a particular "style."

Slowly I began to study, to work out solutions to problems of color and composition in the same way I might have tried to give answers on a geometry quiz. At three in the morning I sometimes slid from bed—trying to keep Will from waking—and went to the easel and worked under false lighting, trying to get the color right on something I had started the day before. Sometimes I didn't paint at all, only primed canvases half the night; the next morning there wouldn't be anything to show for my work but a lot of splattered gesso, but I had been painting all night in my head. Scenes and faces passed across the big surface as if they were on a movie screen. See the twisted hand of an arthritic person: how do I get the knuckles out of line? See the blotched pigmentation on the face of a black person: how do I create that kind of skin? For a couple of months I worked on detail, copied drawings Michelangelo had made of hands, went back through all my old art books and read about color theory. I took a life-drawing class from two elderly Russian brothers who taught out of one of their homes and were the best Atlanta had to offer. I had never in my life been more ready to paint; yet I kept feeling there was a need to sit tight and wait for something to boil up and take over.

And then one afternoon when I came out of the C&S Bank on the corner of North Decatur and Clifton, after depositing a check for Will, I saw a man and his family in line at the drive-in window. There was a problem cashing a check—"No funds," I heard the staticky voice of the teller say—and the man was swearing. The three children were terrified and embarrassed and stared mutely at their father, one little boy with a sucker in his mouth. As soon as I got home, I started getting the scene down, working quickly with a turpentine-thinned wash. Will posed as the father, and I coaxed three little neighbors to sit so I could get the correct dimensions of the children's upper bodies. But the anger, the fear, the looks on those faces: I painted those from memory.

When the painting was finished, I went immediately to the next one (Carroll and his ill father), then to another (one of Will's secretary, Josie, and her little girl) until—in less than a year—there were twenty life-sized pictures stacked and hung around the house in varying degrees of dryness. I had never worked so hard, not even in college; but the work was like a fuel, a charge—and made me work that much harder.

Well, I'm gutless, I decided, after my show. If you can't stand failure, an art instructor once told me, then get out.

I stacked as many of my paintings as I could in the attic, took two to Fitz's shop (they're still there), Will hung three at his office, and I stopped. I let the paints on my palette dry into little rubbery hills and valleys. I sent off for applications to the local colleges, thinking I'd go back to school and get a degree in art history and later teach.

The portrait painting came about purely by accident. A neighbor saw one of the pictures from the show and asked if I'd paint his mother (he liked what I did, but he sure had no interest in someone yelling at a bank teller). It was certain work. Clients demanded little of me other than, Make it look just like Harry. And once we moved to the new house and word got out in the neighborhood, all the families wanted a portrait of someone. Children with cocker spaniels were big; little girls in riding outfits; pretty, young, smooth-haired mothers in linen dresses. See the happy faces. See the prosperous families. See the boring artist. It was lucrative, all right: I paid off all my bills from my years of being alone and I bought my brand-new white Chevy LUV pickup truck that bumped over the hilly streets of Atlanta carrying my stretched canvases and portable easel. And I helped buy this house.

But it became difficult for me and my clients to see portraits in the same way. I began working harder and harder trying to get the personality of the person down; the trouble is that most people don't necessarily want to see themselves the way they are—their main objective is to look good. And the more unhappy I became with what I was doing, the more difficult it became to let pictures go. I almost always thought each portrait was lacking in some way, that there was something else I should have added, another level I should have seen. Often I'd even go back to a client's home and (an intruder now, no longer a part of the family as I had seemed while working there for two or three weeks) ask to make the changes. Most times the family would look at me as if I were crazy and then sheepishly, suspiciously, take the picture down from its hooks and let me make my changes. Others refused, said their portraits were exactly the way they wanted them, and politely asked me to leave. But whether the changes were made or not, I was rarely satisfied. Displeasure accompanied me as predictably as my paints and brushes.

It was Will who helped me see I could stop. For three weeks I had been painting the portraits of four siblings, ranked in age from four to thirteen. Except for the youngest, the children wouldn't speak to me (there were only mumbles at the ends of my questions; rolled-eyes punctuated my sentences), and they quarreled among themselves. The mother, whom I would not allow in the room where the children posed, lurked at the edge with a chair pulled up in the foyer so she could listen and tiptoed in from time to time asking in a whisper if I would just let her "fix this little piece of hair." And she would pull a blond strand out from behind the thirteen-year-old daughter's ear to hide the four pierced earrings that were lined up neatly on one creamy lobe.

One afternoon, after a particularly long session with this family, I came home to "American Pie" blaring out of the radio. "Poor old Buddy Holly," Will was saying to nothing but the kitchen walls. "Died in a plane crash with the Big Bopper and Richie Valens." He is always doing this kind of thing, giving out not only the name of the creator or performer of some golden oldie, but he also knows who the song is about, sometimes even the date it was recorded. When the song got to the part about *the day the music died*, Will said, "February third, 1959."

I threw down my canvas bag of paints and said, "Can we

turn that thing off?" Will put down the newspaper he was reading. It is not uncommon for him to be doing two, sometimes
three, things at once: reading a book and watching a movie on
the TV, talking on the phone and balancing a checkbook, carrying on a conversation with me while listening and singing
along to music.

He turned off the radio and said, "Okay, what's wrong?"

Somebody else might have said, Hey, don't come in here
yelling at me. But not Will; he'll never get into an argument
until he has gotten to the bottom of what's going on.

"Nothing," I said. He didn't say a thing, just kept waiting
for me to tell the truth.

"Okay," I said, "I'll tell you what's wrong. That crazy
woman brought in a piece of fabric—a nice little piece of chintz,
a real nice blue—and asked me if I would mind changing some
of the colors in the picture, that she had decided to reupholster
the sofa. She *wants-me-to-paint*," I emphasized, "a picture that's
going to match her damn couch."

"Don't do it."

"I told her I wouldn't."

"No, I mean the whole thing. The portrait. The commission. Don't do it," Will said.

"I can't do that."

"Why not?"

I would have complained and moaned and done that portrait and made everyone miserable. But Will, he showed me
there was no reason to do something that was unreasonable;
no one was going to make me.

The next day I returned the five-hundred-dollar deposit
the woman had given me, called and canceled the other three
commissions I had lined up, and tried to think what it was I
should do next.

That's been almost two months now. I've tried to stop altogether, tried to stop calling myself an artist at all. I've secretly
filled out applications—for school again and jobs. But then I'll
see something, the way light falls on a leaf, the way the waitress
Kitty's tattoo is punched across her skin, and I'll find a pen and
a piece of paper and start drawing.

I can't stop doing it. At the same time I can't make myself

believe in its importance. It isn't like what Will does, talking to powerful people, getting things done, making money. It isn't like what Henry does, outside all day, trying to change the weather. It's not even like what Carroll and Carter do, creating something that someone has asked for. What I do is what most people think of as a hobby. It's just these things I do with color and marks and scratches. So I sneak to the Waffle Hut every morning, or I stay home all day and think about the hard-working people in my family.

There's something else. They all think I'm acting strange because Will and I can't make a baby. All around me people are trying to get pregnant, not just me: women who waited too long and now half the lining of their uteruses is sloughing off; women who married men sometimes only a few years older, but who were married before and had their families when they were in their twenties and now can't or won't have their vasectomies reversed; women who have no husbands at all, but just want a baby. It's like an epidemic; otherwise healthy women who can't have children. The thing is, I never think of myself like those women you read articles about in magazines. Because I *had* a baby before. I had Angela Diane. I didn't wait until I was in my mid-thirties because I was busy doing something else. I waited because Jay and I divorced, because it was years before I found Will, and by the time I found him, endometriosis had already set in.

Sometimes I wish the problem was Will's. That he had a little snipped tube that we could sew back together and pray for sperm replenishment. But Will's got a truckload of sperm, strong little swimmers who could populate half of Georgia. No, it's me. I've taken my basal temperature for months, drawn those little sharp arrows on my daily chart every time we make love, trying to calculate the perfect time for conception like someone predicting success by the alignment of the stars and planets. The doctor pumped dye up my tubes; stuck a little periscope through my belly button and tried to zap the endometriosis. And now I'm taking these male hormones that the literature says could lower my voice, cause facial hair and weight gain, and make me slightly moody.

I don't look and sound like Will yet, but my face is swollen from water retention caused by these pills. And sometimes I can't muster enough energy to put a stamp on one of the bills he has written a check for the night before. It sits on the table by the door and he comes home and I expect him to say, "You didn't mail this today?"

Enablers. That's what they call those people close to alcoholics who actually make it possible for the alcoholic to keep drinking. Aiding and abetting. It comes out of love, I think, in the beginning. That's what Will is to me, my enabler. I keep thinking he'll come home and say, This is all you've done? But he never does. I say I can't seem to work, and he says, What you do is tough.

What is it I want? For Will to put his foot down? Maybe for him to get to the bottom of whatever is my problem the way he does with everything else?

I don't think Will can. I think he is like those loved ones of alcoholics. I think for once he doesn't want to dig too far because he's afraid of what he might find.

I'm afraid too. Afraid I'm too far gone, that I'll never get my confidence back. That I'll start hiding in this house and never come out. You read about people like that. I heard one time that even Jackie Onassis had a couple of relatives who couldn't face the world, stayed locked up in some old house, just them and their cats.

It feels as if I'm moving slower and slower. Everyone is speeding up and I'm slowing down. Like an old drunk walking in a fog. Like some of those men I see in the mornings at the Waffle Hut, who've never been to bed, who come in for their cups of coffee trying to sober up. If something doesn't happen soon, I'll have slowed down completely. I'm going to be down on my haunches, crouched in a doorway, looking out.

Marilyn: 1986

"She's fattened you up, I see," was what he, Olin, said when I came home after all those months away. Then he raised me up on my toes an inch or two with a hard slap to my behind, and laughed like he does. Ha ha. Normally, I would have shown him my teeth, screamed something, held up long nails. But my nails had been eaten to the quick those last couple of weeks. I went to the back room, lay down on that lumpy, damp bed and heard Mama say in as bold a voice as she ever used, "Let her alone."

When I was sixteen, I lived with my mother's sister in Kentucky, September through March, my junior year. No one knew me. No one at home, save Mama, knew why I was away. I'd been in some trouble more than a few times, out late drinking wine coolers, getting caught smoking a joint in the girls' bathroom at school, stealing ice cream sandwiches out of a Mini-Market freezer and once a pair of high-top sneakers from Kinney's. That's what they thought it was about, my going to Kentucky. Reform. That Mama's beautician sister in Paducah was going to reform me. Aunt Abbie.

I lie on the couch, eat Doritos and Snickers.

Abbie comes home at night, smelling like chemicals—permanent solutions and hair dyes—and carrying bags of things she says I ought to eat. Cheeses, grapefruit, oranges, bananas, liver. She has this pamphlet from the county health department, and every day she shows it to me. "See, it says here you need servings from each of these different food groups. You need to be eating cereals. Whole-grain breads. Baked potatoes. Dairy products."

The bananas she buys for nineteen cents a pound turn black in a milk-glass bowl in the kitchen. I eat chocolate. Pour salt on my fingers and lick it like sugar. Drink Pepsi by the gallon.

During the day the TV is never off. Game shows and soap operas. Reruns of old shows I watched when I was little: Andy and Opie; Lassie; Mr. Ed. That channel with only news on it. One with children's shows: cartoons and *Sesame Street*. Big Bird asks questions, I answer.

But every night when Abbie asks questions, my mind is soggy from all the TV. Thoughts moving up and down on the ridges of my brain like it's all in slow motion. Sometimes it's hard to speak. My tongue moves so slow too, as stiff as a broom handle.

First, it is only a movement like butterfly wings. Just this tiny little sweep of a wing.

But it gets stronger. This thump like a cricket, maybe, or a grasshopper. Then it is a full-fledged rabbit kick.

Sometimes Abbie and I watch TV at night and even she will see it. An elbow. A knee. "What do you have in there? A soccer player?"

Abbie tries to get me to go to church with her and pray. I don't want to hurt her feelings, so I go. But the preacher, when he sees my stomach, looks sideways at me and shakes my hand like it's a vegetable gone bad in the refrigerator. I can tell by the touch of that hand that he's not going to say one prayer over me. His prayers are too expensive to waste on this girl and her belly. I make up excuses when Abbie wants me to go back. Tell her I'm dizzy. She touches my hand like she's just made a biscuit. Pat, pat.

She is soft and round, built like Mama. Soft round face, pink, the cheeks like warm peaches. Hands so small they look like something on a doll, but chapped and cracked from working in shampoo all day. I hear her whispering to Mama on the phone. "No, she's okay, honey. Leave her alone." She has to stand on her toes and reach to hang up the receiver. On the wall under the phone is a penciled list of numbers she calls: the women at the beauty parlor, the preacher, Mama, and the brothers. When Abbie sits all the way back on the sofa, her feet don't touch the floor. She wears tiny patent shoes with a strap, like you see on little girls dressed for Sunday school.

Glasses of milk handed to me with those little hands. "Drink it, honey," she says. I nod, but then when she leaves the room I run with the glass to the sink or the john.

The lawyer comes with the couple. He is a dentist; she's a school-teacher, thirty-one years old, wearing braces and rubber bands. She's tall and dark, her straight, thin hair pulled back with one small silver clasp. At first, I feel sorry for them, they sit so close together, her knees (big as hub caps) pressed together so hard. Then they start. "We have so much to offer," they say. They must say this five hundred times. They show me pictures of their brick house, the swimming pool, their cars. They are hik-ers, they tell me, and bicyclers. They read lots of books and go to movies and have hundreds of friends and have been to En-gland once.

They will pay all the medical expenses and the hospital bills. They show me where to sign.

I can't keep my eyes off her mouth. Every time she speaks or smiles, those rubber bands snap and stretch. I think that if one pops off, the jaws on that long face will fly apart.

They are excited that she and I have the same skin coloring, the same color of hair, about the same height. They tell the lawyer he has done a nice job. His feet tap linoleum; Abbie's tap air.

Little silver cage strapped to the front of every tooth; I think about asking how she gets stuff out of there. With a toothpick, maybe, or a pencil?

They spread the papers out in front of me, show me where to sign.

I only leave the house when I go to the doctor. And when we come back and open the door, the smell of the house always shocks me. It's like walking into a closet that has not been opened in years; I wonder if that's the way I smell when I pull my blouse up over my stomach and the nurse rubs that cold gel on me and runs that black instrument over me, listening for sounds. Wonder if it's in my hair. That smell like old coats and mothballs.

Each time Abbie climbs the five steps to the back door, she has to reach for a kitchen chair and rest before she can get her breath. That's what she says: "Just let me catch my breath."

Usually I fall asleep on the couch with the TV going. Abbie comes in in the middle of the night after the station has gone off the air, turns off the set, and covers me with sheet and blanket. But the night it happens, I go to bed early, before ten. "You all right, honey?" she asks me.

I tell her I'm fine, but I feel restless, fidgety. And as big as I am, I feel almost weightless and empty. I get in bed and the sheets irritate me so that I kick and turn trying to get comfortable. Stretching to turn the light off, it happens. It is like someone has turned a hose on inside me, and the water gushes. I remember Mama talking about the doctor having to break her water both times; she made it sound like a trickle, a leaky faucet. But mine rushes so that I say, "Oh!" then call for Abbie. She helps me to the bathroom, my water still flowing. It feels like I will never empty, like I could water acres with what's coming between my legs.

I sit on the toilet while Abbie talks to the doctor. He says we'll probably want to get to the hospital by early morning, as soon as the contractions are five minutes apart. But the pains start immediately and do not let up. She helps me into the front seat of the Rambler, and dressed in a big clean gown—one of Abbie's—and covered with sweater and coat, I feel like an overstuffed travel bag. Big, padded; folding and unfolding.

She drives me up to the big new hospital, Lourdes, it's called. Abbie laughs at that, the name, but I'm not sure why. She runs in, holding her chest to keep it from bouncing as she runs. They tell her, "Around back!" and the Rambler squeals as Abbie takes the corners too hard.

I have gone to none of the childbirth classes; I did not want to hear them talking about breathing and pushing. I was too ignorant to be scared.

But now the pain is terrifying, and the nurses are too busy with other women to help me. Out in the hall I hear the words *full moon* and *they're dropping like potatoes*. They give us a room and pads and a nightgown and rush out. Abbie closes the door and helps me into the gown. But it takes forever since I have to keep stopping and stooping because of the pains and I keep having to pee. I am peeing buckets.

I am standing barefoot on the floor, folded over myself; when the pain stops, I lift my head and ask Abbie if I'm going to die. She shakes her head, and I think, *She's* scared. I think, I should take her home and stop this mess. But the pains come back and I see that this is not going to stop. It is barreling, tearing me apart.

Twelve hours, they tell me; but it seems shorter and longer. Time has gone screwy and so has my brain. When the pains come, I do not scream but I about break off Abbie's hand. She starts for the door to use the bathroom and I cry for her to come back. When she touches me, I yell, "Get your hand off me!" When the pain is over, I stroke her little arm and say I'm sorry. Apologize and yell. Apologize and yell.

Centimeters is what everyone talks about when they come in and stick their hands between me. I clamp my knees over the pain, and they pull them apart and say it is time, I must push. "Didn't you take the childbirth classes?" someone asks me. "Didn't she take the childbirth classes?" someone asks Abbie, but she can't speak, either. We're all going to die if they don't get this out of me soon, I think; all three of us, me and Abbie and the baby, are going to roll up and die.

I have to be taught to push. When I do what the old nurse tells me, it feels like I am shitting my guts. Each time the pain starts to cut, she starts counting and I push. The push helps the pain and I push. And push. And push.

Return on the dollar, that's what Olin is always talking about. Return on the pain. It is the easiest thing I have ever done in my life. It is nothing. Nothing. Nothing compared to the return.

I do not let the couple see him. They stand outside the nursery for hours, tap at the window, ask the nurses to turn his crib around. But I do not let them in my room, I will not let her touch him.

The nurse puts him to me and she says, "He be a piranha."

She shows me how to express the milk so my breasts won't hurt so bad. But I'm afraid if I pump it out, I'll use it all up; and she has to explain that the more milk that is pumped out

means the more there will be for the baby, and not the other
way around like you would think. I express my breasts until
those big, hard, painful rocks are soft and limp; I try to pump
them dry, and the nurse says, You can never really empty them.

I eat everything that's put on my tray: green beans, chicken,
Jell-O. I drink all the milk and ask for more. He watches me
with those black eyes while he nurses, and I tell him I'm sorry
I didn't do such a good job of getting ready.

Every day they knock. I hear her say into the door, "You've
got to let us have our baby." But my heart is as cold as hospital
metal.

Abbie and I take him home in the Rambler, the heater
blowing hot on my knees, church music on the radio. She has
borrowed a bassinette from one of the girls at the beauty parlor.
It sits high—white and lacy—on its metal legs like some large
white bird beside my bed.

The couple and the lawyer come round to our back door.
I let them sit in the living room while he sleeps in the other
room. She sits on the couch and says how long they've waited.
All that silver in the mouth; face like a collie. I hear the lawyer
whisper how they cannot push me; I see the looks. Abbie brings
in a plate of sugar cookies and moves among us like a pillow.
They tell me I'm breaking a contract, going back on my word.

Abbie puts the plate down on the television and tells them.
"We've decided to keep him," she says.

I do not listen to the rest. I leave her with them and go to
my room and put him in the bed beside me. There is loud talk
and crying and Aunt Abbie shooing them out like birds. When
he nurses, he makes the same sound I made during labor, but
softer. *Nnnnnh, nnnnnh, nnnnnh.*

Mama sends me secret money, and we buy a blanket and
diapers and a little blue outfit with a matching hat and suspenders. My breasts fill up like they're hooked to a faucet. Every
morning the sheets and the top of my gown are wet. The milk
flows and he drinks it. "He be a piranha," we joke.

Every day but Sunday, Abbie goes to the beauty parlor,
washing and curling women's hair. She comes home sometimes
at lunch, bringing me a can of soup, or lettuce and three-bean
salad and cottage cheese from the salad bar at the grocery store.
She likes to hold him while I eat. "Doodle bug. Doodle bug,"

she sings and circles her finger in the air. And then she drags
herself back to work, and every night she brings home dinner
and sometimes more diapers. She stands at the stove, singing,
"Doodle bug doodle bug, I love you. Doodle bug doodle bug,
you mama loves you too."

I roll him up in blankets so he's as stiff as a papoose and
push him in the secondhand stroller to see the girls at the Kut
'n Kurl on warmer days. They say, "Look at that hair!" and
pass around the tight bundle. The only things that move are
those two black eyes.

He is one month old, and we have planned a party. Aunt Abbie
buys candles for the cake, and a squeaky toy, and has borrowed
a Polaroid camera from one of the girls at the beauty parlor so
we can take pictures. I am changing his diaper, putting on the
suit with the matching hat and suspenders, when the owner of
the beauty parlor calls.

It is about Abbie, can I come right over? But when I get
there, she is gone. A couple of the girls are in back, sitting on
the edge of the old couch next to the coffeepot and refrigerator,
holding their heads. The customers are standing in two tight
circles, whispering to each other. One of them has only one
side of her head covered in rollers. Another has had part of
her hair brushed smooth, but the rest sticks out from her scalp
like white cotton candy.

There is a policeman there taking notes, and I hear the
owner giving details, talking into a handful of wadded Kleenex.
One of the girls had talked her into getting her hair done. Wash
and set. She was so tired, I hear. Needed the lift. She fell asleep
during the washing. And then again when she was getting rolled
up. Would open her eyes, and laugh, say, "Ooooh, that's so
relaxing, honey, you're putting me to sleep." They put her
under the dryer, set it for half an hour. And when the buzzer
went off, she just sat there, her hands clasped together on top
of a copy of *Family Circle.*

"That big old overworked heart of hers must have been
sloshing around in there like a washing machine," someone says.
Then it went into a hard spin, and stopped, her head in a
forward tilt under the humming hair dryer and her feet three
inches off the floor.

* * *

People think you do things—go to bed with boys, want a baby—because you want somebody to love you. I've had people love me. That's not it.

Once I made love to a boy so many times in one night that it somehow pushed air up inside me, and when he came out the last time it made a sound like I was farting. I tensed the muscles down there, but I couldn't stop it. I laughed so he'd think I didn't care, and then I said, "This always happens."

When I walked into the living room that same night, my lips and chin looking like they'd been rubbed with Brillo, Olin folded himself forward in the La-Z-Boy and said to Mama, "You'd better get me one of those Hefty bags, Mary, 'cause there's trash in this house."

The four brothers and Mama come from five different points to Kentucky.

All of them—the Keedy boys—have been named for American presidents: Thomas Jefferson, Abraham Lincoln, Theodore Roosevelt, John Quincy Adams. I've heard this story since I can remember. I've also heard: "And we got named for First Ladies." Abigail Adams and Mary Todd Lincoln.

Abbie was sixteen and Mama just twelve when Grandmother and Grandfather Keedy died within a few months of each other. It happened so long ago and the children were all so young that no one really knows what happened. A hole in the heart for one of them, it's guessed, and a burst appendix for the other. But no one knows for sure. These two illnesses are discussed when the five gather, and it's speculated that Abbie may have inherited the faulty heart, although some of us know better.

Only Abbie was left in the house in Griffin to care for herself. The others—Mama, Jefferson, Abraham, Teddy, and John Quincy—were sent to the children's home in Atlanta, most of them too young to stay at home and too old for anyone to want them. "Used merchandise," Mama used to say; that's what it felt like she said, when year after year no one took them. It was only Teddy and John, four and two, who got placed in homes.

Abbie married a Kentucky boy right away and moved first to Bowling Green and then to Paducah. Her husband died young, but she stayed on there. And the rest of them, spread out all over the country (John Quincy in California, Teddy in Carolina, Jefferson in Louisiana, Abraham in Pennsylvania, and Mama in Georgia), hardly knew one another.

But when they get together, they all talk about Abbie. "Little mama," they call her. She wrote them all, no matter where they were, and sent them each a crisp new dollar bill on each of their birthdays every year till they were grown and married.

They sit around in Abbie's crowded living room, sitting on chair arms and on the floor, and none of them is alike; they don't even sound like one another (except Mama and Abbie) because of the different places they've lived and the different ways they were raised. But all of them are short and thick-bodied, even the men (when I had thought it would only be the two sisters). They are all Keedys, big-hearted and easy to grieve.

It's Olin I took after, the reason I have this height. And it's my brother, Will, who has the Keedy blood.

The brothers leave, and it is me and Mama. Ever since Abbie died I have been nervous. But Mama has said nothing, made no indication. It is only after the last of the boys has left that she says, "We're going to have to do something."

Going through Abbie's things she has found the bill from Lourdes. More than one thousand dollars.

I tell her I'll work with her at the restaurant, put the baby in a playpen, and help her fry chicken and make meat loaf, dish out mashed potatoes. I'll pay it off.

She shakes her head. You've got to finish school, she says. But that's not it. That or the bill.

Mama won't say it. She never will. Won't say she's scared to death of Olin, scared of what he'll do if I come home with a baby.

She's the one who calls the lawyer. I hear her speaking in Abbie's telephone, reading him numbers off the bill.

I never leave the room. Won't come out. Someone takes him from his bed and he doesn't even cry.

* * *

Every day Olin jokes. "Looks like she's so mean she killed old Abigail."

One time Mama answers, "Oh, shut up!" Then she lowers her eyes. I wrap my arms around me so he won't make fun of where I carried the baby's milk. "Grown in places, I see," he says sometimes.

It is spring. The school counselor is going over my records, but I won't pay her any attention. She is stupid, dumb. What does she want me to do, apologize? I take a pencil out of my bag and write on my tennis shoe: SUCK.

She says, "I just don't understand, Marilyn. You're plenty smart. Your test scores show it."

I think maybe I ought to say the word out loud. Suck! Make her jump.

"What is it, anyway? Can't you tell anyone what's the problem?"

I switch shoes, start writing on the other one.

"Damn it!" she says, bangs her hand on the wall. Then she sits, says she's sorry. "I'm sorry," she says again. "But Marilyn. Marilyn, you've got so much to offer."

I don't know why, but her saying that changes me. I can feel myself changing inside. At school none of the girls are like me anymore. They are either rough and hard like I was before, talking trashy and getting into trouble. Or they are clean and tight-hipped, wearing uniforms of the drill team and the cheering squad, trying to make the sororities. But me, I'm not like any of them now; I am older, walking somewhere above where they are walking, speaking in a slow, quiet voice that is different from all other sounds. I study for the first time. It isn't hard. One hour or two in the evenings and I make all A's easy. In the afternoons I file charts at a doctor's office near the school. I don't run with anybody.

"Uh oh, Mary," he says. "Clean up the conversation, the Brain is home."

I don't show him my grades anymore. When I do, he says, "Oooh! I guess you're going to go to college too, like big brother Will." Then he stops smiling and says, "Well, don't count on any of the money coming from here," and he taps at the pocket with *Olin* written on it in shaky red letters.

It's Will who pays my way, who writes the check to the Admissions Department at the University of Georgia every quarter. They tell me I need to decide on a major, what will it be? They say, "How about marketing?" And I don't even know what that means.

I make good grades, but I don't care. Not about business courses, not about any of the things the other girls do. So I drop out after the second year, get Incompletes in all my classes. Will thinks I'm no good and lazy. He comes to the apartment in Atlanta where I've moved in with this boy I knew from a band that sometimes played at the college. "Marilyn. Marilyn, you've got to make something of yourself," my brother says. And Olin, Olin just laughs. "I could have told you she'd never be nothing."

He is ten years old now.

The dentist, I don't know his name, don't remember if they ever said it. Sometimes I spend hours phoning dentists in Kentucky. I call their offices and say, "Yes, I'm calling to see if Dr. So-and-So got his son's pictures in the mail. Which son? Jackie? The one who is six [seven, eight, nine, ten]? Oh, I must have the wrong Dr. So-and-So then."

Sometimes I've gotten a dentist with a Jack or a Jackie, and I'll say, "Oh, he didn't get the pictures, then they must have been sent to the school. Which school would that be, do you know?" Sometimes they say, "Who is this?" But a couple of times they've given me the name, and I've driven the seven hours to Paducah and waited outside a school until a group of children come out who look his age. And all of a sudden I'll yell, "John F. Kennedy!" to see if one will look up. But all of them look at me and I get scared. I look at all the faces, but there's no face like me looking back.

My best feature has always been my teeth. They're straight and long and since I've never smoked anything but a little pot and never drank coffee or tea, they're whiter than most folks'. I guess that's something. I never needed braces like the other kids. Sometimes in secret I'd fashion a paper clip into a curve that would slide over my front teeth and then attach it to a wad of gum or a piece of that flavored paraffin kids used to chew; the wax would conform to the shape of the roof of my mouth, and I'd talk with a little lisp like the rich kids who wore retainers. This was just in secret though; I kept it hidden in the top drawer of my dresser and only pulled it out when I was alone.

There's a boy somewhere with a black stare and white teeth, not needing the one thing his adopted daddy can give him.

I sell artists' supplies at Sam Flax. Will got me the job, he and his wife, Eleanor; they knew the manager. Eleanor comes in from time to time for her paints and brushes and things. You can tell she'd just as soon not have to talk, but she does anyway and is always full of questions for me. Everything going okay? Working hard? Those sorts of things. But you can see what she's really thinking when she looks at me: No good. Selfish. Lazy. She thinks I'm nothing next to Will. She's right, I am.

I borrow money from him from time to time, every few months when I'm low on the rent. It would be easier to take from someone who doesn't make it so easy; but Will's got a Keedy heart at his center and he'd give you anything. That's what makes it hard, because Will's so good. But I go ahead and ask for another handout every time because I'm not ever going back. Not ever going to live in the same house with Olin.

Mama would like to get out, too, but she never will. No matter what he does, she still pulls herself up when he comes into a room and gives him the best chair. Still puts his dinner in front of him every night, even though she's cooked two hundred other meals before she gets home to cook his. I think she'd go crazy if she didn't have the restaurant. People come in there for lunch and know her and tell her she makes the best fried chicken and potato pies in the world. She does.

Before the restaurant, she used to take in children. Foster kids, three and four at a time. One time we had seven: all ages. He let her because of the money. It wasn't much, but since she had her garden, he was able to keep most of what they paid her to buy food. They slept all over the place, on quilts and mats she lined up at night in the kitchen next to the warm oven, and the smallest one sometimes in the bed with her and Olin. There was always some child with a runny nose and pinkeye, always one falling on the furnace grate in the hall and scorching his hands and knees. She started taking the fosters in before she had me, when they thought Will was going to be an only child because of all the miscarriages. There were four or five of them, some that came so early in the pregnancies that they weren't much more than bad periods, others that went almost full term and resulted in tight little babies falling out of her weak cervix like they were just falling off her lap.

There must have been thirty or more fosters over the years. Some of them still come back, bring their own children to show her. Sometimes I felt Olin didn't know me from all of them. *Isn't there anyone in this house that doesn't have a runny nose?* But he doesn't look at me.

Sometimes I pretend I'm one of the fosters, that I've got a rich, kind father somewhere looking for me. Sometimes one of the girls and I will play we're sisters. I could be a sister to one of them as easily as I am to Will. He's so much older and never home, and when he is home he and Olin move from room to room like opposing pieces on a game board. Olin messes with him less every day though. Olin's still bigger, but Will's bigger in the head.

The standards for foster children got more stringent over the years. There had to be a bed for every child and x-amount of rooms and baths in a house for x-many children. And then one of them told a social worker he saw Olin hit Mama. She denied it, but it's hard to cover for someone when skin turns blue and yellow.

That's when she decided on the restaurant. She and Olin owned the building (an old service station) next to the house and had left it empty for years. Boxes and Christmas decorations and old jars and tools, mattresses got stored in there. We used to go in there and hide, lie on the smelly ticking and play we were wounded and dying. One time one of the older foster boys got on top of me and jabbed his tongue in my mouth and held it there for nearly a minute. I ran back to the house squalling, but Olin was there with her, and when he asked what was the matter all I could say was, Nothing.

She talked to him for over a year about the restaurant before he let her do it. She sold pies and breads to other places around town and saved her money, enough to have a kitchen put in and paint the floors and bring in metal chairs and tables. He laughed at her at first, but two or three days a week he sits over there and talks to his buddies while they eat their lunch, a toothpick hanging out of his mouth while she serves the food she starts cooking at seven in the morning. All summer she grows squash and tomatoes and okra and greens. On summer nights she cans, her hair sticking to the back of her wet neck; and all winter she cooks what she put up six months before: circles of limp yellow squash swimming in round plastic bowls; peas, greens, okra, stewed tomatoes. Sliced tomatoes and sweet onions. Biscuits and cornbread. Sweet potato pies, banana puddings, toasted pound cake. Home Cooking by Mary Todd. It's going to kill her.

She's had a staple put in her stomach to help her lose weight. It helped at first, but now she's as big as she was the time before she went to Weight Watchers and won the gold star. High blood pressure, like Abbie. Same flush in the cheeks. Falls asleep anytime she takes her feet off the floor.

Will and I worry, try to get her to slow down. I say, Did you take your medicine?

What I don't say is, Why did you let them take my baby?

People say you change after you have your own child, that you're more understanding because for the first time you realize what your parents did for you. That's not what happened to me.

It went back further than that when I saw those black eyes and understood it all, not just to when Mama and Olin were young and raising children. But back to when they themselves were babies like Jackie. I never picked up a book about childbirth or raising children before he was born. But after I saw him, in that first month, I had Abbie get everything she could find for me at the library. And all those books, they talked about how much damage can be done to babies, permanent damage that lasts their whole life from what happens to them when they're still in the cradle. You can believe it when you look down at one of those little things. Anything in the world could be done to them and even by people that aren't altogether mean or crazy. Olin was raised by an uncle. He might have been left to lie in a baby bed for hours, squalling, not picked up till he was nearly drowning. He could be trying to walk and falls, and someone behind him just laughs. He could be a tired toddler, out too long in public, with someone jabbing at him and saying, Shut up! Shut up, stupid! Someone could hold him out over a deep hole and say, You don't stop, I'm going to drop you. They could say, You're a bad boy and the devil's going to eat you. Who's going to arrest anyone for that? That's what I remember sometimes when he opens his mouth. Who did what to Olin?

I never knew about the Lindbergh baby until a couple of years back when they had a special on the television. Maybe it doesn't seem so bad, just another child among millions, until you think about the horror of it. They just put him down to bed, in his own bed, and when they went back to check on him, maybe to put on an extra blanket, he was gone. I've played that out a hundred times. She goes over to cover him up and when he isn't there she thinks: *The nurse has him. Or Charles.* He's got to be somewhere. Because the brain doesn't let you think that babies can be gone from their beds and then gone forever.

Sometimes it feels like Jackie is dead. One time I filled out an employment application and where it asked about children, I checked the block under *Deceased.* I wasn't lying or trying to kid anyone, it just felt that way, like he died as a baby and went away with Abbie.

Mama and the foster children: that's helped me understand some things. She saw that most of them made out all right, and I guess she thought maybe you could trade children around, like a jar of tomatoes for one of peaches down on one of those shelves in her root cellar.

The thing is, that's not true. There are whole shelves of emptiness in this world. Mason jars with nothing but air in them. Worse, there are busted-up jars everywhere, shards of glass that can kill you.

I didn't even have a name for him, hadn't even thought about it. Then when he came and they kept asking, I knew it couldn't be just anything. Not just Billy or Bobby. I remembered about Mama and Abbie then and the brothers, and I remembered that picture of JFK that hangs in the restaurant, one that Mama traded something for with one of the black girls that washes dishes. I was too young to remember the assassination, but I've seen those pictures and films and heard Mama talk. That's what I wanted, John F. Kennedy Turner. And it was Abbie who said, We'll call him Jackie.

We left most of Abbie's things in that house, and Mama and the brothers turned it over to a real estate broker. When it was sold, they divided it up among them. Just a few thousand dollars. Not much return on the dollar.

Mama took some of Abbie's clothes. She still wears an old blue car coat with little wooden fasteners that look like barrels instead of snaps or buttons. We left nearly everything else. Locked the back door with that box of birthday candles and the borrowed Polaroid camera still sitting on top of the refrigerator.

Will: 1987

$\mathbf{M}$y mother's wrists are like a baby's: no wrists at all really, the bottoms of her arms wider almost than the hands themselves. The ankles are the same way, those short heavy legs packed down to the ground, flattening her feet. She's gained all the weight back, and more. But what can you say?

We're here for Mother's Day. I called and said we'd take her out, but she wouldn't hear of it. "When my children are home, it's a sure thing nobody else is going to feed them." There's a platter of fried chicken out there on the stove, piled with enough breasts and legs to feed a dozen people instead of just the five of us. She's fried extra for all those who are bound to stop by during the afternoon, bringing potted plants and snapshots of their children and little glass jars of candy for her. Sixteen Mother's Day cards fanned open and standing on top of the television: pictures of roses, bonnets, picket fences, baskets of flowers, hands in prayer, a photograph of a woman looking out an open window. Hallmark: buck twenty-five's worth of emotion. One of them, that white fence, is from Kate.

The envelope's been thrown out, and I don't dare ask Mama if she noticed a return address. The last time we talked, Kate was in L.A. That's been six or seven months, much longer since I've seen her. But she calls once or twice a year, mostly to ask if I know anything about Rita.

The first time Kate came to live with us she was about nine or ten. That black hair cut like a boy's. She was built like a boy too, straight as a picket. Like most of the others Mama took in, her parents weren't dead. At least not her mother, Rita, who was always either down on her luck, broker than a busted piggy bank, or clawing the walls in some rehab center, drying out.

Kate would stay with us long enough for Rita to get herself pulled back together. Then Rita, not that much older than some of the kids we kept, would come pulling up in front of the house honking the horn of a new boyfriend's long car or packed into a bus full of guitars and musicians, finally hooked up with a band that was going to take her to the top this time. She did land a job as backup singer with a decent group or two, and several times she was the opening act at country-music festivals. On those return trips to pick up Kate, she'd be decked out in a new outfit, her legs thin as straws, sucked up tight in boots and jeans; I've never seen legs like that, so long they looked as if they'd go on forever. Sometimes her hair would be a different color, and sometimes she'd tell us to call her by a different name; *Lydia* it was one time, and another time, *Lenore*. She'd hand out autographed pictures of Jerry Lee Lewis and Willie Nelson to the other kids, Kate standing there like all the rest of us, amazed and awed. Even when Kate was grown, long after we had married, she would swear she was going to sue some former rock star or his estate because she had just figured out that he was the one who was her father and had left poor Rita. It was Elvis, of course, most of the time, or Hank Williams, or even Jerry Lee. I never knew whether the idea was hers, or if the stories originated with Rita. But when Kate was a kid, I'd see her holding up next to her face pictures of some singer and pointing out all their shared features.

There actually *was* a little white wooden fence around this house once, until one of the older boys busted through it with a dirt bike and we had to knock the rest of it down and haul it off. That's what it was all about with Kate, I know. Her picture of a picket fence, of somebody having a mother who handed you something other than a pack of cheese crackers and Twinkies for lunch and breakfast. That's what she thought we were, bacon and eggs and peas and carrots, bedtimes at a regular hour, and a zip code that kept that same line of numbers year after year. That's the funny part, every other household I ever saw looked as if it were the perfect family to me. I wanted to be like all those other kids from school, whose fathers played golf over at the country club, where they all got dressed up every Sunday morning in gloves and ties, and went to church, where no one woke up in the middle of the night to the sounds of people yelling.

Of course that was just the one side of Kate, her wanting what looked better at our house, in comparison. The other side was off chasing Rita, wanting to be just like her, who wouldn't feel right if she didn't spend most of her nights in a car or a motel.

And I have to admit that it probably was Rita who caused me to be attracted to Kate. I grew up in a crowded living room in this same house, with half a dozen foster children all around to keep me company because Mama didn't think she could have any more of her own. The room's full of us, and Mama's standing at an ironing board in front of the TV, watching *American Bandstand* from Philadelphia, crying because Ray Charles was lip-syncing so sweetly. If we'd had money, Mama would have gone to see Elvis or Patsy Cline or any of the others like some people did. Music was the one thing, the only thing, that could lift her out of this cracker box and take her places.

And then there came Rita, looking just like one of those people we sang along with. She once had a poster made of herself, and another time sank everything she owned into paying for cutting a record. She had a voice like an angel and a rubber-band body—tight and springy one minute, limp and dangling the next—and, in the beginning, one of those sweet oval faces. But so did a thousand other girls; whatever it takes to shoot a person into that thin strip of space that makes them a star was not there. We did not know that though. We always believed, when she told us, that Rita had made it.

When I was a kid, I could always get away from the house without anyone noticing. There were so many others that no one was bothered that I was off by myself, riding my traded bicycle all over town. Staying all afternoon at the ball field, sleeping over at friends' houses. The things I was allowed to do, with no one worrying: climb out on the far limbs of the old oaks in our neighborhood, scooting back down with armloads of mistletoe to sell every Christmas; pedaling way out on the far edge of town, selling *TV Guide*s door-to-door to strangers; staying out long past dark, watching for bats in the culvert that ran behind the house. Friends were jealous of my freedom.

Sometimes still, I like to sneak out of the office in the middle of the afternoon and go see a movie, or maybe wander around in a mall eating a vanilla cone, just slip out like I'm still on my old blue Racer and no one knows where I'm going. I like that on vacation, too, for it to be as if Eleanor and I are lost somewhere and no one knows where to find us. It drives her crazy though. She (the one who can't stand a telephone!) gets uneasy anytime we're somewhere her family can't get in touch with us if anything were to happen.

They're as different as two people can be, Kate and Eleanor. And being married to one was nothing like being married to the other. It's difficult for me to believe that the same word, "married," can be used to describe two such different things.

With one, it was like holding a child's hand at street corners, trying to keep her out of trouble, scared to death all the time that something was going to hurt her. When she came back to visit after being gone a year, she looked just like that—like she needed someone to take care of her. And I was the one who happened to be there when she most needed a hand. I didn't know it until later, but I was exhausted all the time when I was with Kate. Exhausted and anxious.

With Eleanor—with Eleanor, it was like it was the first time I found home. Not picket fences like Kate was looking for, but a place on this earth where I fit, where I could take a deep breath and never be afraid of running out of air. People think (Eleanor thinks) that because she can be so quiet and holds back and seems to have the self-confidence of a snail, and that because I talk a mile a minute and come on like a bear with a sore behind, that it's me who holds things together, me who is taking care of Eleanor. What no one knows but me is that it's Eleanor who holds me steady.

And, like James Taylor says, she's the only one who can move me. J.T. Out of his mouth come all the things I'm thinking. That skinny old boy from Carolina, looking like he works in a sawmill and putting words together that make grown men cry. *Don't let me be lonely tonight.* There it is, J.T. on the guitar, Lee Sklar on bass, Brecker making the saxophone cry.

* * *

I got into this business by accident. All the other smart boys in my class were planning on being lawyers. That seemed as good a thing as any to me, because I sure didn't have Mama or Olin pushing me in any direction. I took all that political science and history, and I was working two jobs, before and after classes, saving up for law school. One of the things I'm best at is talking, and when my number came up for the draft, I talked my way straight into a six-year hitch with the reserves. I did basic, hated every minute of it and every idiot S.O.B. who took particular pleasure pulling rank on those of us whom they called Joe College. I hated the weekend every month, too, especially after Kate and I were married and I didn't know what she'd be doing when I got home on Sunday evenings. But it kept me out of Southeast Asia and helicopters. It also showed me some other things I'm good at. Getting things done; being in charge.

A lot of guys move in packs, stay so close you'd think they'd smother each other. I never have. A pack will slow you down. So when the others would sit together drinking, bellyaching about being bored, I'd think of entertainment. I became the Picture Man, the guy who smuggled in porno flicks and showed them at the PX after hours. They thought Picture Man was a miracle worker, getting something different every month: *The Devil in Miss Jones, Behind the Green Door,* all that crap with Annette Haven and Linda Lovelace and John Holmes. I handled it all: the beer, the liquor, the popcorn, running off the tickets, getting my hands on a projector, collecting money, keeping it all quiet and me out of trouble. Those boys would sit down there drinking, whooping it up, letting out their energy in hoots and whistles until they could get somewhere private. I liked being the one up there running the film, the master of it all, the one who got congratulated.

Over one of the two-week stints in the summer, I got tired of running the projector and lined up live entertainment. First, it was just Rita and whoever she was traveling with at the time. But later I found someone who knew someone who knew Gladys Knight and the brother and cousins back in Atlanta. I had guys selling off stereo equipment and jewelry until we got enough money to get her and the Pips to drive up to Augusta. I'm fast on my feet, real fast; and with this mouth of mine I can talk pretty smart people into just about anything. I was good is what I'm saying. And I liked it. When you're twenty-one and you've bluffed your way into speaking person-to-person on the phone with people who have their pictures on the covers of record albums and *Rolling Stone*, being a lawyer no longer holds much excitement. That's how I got where I am.

Turner Entertainment in a downtown Atlanta office. Sometimes people call and think they've got that other Turner; I've got a drawl good as his, and so I play along and then come home and tell Eleanor about it; a couple of times I've worked out a deal before they realize it's me who has them hooked on the other end of the phone. We live in a nice house in the right part of town, drive a nice car, know big-time people, names you would know. I need it all, *need* it the way some people need coffee or cigarettes; maybe even the way some people need air. But none of it, not a bit, means a thing without Eleanor. And that's where the danger lies: needing two things so badly, and knowing those two things don't necessarily go together.

If Eleanor had her way, we'd have things as plain as a plate-glass window. No frills, no fancy cars, no big house. No money. *I'd* give it all up if I couldn't have Eleanor. But what would I be? Eleanor just wants us to slow down, be quiet. I try, but I can't. I'm running. Running. Running just as fast as I can, from failure.

Eleanor helps Mama stuff the deviled eggs. Little cubes of sweet pickle poke through the yellow she spoons into each shell. The women's talk is like some background music, nothing you have to listen hard to but something that is soothing, keeps out the quiet. I am not expected to help with any part of the meal, even by Eleanor. Here, I sit back in the old vinyl chair and read the paper, listen to the talk, eat the snacks Mama wordlessly hands to me, acting the part of a Southern male, a role I would play nowhere else in the world.

Mama and Eleanor like each other, but then Mama likes everybody. She's still got the big framed picture of me and Kate on her bedroom wall. She would never think of taking it down, and at the same time she would never think of it being an affront to Eleanor.

Nothing in this house ever gets thrown out. I see the same

threadbare dish towels that were used here three decades ago. What isn't used is washed and folded and stacked in boxes that line the bedrooms, fill up every closet. In the dining room are cases of ketchup, Coca-Cola, and Dr. Pepper, supplies she has run out of room for over at the restaurant.

Mama is telling my wife and my sister about Siamese twins she read about in *Star*. "Connected at the skull," she says. "Can you imagine?"

Marilyn draws on her cigarette and says, *"Mama."*

"It's true, they are. And you know there's not a chance in the world those little things are going to make it."

"Well, I keep thinking about that little boy," Eleanor says.

"Which one?" the other two want to know.

"The one who had to live in that bubble."

"Lord," says Mama, who is cutting up the eggs that didn't peel well enough to be deviled and is raking them off the cutting board and into the bowl of potato salad.

"I read an article about him the other day while I was waiting at the doctor's office. It was kind of a look back at his life, and all he and his family went through. There was this picture of him where he's walking around in that thing, with hoses hooked up, and he looks like this little astronaut. It's the saddest thing. Him living his whole life that way."

Eleanor's voice plays on—steady yet invisible, as if she is blowing glass. I am aware of it all around me, it's comforting, and I imagine being in a bubble myself. Mama nods occasionally or shakes her head at how awful something is. But Marilyn is quiet, just keeps rolling her cigarette into the lid of a pickle jar.

"I just don't know how they stood it. Not ever being able to touch him or hold him."

"Oh, I know it," Mama says, and then in the same breath adds: "Marilyn, run over to the restaurant, honey, and bring me back some celery."

Marilyn just keeps rolling.

"Did you hear me, honey?"

"Huh?" Marilyn looks up weak-eyed at Mama.

"Celery." She holds up her knife and waves it. "Run get me some out of the Frigidaire next door."

Slowly Marilyn stubs the Salem, rubs it harder than you would need to stop the burning. Then she goes out the back door, reaching back with the heel of her sandal so the door won't slam. She's wearing a blue-jean miniskirt and her legs are the color of caramel from going several times a week to a tanning salon. I watch my wife watch my sister and know Eleanor disapproves of it all. The bought tan, the false nails, the cigarettes, the lack of initiative.

In many ways, though most people wouldn't guess it, Eleanor and I come from the same mold. Both the oldest, both overachievers at an early age. Me in sports, she with her art. Both making all A's. Eleanor is ambitious too. Sometimes I think maybe even more ambitious than I am. But Eleanor just wants to achieve different things. Every time I set foot on a golf course or in a country club, I'm afraid there's going to be someone there who's going to tell me I don't belong. But Eleanor, she wouldn't join a country club if you paid her. I believe Eleanor would rather die than belong to a country club. I know she'd rather go hungry than for you to think she did a bad job.

So you see, that's the difference: I'm working for position and Eleanor is working for praise.

That's why she can't understand Marilyn. Marilyn doesn't seem to be working for anything. Not success, or praise, or self-satisfaction, or anything. She only stays at one thing until she moves to another.

I worry about her the way I used to worry about Kate. But at least Kate, even if she didn't care where she was, cared about where she was going. She had a plan, even if it was cockeyed and crazy, even if it changed every other minute. But Marilyn, Marilyn doesn't have a plan and doesn't want any. She is just there, like a case of ketchup or a piece of furniture, and doesn't much care where you put her. That's what kills Eleanor. It's what kills me, too, because I don't know what to do about it.

I know about the baby; Marilyn's. It wasn't hard to guess. She came back after those months in Kentucky with her face puffy and Mama treating her so carefully. Maybe others knew, too, because she was changed, hardly ever said anything. Maybe even Olin guessed but didn't want to know, was only halfway hoping someone would slip and tell him when he picked at her.

I never said anything to either of them, her or Mama, until a couple of years ago. This boyfriend she had been living with called and said we'd better get to the hospital, that Marilyn was fine now but had had a close call with some intestinal thing. Mama and I guessed what it was, but didn't say anything to each other. It was only when Kate heard and called and said, "What did she take?" that I admitted anything.

Of course I got my back up like I do and said, "What are you talking about? She didn't take anything."

"Oh come on," Kate said. "I've been expecting this for years. So what was it? Sleeping pills?" And she rattled off a list of pharmaceuticals as if she were drilling in Latin. Kate is one of those people who knows drugs the way some people know the names of flowers or birds. I've never taken more than an aspirin or two in my entire life, but she remembers the names of prescription drugs better than most medical students.

It was while I was driving Mama home from the hospital that I asked her about the baby. "If I could take one thing back," Mama said, "it would be that. I should have let her keep him."

I'd always only guessed before, but to hear her say "him" grabbed at me. There was a boy somewhere of Marilyn's. "She wanted to keep him?"

It was the first time in my life my mother ever looked at me like I was stupid.

"I thought she would be like all those young girls I saw trying to make it without any help and ending up handing their babies over to people like me, coming back every few months and hauling them off again, trying to make a go of it. I thought I was doing the right thing."

"You did, probably."

She was rolling the hem of her sweater between her fingers and shaking her head. "I should have packed up both of those children and brought them back from Kentucky and helped her raise him. I should have told Olin to go jump if he didn't like it. But I didn't, and I did wrong."

I never told Eleanor. It's not the kind of thing we would normally keep from one another. But Eleanor lost a baby once, and ever since we got married she's been trying to get pregnant. I didn't know what she would think about Marilyn giving up a baby.

*   *   *

She's leaving, Eleanor is. Going to New York.

Her friend Carroll called and said he was going to Paris at the end of the summer or early fall, and he wanted to know if she knew someone who would lease his apartment for a couple of months. When she told me about it, she was nervous, I could tell. "I don't have to do this," she said. "And I won't if you have any problem with it at all. It's an awful lot of money." But I told her that of course I wanted her to go. It's a good opportunity, I said, a chance for her to finally get immersed in her work again. She's not going for three or four months yet, and I've practically packed her bags.

Quiet hurts me so, rings in my ears like pounded metal. Maybe it's from growing up with Mama's music, with voices clashing all through the night. I can't go to bed at night without the television going, can't drive in the car without the radio on.

I'm already scared of the quiet when Eleanor's gone. Kate and I used to sleep with the TV on; I was usually the one who'd wake up in the middle of the night and turn it off, then go back to bed. Kate slept the way you see children sleep, arms and legs sprawled out, thrashing about, sometimes talking. I used to answer her when she'd talk, ask her what she'd said. When she'd hear my voice, she'd get still and quiet, and then go back to sleep without saying anything more. Sometimes she'd sit straight up in bed. Once when she bolted like that, she stared at the wall, like she was staring at someone, and said, "I won't let you." She didn't remember anything about it in the morning.

Four or five times we went to places where Rita was drying out. When we'd get there, Rita would pace up and down the room, talk constantly, move those long hands and fingers as if she were playing different musical instruments. "Hey, I'm fine. Fine. I've got this gig worked out for the weekends, and got this guy who's going to give me voice lessons during the day. Maybe I'll even find another job for the mornings."

"Do you hear what you're doing? You're setting yourself up again," Kate would say.

But Rita would just shake her head and pace. "No, babe, I've got it under control. I'm fine. I'm okay."

The last time we went to visit Rita, to a little place in Texas, Kate stayed on in the motel room we'd rented, said she was going to just stay a few more days. I knew then, though, when I left her with the Honda and flew back to Atlanta, that she wasn't coming. Even when she called from all the different places, saying she was only going to follow Rita another week or two, to make sure she was all right, I knew she wasn't coming home.

I drove out once more, this time when they were in Tennessee, and made sure she had money. Kate was waiting tables at a place near Opryland, and she and Rita had an apartment together, though it was the mother who came and went like a wild teenager and made Kate sick with worry. Rita had gotten to where she wouldn't eat any packaged products anymore or hardly anything in a restaurant. She was afraid of nitrates and preservatives, and she drank bourbon like it was water.

There was no fighting or arguing between me and Kate. She just stayed. And I was relieved to let her—maybe the way Mama always was when someone from the agency came to pick up one of the kids. You're just so relieved not to have the responsibility anymore, even though you know they may not be in the best of hands and even though you know you'll worry.

I used to dream about Linda Ronstadt, dream she'd come to me for counsel. Ask me what songs would be good for a new album. I'd take over her business, protect her from all the hangers-on and groupies. I'd rush her off the stage after a performance, the way they used to escort Elvis. I took care of her in every way, and then late at night she'd hold me.

When I was in high school, Mama cooked me steak dinners after every football game. Everyone else would have eaten, but when I got home, she'd set the table again, bring a baked potato from the oven, cut it down the middle, and fill it up with margarine. She'd put a T-bone in the skillet and sear it, and then put it on my plate and sit beside me while I told her about the game and ate.

Marilyn and the fosters hardly ever made good grades. When I brought home my A's, and Excellents in conduct, there'd be some kind of pie waiting for me on the counter. Peach or sweet potato or pecan, or maybe a lemon pound cake.

I'm a small boy, four or five, and when I fall or in some

other way hurt myself, Mama wraps me in her arms, holds me against her on the couch, and gives me licorice or Tootsie Rolls.

Eleanor is going to New York. And I am hungry.

Olin used to knock me around. Shove at my back from behind, threaten to beat me. Then when I was twelve, and the biggest boy in the class, I pulled my fist back and told him if he ever hit me again, I'd kill him. He never touched me after that. Even when I never grew any bigger. He's still four inches taller, but I backed him down once and never had to do it again.

What Olin does now, on the rare occasions they come to visit, is knock my possessions around. He'll look at our foyer and say, "This is an add-on, isn't it?" He'll walk along the fence in the backyard, then come inside and ask, "How big's your property?" Just under an acre, I tell him. "I've got two acres and a half."

I met Fitz, Eleanor's former mother-in-law, in the apartment over her store. Fitz is as crazy as a coot, and I love her. And because of how Eleanor feels about her, I never thought much about her being Jay's mother. Not until the day Eleanor and I were driving in the neighborhood where they all used to live, and in front of this house, she said, just in passing, "That's Fitz's old place." It was practically a mansion.

Eleanor doesn't care about the size of that house or any other. But I do. Sometimes it hits me that I'm more like Olin than I'd ever like to think.

I make more money in a year than he makes in seven. I've known it for a long time, maybe forever: size is important to me. I cannot live little.

In early September, the year before we were married, Eleanor and I stayed for a weekend on this little driftwood-strewn island near Hilton Head, South Carolina. A buddy of mine had rented a house there for the week, but because of a sick relative, he had to leave early. He called and asked if I wanted it for the last three days. I had this convertible then, an old Austin-Healy, one I bought for almost nothing and then put back together myself. Eleanor and I drove all the way there with the top down, a hot humid wind slapping at our faces the whole way. We were already burned when we got there, from the drive, and looked as if we'd been at the beach for days.

That house felt so good. My friend had left the air conditioner on high, and the place was like an icebox next to the way it had been in the hot car. We had seen a seafood shop on the way in, about a mile or two away, and since we were too tired and burned from the ride, we decided I'd go buy shrimp and we'd eat in that first night.

When I left, Eleanor was getting in the shower. I went to a liquor store first, bought us gin and limes and beer, and then to the seafood place for a pound and a half of six-dollar shrimp. Again, when I walked in that door, it felt so good. Cold and clean. I put the groceries down in the kitchen and called out to her that I was back. I was pulling beers from the six-pack when I heard Eleanor behind me.

Her hair was still damp and curling around her face. But she had put on this blue gauzy dress that hung from her neck, exposing her shoulders. And she had put on makeup, a little blue in the corners of her eyes; lipstick; and she was wearing perfume.

Other women had dressed for me, fixed themselves up for going out to parties. And so had Eleanor. But they had done it only when we would see other people. This hot night in September, we weren't planning to step outside that door. Eleanor hadn't done this for anyone but me.

It made my throat throb. I turned back to the refrigerator, and asked her in a tight voice if she wanted a beer.

Maybe some of that gin you've got there, she told me. I put the ice in the glasses, poured the gin, the tonic, cut the lime—all with my back to her, not saying a word. I gave it to her the same way, cold as the drinks and that room.

I was fiddling with one of the other bags when she put her hand on my back and said, "What is it, Will? What's the matter?"

I couldn't speak. Couldn't move. She was hurting, I could tell, but I still couldn't say anything. I was afraid that if I spoke, my words would knock together like marbles.

"You're sorry we've come, aren't you? That's it?"

I turned around and just shook my head. She was beautiful, and for no one but me.

"No one ever did that before," I said.

I'm not the kind of man that women talk about, and I guess not the kind they think about. Not the kind most people would picture holding a beautiful woman in their arms. "No one ever dressed and made themselves up like that for me," I said. "Just for me."

Eleanor took me to her, and moved so gently, as if she thought my body were bruised or burned. Her fingers swept over me like the coolest breezes, like waves from a deep cold source. She caressed and held and licked and loved, and pulled me inside her and held me there. I felt the way I did those couple of times I had gone skinny-dipping; everything that touched my skin was lovely, like floating silk, like water.

The package of shrimp stayed so long on that counter that we were afraid it had spoiled, and we threw it out. Later, we found crackers we had brought along in the car and ate them for our supper.

I am a man with large appetites. During that one weekend in September, Eleanor filled me up.

We came back from the little island with people talking about our tans, and we hadn't stuck one toe on the beach or in that dark ocean.

I love to watch Eleanor put on her face. That's what she calls it, putting on her face. She draws a flesh-colored pencil under her eyes, and her breasts hang over the sink, not so far from the water. Sometimes I go into the bathroom when she's doing this, pretend to be hunting for something in the cabinet behind her (tweezers, Band-Aid, aspirin) and then turn around and cup her breasts. Or her tail. I hold on for dear life, and she says, "Will you get out of here, Will?" When we were on our honeymoon in Brussels, and a snowstorm came up (the Flemish people we knew said it was unusual, hardly ever happened there), Eleanor and I walked so long and so late in the snow that we were nearly sick. That night, naked, she had leaned over the hotel sink, all these red angles and roof lines out the window beside her, with a towel over her head and breathing in steam to keep bronchitis from dropping down into her chest. While she was leaning there, I snapped a photograph of her from the bed. She didn't know I'd done it until we were home and going through all the pictures of the trip, sorting them out city by city. "What is this?" she said. "Honey buns," I told her. My sweet baby's behind. I keep that picture tacked up on the inside of my closet, just above the shelf where I put my wallet and keys every night, Eleanor's tight fanny riding high in the air.

She puts mascara around the eyes. Pink on the cheeks and a different powder over the pink (all this is done with a big, black-bristled brush). More black around the eyes. The hair comes down (yellow, brown at the crown). A fingertip full of shiny coral goes across the lips. She stands back, squints, frowns, paints more powder over the cheeks, and quits. God, the act of all that. It goes to my very center. But I never let her know how deep it goes, how it touches me to see her naked, so vulnerable, so trusting like that.

Whenever my wife is away, I move to her side of the mattress, use her pillow. I don't tell her this, don't dare tell her the other things: touch the white robe that hangs from the hook in the bathroom closet; open the drawers containing the soft rows of folded beige, white fabric, stockings rolled and stored in a plastic bag, little empty perfume bottles that roll to the back of the drawer when I close it.

Olin and a neighbor are outside working on a car. They are bent up under the hood, and over them, in the ivy-choked oak trees, squirrels flick their tails and climb, their skins smooth as chamois. Mama is going to hold dinner until Olin is ready. She spoons potato salad into a scrving bowl, asks Marilyn to set the table. She stretches Saran over the huge platter of deviled eggs. But she keeps out six or seven and puts them on a little chipped saucer.

Eleanor begins telling her about New York. Why she is going. Where she will stay. Mama says, "That sounds interesting, honey," and hands me the saucer.

I don't believe I've ever been in this house when the TV wasn't on. Its sounds and the voices of the women play on. I pick up the eggs, one by one, and eat them.

Eleanor: 1987

⸙

Sometimes things stay in your brain so well it feels as if they've been sealed in there with cement and metal. Very often they're the things that, if you were watching after a child, you'd never expect to be the things she would remember. The summer I was eleven and spent with my aunt Kathleen and uncle Jim in North Carolina, while CoraRuth and Henry lay in hospital beds in two different cities recovering from the injuries of an automobile accident, small incidents became embedded in my mind forever, so sharp and real I sometimes believe I can reach up and touch them.

My cousin Sis's toes. They are always bloody and raw, or else scabbed over with little layers of dry, peeling skin. My aunt and uncle live near the bottom of a hilly street, the last house on a corner, and my cousin Mason and I take turns pushing his bicycle up the street and then riding down again and at the last minute making a sharp left off the sidewalk and sliding into a thick soft pallet of pine needles. We see who can ride the longest with hands and legs held out, balancing against air, our hair and voices blowing. Sis is much younger than either of us, and Mason won't let her on the bicycle because he says she's too small although she's long become too big for her tricycle. But she follows us to the top of the hill anyway, pushing the trike from behind. When she gets to the top, she picks up the tricycle, struggling with it, and points it down. She leans forward, her knees on the piece of metal that goes between the back wheels, and she gives herself a good push, steering with her arms hunched over the seat and her hands up on the ribboned handlebars. The pedals go around and around with nothing riding on them. Sis has no brakes this way, and so she drags her toes all the way down to make sure she doesn't run off the curb at the end of the sidewalk. Aunt Kathleen bandages Sis's toes every night after our baths and tells her she's going to have to wear shoes tomorrow. But the shoes always come off, and so do the Band-Aids, and Sis's toes stay so ragged and raw I don't know how she can let anything touch them.

Aunt Kathleen cries all the time. I hear her talking on the telephone, and I sneak into the kitchen to see who she's talking to. She speaks in whispers when I'm around and touches the hem of her dress to her eyes. It was when I overheard people talking in the halls of the hospital before I was released that I learned my sister Diane had died in the car wreck. When I hear Aunt Kathleen crying now at home, I think it means someone else has died, Mother or Henry, and she must be too afraid to tell me. And I'm too afraid to ask.

I go outside under the trees and chew on pine needles. They taste sour to me, like pickles.

Mason and I go to Bible school. Aunt Kathleen drives us there and drops us; as she pulls away, I watch Sis's long face in the back window of the station wagon following us. Mason has nothing to do with me here and sits with the boys. For three weeks we study the Miracles of Nature. We collect leaves and flowers and draw pictures of birds and grasshoppers. We stick a lima bean in a jar and give it water, and we watch it sprout a long, pale whisker.

On the final day of Bible school, parents are invited to attend our graduation presentation and hear about all the things we have done. Henry is coming, they've told me. Someone is driving him up from the famous university hospital where they put people's bodies back together. I haven't seen him in weeks, not since the accident.

My part in the program is to explain about the lima bean. I am to show how we slid it against a piece of curved cardboard in the jar, and how it sprouted after a few days in the water. I learn everything I am to say, and I practice it over and over.

All I can think about is Henry, and what he will think when he sees me. He isn't there when the program starts, and I start worrying. I am sitting on the stage with the others when the door in the back opens, and someone with a large head, with a face that is blue and yellow, and with two short bars of metal sticking through the skin of one cheek, walks in. A third bar runs between the other two and holds them together, like a television antenna. Everyone turns around and stares. He and the man who walks with him find chairs. And the teacher calls my name and directs me to the center of the stage. I'm holding the jar with the bean in it. It's cold and smooth between my hands. I don't say anything. I am frozen. I can't look up, afraid I will see Henry. The teacher leans toward me and asks a question to get me going. I can't nod or shake my head. She kneels beside me and helps me hold the jar and begins explaining, speaking all my parts. She has one hand on my shoulder and one hand on the jar. And when she is finished, she takes my hand and walks with me across the stage and past my chair, down the steps and out the door.

My mother is in another hospital across the state. When we go to visit her, we have to drive across mountains. I get carsick every time, and Aunt Kathleen has to pull over and let me throw up in a ditch on the side of the road. When we get to the hospital, my new dress smells of vomit, and I start to cry. CoraRuth will see that I've ruined my clothes again, I tell them. I lean against the wall in the corridor and refuse to go inside the room where my mother's legs are floating in slings, held in the air by pulleys and girders. Someone pinches my arm and calls me, "Selfish!"

In our living room back home in South Carolina, there was a large, black square-shaped furnace that took up half the space of the room and made a noise like traffic. During winter, the rest of the house always stayed cool while the living room was steaming. When my mother had sick headaches, I put baking potatoes on the top of the furnace and cooked them there so she could eat them. I brought her washcloths from the bathroom, and put them on her forehead, and tried to keep my sister and brother quiet.

I hid behind the furnace on school nights when I was supposed to be sleeping and Diane was in the living room with Mother and Henry watching television. I crouched there until

CoraRuth, still on the sofa, would say, "Go on back to bed, Eleanor. You've got school in the morning."

When Mother and Henry are released from their hospitals and we are back home, the furnace has to be removed. They take it out in sections, its pipes and hoses hanging loose like the body parts of a murdered animal, a stiff black elephant. With it out of the room, Mama can maneuver the wheelchair past where it used to be and push down the hall to her bedroom.

She goes from the wheelchair to two silver crutches. They have white rubber handles that she grips, and metal clasps that fold down and hug her arms. When she no longer needs the crutches, my friends and I sometimes take them from the hall closet and play with them, pretend we're soldiers and nurses. But mostly they are propped together in the back corner, the door closed, and they stay there over the years, silent and still as family skeletons.

The day before our accident, my mother had bought four bottles of liquid vitamins for me and Diane at a Rexall one-cent sale. At the moment of impact, I fell off the backseat and landed on a broken bottle. It cut a very small jagged question mark on my left knee.

They say I am the one who gave the police our address and the names of our nearest relatives. All I remember is something jerking tight little stitches in my knee.

While I am in the hospital, different people take turns staying with me. When my aunt and grandmother and my mother's cousins aren't around, it's one of the secretaries from Admissions or one of the volunteers. But on the day they send Cora and Henry to different hospitals, both in North Carolina where there are special doctors, it is the woman from the pharmacy. We sit outside her office at a long table, and she lets me count pills into dark bottles. The pills are long and brown and smell like metal. Vitamins, she tells me.

I have dreams of my family from time to time, but in them no one has ever gotten any older. I am always eleven or twelve, taking care of my brother, and Henry and Cora are never old like they are now, but young and in a hurry.

My brother is a grown man, with children of his own. But in my dreams he is always a toddler, who is being carried on my hip, who I am responsible for, who I have been told not to let get in trouble.

Last night I called my parents and told them I was going to New York. I explained how my friend Carroll was going to be in Europe for a couple of months and that it was such a perfect opportunity. How I would be able to get so much work done there, how the city will be stimulating, how I've needed this kind of time to myself.

My grandmother's maiden name was Painter. That has always been like an omen to me, like a sign that this is what I should be doing. I paint in my dreams sometimes, work out problems that can't get worked out when I'm awake and really painting.

Henry is silent on the phone. I can't even hear him breathing. I try to explain that in Atlanta, art is considered a hobby. That in Atlanta, art is something that is done on the *side*, whenever everything else is taken care of. Atlanta has its beauty, its trees, its new buildings, its furniture and cars. But in Atlanta, if your work is other than buying and selling, you are thought of as odd. All this makes sense to me when I say it to myself, but when I try to say it to a practical, hardworking man like Henry, it sounds so hollow and silly.

CoraRuth asks me a hundred questions, and for every one I give her an answer that ten minutes earlier had seemed sane and steady. Now, for every word I speak, I feel a pinch and hear a silent "Selfish!"

I end the conversation, saying I'm going. But when I am off the phone, and there are no more voices, I hear the distant rattle of old metal. Of crushed jaws. Broken legs and fingers and rib cages. On my tongue I taste iron and sour pine. I see roots and hair, raw skin, frightened children, and the tiniest human scar in all of America.

The telephone receiver rests between the cradle and my hand. And I have forgotten why it is I need to go anywhere or why anything other than these few things is important.

CoraRuth: 1987

ﾧ

Well, we were worried to death when we found out she was going up there. All alone like that, staying in a place on the ninth floor of this big building. It's not even an apartment building, or a hotel. She said they used to make women's hats in there! I thought, What in the world? Her not knowing a soul. Not having a car. How was she supposed to get around? We hear the news, know the kind of rigmarole that goes on up there, what happens to people on those subway trains.

I said, "Now tell me again why it is you're going." She just said so she could work. I thought maybe she was going to do landscapes of New York City, the Statue of Liberty maybe, the Empire State Building, those sorts of things. But no, she was going to paint people. "I don't understand," I said. "They've got some kind of different face up there than we've got down here? You've already painted every interesting human being in Georgia and South Carolina?"

"Mama, it's not so much that I'm going for something *to* paint, but for a concentrated period of time to work without any other demands on me. Any other responsibilities."

"Well, yes, I guess all those youngins hanging on you every minute does make it hard." I don't know why I let things fly out of my mouth like that. I could have kicked myself the second I said it, what with poor old Eleanor trying to get pregnant like she is. I felt terrible. It seems like this temper of mine gets worse instead of better.

But tell me. What *does* she have hanging on her? What kinds of responsibilities? When I was her age I'd had three children, cleaned house every day, cooked three—sometimes four—meals a day for a meat-and-potatoes man and three finicky little ones, and I kept the books to Henry's business on the side, helped hire some of the migrant workers. Sunday school lessons, PTA meetings, Christian Women's Club, choir practice, Girl Scouts, Boy Scouts, art classes, piano lessons, drama club, Little League, Henry's softball team, a million pairs of socks and underwear and grimy pants legs to wash. Sewed uniforms and costumes and all my kitchen curtains. Mopping, ironing, cleaning. Putting up preserves and jellies every summer. Shelling nuts and baking every fall.

Sometimes I wanted just five minutes alone, a chance to go to the bathroom without one of the kids or Henry or Mama sticking their nose in asking where something was. One time when Lucas wasn't but about two years old, he saw a picture of a woman taking a bath in a magazine, and he asked, "Where are her little children?" It was the only chance I ever got of getting a bath myself, with one of the babies in there with me. It seems like with children you're just tired for years. In fact, you begin to forget what being rested is like, how it is to sleep all the way through one night or not to go to bed with a washing machine full of clothes and a house that still needs picking up. Just five minutes. That's all I wanted sometimes, to be able to close my eyes and not worry about some child getting hurt or into something. Five minutes without anyone pulling on me, without any noise.

It wears me out now just thinking about it. But what did that girl have to worry about? I didn't see what she had to fly all the way to New York to get away from.

Unless it was Will.

I was glad she let pass what I had said. I didn't have the energy all of a sudden to get into it with her. Everybody was quiet for a spell, and then she said, "Daddy, are you there?"

He mumbled something and I said, "Speak into the receiver, Henry!" Sometimes that man can plain tie a knot in my nerves.

I know how to spot trouble, but I hadn't seen anything blowing up between Eleanor and Will. It made me wonder if I hadn't been paying attention lately or if I was losing my power of concentration. Losing my gift for sensing things: infidelity, economic disaster, thundershowers.

You could spot it a mile away, when it was happening with

her and Jay. Looking at them was like putting salt on a raw place. She got down to about a hundred pounds, even after having been pregnant and for about a year she and Jay both looked like death warmed over. They didn't talk, they didn't touch. It was awful. But I hadn't seen anything like that with her and Will. Every time they came up here, he about ate her up. One time Henry even said he didn't think it was natural for a grown man to carry on that way about a woman.

So I didn't know what was up. Nobody said anything, but I guess we were all praying that she wasn't going to turn out like Henry's cousin Winnie. The woman lives over in Nashville, dyes her hair auburn, and has been married four times. And her a college professor! A couple times we hadn't even heard she'd left one husband when we find out she was hooked up with another. One time it was even a preacher. But he was Episcopalian, and Lord knows they don't count.

You hear about how certain strains of people run in families, like alcoholics or dope addicts. Like I said, me and Henry didn't say anything, never mentioned the name Winnie, but you could tell we were both walking around the subject like two people circling a dead cat. Nobody wanted to touch it.

To tell you the truth, I carried on that night on the phone. I should have let the whole thing go, said, Good Luck, and Go on up there, and Have a good time. But I couldn't. I said, "I guess this is going to cost poor Will a pretty penny."

"Mama," she said. "I told you, I'm staying at a friend's place who's out of town. My friend Carroll."

"That hippie fellow?"

"Oh, good grief, Mother. This is the nineteen-eighties. He's not a hippie."

He was too. I'd seen him. One time he was even wearing an earbob. And he was scraggly and sloppy and never put on a thing but a pair of dirty blue jeans. Always acted like he was on something. If that wasn't a hippie I didn't know what was. What was Eleanor thinking, going up there and staying in that kind of person's apartment?

"What's Will going to eat?" I asked her. "What's he going to do for his supper?"

That got her to laughing. But before we were through, she was bawling. Of course that was nothing new. I've said this before, I guess, but that girl is good at crying. The whole time she was growing up she'd haul off up to her room sobbing like she'd been hit (*which* she never was!) when nobody had done anything to her but say good morning.

Well, you never really know your children, never really know what they're thinking. But Eleanor is worse than usual. She's always been a peculiar child. Just different. Spent all that time off by herself, out in the woods or up in that room of hers. Never played with dolls and clothes and cutouts like a normal girl. Didn't care about parties and little frilly things like you'd think she would. Never even had but one close girlfriend. She just wanted to come home and paint or ride around with Henry in that truck. I guess I should have taken her somewhere to let somebody check her out, if we'd had the money.

I don't know what gets into her head about stuff. I thought she should have stayed with Jay; I told her so too. (Not that I don't think Will's a good man, a fine provider. And not that once or twice I myself haven't wanted to jerk a knot in Jay's tail. It's not that.) But nobody's life is perfect, is it? It's not like Jay was a rounder. Or a drinker. He's not the type. And he sure never did anything like hit her—I'd have boxed his ears if he'd ever tried! No, Jay just didn't have a lot of get-up-and-go. But no law I've ever read says that's a crime. My policy is, you live with whatever you have to.

And then her carrying on with his mother that way. Now that's not natural, is it? Staying friends with an in-law like that? And the way Fitz is, well, she's worse than a hippie. Demonstrating out there at that nuclear power plant with people half her age, wearing her hair back in a braid like she's started doing. Forming that old people's ozone club or whatever it is. I don't know.

It's just like I said, Eleanor is different.

After we got off the phone, I said to Henry, "What do you think's going on?"

He said, "I don't think anything. And I'm not going to think anything."

Well, I know Henry, and I know that's about as close to a lie as he's ever come. Not think about it!

Then he said he was going to go to town and buy a new

carburetor. (He's gotten into the habit of buying spare auto parts lately. Batteries, spark plugs, fan belts, mufflers. I've never seen the likes.)

So there I was left to contemplate our eldest child's ruin by myself. I wondered if she left Will for good, if I'd be able to get away with not telling anyone at the Christian Women's Club.

But guess what? Every time I've talked with her since she's been up there, all she talks about is how much she misses Will. Says she calls him every day. He sends her flowers. She writes him little cards. Says she thinks sometimes she'll never be able to stand it the whole time (she's supposed to stay two months).

I think her being miserable is a good sign. I mean, if she was laughing it up, having a big time, it would make you worry. But if they're so crazy about each other, then there must not be any problem. I think maybe it's got to be what she said, that she's gone up there to work.

Because apparently she is working. Says she's got about five big canvases painted so far. That's a lot; the girl is slow as Christmas. I've seen her keep one painting around for months. She'd be working on other things, too, all along. But she'd go back to that one again and again, trying to get something just right.

You know what I've been thinking? I haven't told a soul this except Henry. But I've been thinking maybe I'll go up there and visit. Well, why not? I've never been to New York, never set a foot above North Carolina. We had plans to take the kids to different cities, up to Washington and Williamsburg and those sorts of places. But I don't know what happened. It seemed there wasn't enough money or enough time, and we never got around to it.

But now it's just me and Henry, and Mama half the year. The children are off on their own. Lucas set up as a doctor, making his own money. We haven't had such a bad year. I'd like to see what kind of food they give you on an airplane. I could stand a little excitement.

I thought Henry could too. So last night at supper while we were watching the news (we've gotten to where we don't eat at the table anymore unless someone's here; we take our meals out to the den on trays and eat in front of the TV), I said to him, "Henry, how about let's hop on Delta and fly up there to see Eleanor."

Why, he looked at me like I was crazy. "What for?" he wanted to know.

"Well, to see our oldest daughter for one thing. And to see the city. Eleanor could take us around, show us things. Do a little sightseeing."

"No."

"What do you mean, no? Just like that, no, you don't even want to talk about it?"

"It's cold up there."

"Well, you've got a coat, don't you?"

It used to be that Henry wanted to go everywhere. He'd bring out that atlas of his and we'd look at it with the children and talk about all the places we wanted to see. China, Hawaii, Mexico. Eleanor wanted to go to Switzerland, because of Heidi. We thought we'd go out west somewhere, Yellowstone and the Grand Canyon. Maybe do some camping. But now Henry doesn't seem to want to go anywhere. Last month I couldn't even get him to drive up to Spartanburg with me to see a crafts show.

"Henry," I said. I wasn't going to let this thing drop just yet. "Henry, let's do it. Let's get us a couple of tickets and go. It'd be good for us."

You know what he said? "Just tell me what our daughter's doing up there in the first place, CoraRuth. You just tell me." He put his tray over on the mantel. "I don't know what's gotten into you women these days anyway."

Well, I think I know what's gotten into Henry. Me. Me and my Powder Puff Mechanics.

A few years back I took this course over at the technical school on what to do if you're out somewhere by yourself and your car breaks down. With the way Henry takes care of vehicles, I needed it. I figured I could show him a thing or two, you know, about his truck. Well, he wasn't interested. Said he knew what a spark plug was, knew how to change the oil. My foot! Henry doesn't know a spark plug from his you-know-what. Thing is, it doesn't matter. The man is good at plenty of things, he doesn't have to know anything about cars. But I figured one of us ought to.

So anyway, I took this class. And then last spring they offered a refresher course, and I took it too because I'd had a pretty good time the first time round. You should have seen some of the women. They were worse than Henry. Didn't know head from tail, and half of them were afraid of breaking their fingernails. So I got to where I kind of explained a thing or two to some of them on the side while the instructor was under someone else's car with an oil pan. I showed them how you could just put a little piece of fabric right on the side of the car after you opened the hood (I carry a piece with me all the time, keep it in the trunk along with the emergency bottle of water and flashlight and first aid kit) and about how you could lean on that and you wouldn't get the first bit dirty. They acted like that dipstick was something they'd been told not to touch back in high school. I told them, "Look, it's just like you're taking the temperature of a baby," and I handled that little dipstick like it had just come out of an alcohol bottle and I eased it in there and pulled it out and said, "See, nothing to it." I told them there wasn't a thing under that hood any more difficult to understand than anything in their kitchens. I told them they worked machinery all day long: garbage disposals, washing machines, hair dryers. Just because it was in a car didn't mean they couldn't learn about it.

Those women just related to me. I kind of made them feel at home there, their heads stuck up underneath the demonstrator hood. (That regular instructor, I don't think he necessarily *wanted* to make it look easy.)

Before I knew it, people started saying how I should be the one teaching that kind of course. I said phooey at first. But then it started seeming like fun. So I talked to them over there at the technical school, and before long I was teaching Powder Puff every Tuesday morning. Then they started asking me if I'd talk to the girls in the home economics classes at some of the high schools. *And* once a month I have a demonstration in one of the malls in Greenville; they bring in a Chrysler and a loudspeaker system, and I talk about how important it is to keep your oil changed and to check the water in your battery. Those sorts of things. Sometimes I wear a pair of white gloves when

I explain how to check the oil; you know, to add some drama to it. They put a little piece about me in the *Greenville County Advertiser*. Everybody's just tickled pink about it. Everybody but Henry.

Well, he's acting plain goofy. Started buying all these car parts he doesn't have the first idea what to do with. And the other day, when I came home from the store, the car full of groceries, he didn't come out the way he usually does when I honk coming down the drive. I had already started carrying sacks in by myself when I spotted him. He was sprawled out on his back on Luke's old toy wagon up under his truck.

"Henry, come help me, honey," I yelled. "I've got sixty-five dollars' worth of groceries out in the trunk."

"CoraRuth, I'm busy here." There I was holding a five-pound bag of potatoes and a gallon of 2% milk, and him not lifting a finger to help me.

"What in the world are you doing, Henry?" I asked.

He sighed like he was perturbed with me. "Changing the tail pipe, Cora."

"What's wrong with it?"

"It just needs changing."

"Yes, but why? Has a hole rusted through or something?"

"It just needs changing, Cora, and I don't have the time to explain to you the reason why."

Well, good gracious. I hauled all those things myself, even the heavy canned goods, and then went on in and started supper.

I've thought about giving it up, Powder Puff Mechanics. But why should I? For the first time since I've been married I've got a little of my own money. I don't have to go to anybody and ask every time I need a dime for one thing or other. And I like it! Like speaking in that microphone, hearing my voice sounding so different, so—*interesting*—as it moves through the mall. I like the way people look at me, ask me questions, like I'm an authority. I believe I could have been something different if I had wanted. A schoolteacher maybe. Maybe even an actress. I saw this poster yesterday that said they were having tryouts next week for the Neighborhood Theater. Believe me, I've thought about it.

I don't have the least intention of hurting Henry. But my

showing somebody how to use a screwdriver doesn't have a thing in the world to do with him, now does it?

Everybody's got to feel special at some time or another, don't they? Men do, I've always known that. But women do too, I think.

The most important I've ever felt in my life was when I was pregnant the first time, with Eleanor. Everybody looked at me different. Everybody smiled at me all the time, even the grouchiest old codgers. Opened doors for me everywhere, scooted up chairs for me to sit on. Offered me something to drink, let me use their bathrooms. And it wasn't only because I was as big as a two-ton truck and had a head pressing on my bladder. It was because they knew it was all a miracle. The first time I went out again by myself after the baby was born, I thought, Now no one knows I'm special.

When I got my children, I lost big parts of Henry.

Don't get me wrong, my children are the best thing that ever happened to me. But there sure have been times when I wished, just for a little while, it could still be me and him, that we could get in a car and go somewhere and he wouldn't be filled with worry about money all the time. It seems like as soon as we had the babies, money was the thing that occupied so much of his mind. I guess it was the responsibility, of being a breadwinner and father and all. Well, children change you, that's for sure, and they took parts of him away, my Henry. And now I'm determined to get some of those pieces back. Pieces that got misplaced over the years with car payments and mortgages and bank loans against the taxes. Pieces that got carried away with every child. Some of them won't ever come back to me, I don't guess, all those pieces that were there in the beginning when I first met that dark-headed, silent boy. But parts of them might, parts that aren't dead or lost but are just hidden somewhere under piles of paperwork.

I've decided something. I'm going to buy those two tickets for me and Henry. At first, I thought, Well to heck with him; I'll go by myself. But now I'm thinking Henry really wants to go, he's just scared. So I'm going to buy the tickets and hand them to him and say, We're going. We won't bother Eleanor. I'll get us a hotel room somewhere. And he can't say a thing about it; I've got my Powder Puff Mechanics money. And I'm going to take my daughter out to lunch. Buy her a present. Not for an occasion. But just because I want to.

This is the first time in my married life I've ever done anything like this. Henry's the one that says what we're doing, and I always go along with it. I don't always like it, and one way or another I get around to letting him know I don't like it. But still, I've gone right on along with every one of his plans. I'm not going to argue that a man shouldn't be the head of the household and all that. But sometimes, if you know something isn't going to work out, isn't it more honest to speak up and say so instead of sitting there stewing because he's the man and ought to know better?

There's something else I've decided. We ought to sell this house. What do we need all these rooms for? All these floors to sweep and windows to wash.

For years we've been talking about remodeling, adding on. But that staircase still has the same old coat of paint. The commodes run all night, no matter how many times you go in there and jiggle the handles. The plaster's cracking. When in the world do we think we're ever going to get around to remodeling? Why would we think we need to add on?

We've talked about dream houses too. Sent off for plans. Huge houses, bigger than this. I don't want it.

No, I've decided I want a little place, just enough room for me and Henry, a room for Mama, and an extra bedroom for when the children come home. Nothing fancy. Just a simple place with one big room with a fireplace, where we do all our living. And I want a kitchen the size of a postage stamp. I tell you what, I'm tired of cooking. All those meals, and Henry the type that turns up his nose every time you try to slip something in on him like a little piece of cauliflower. He can cook his steaks in that fireplace, and I'm going to use that little kitchen of mine for whatever I want to. Maybe for nothing but boiling tea water. Making that sweet-smelling stuff out of rose petals.

Everybody needs some time to themselves. I do anyway. I've had thirty-some years of needing time to myself. Even now, with poor old Mama running that TV all afternoon watching her soap operas. Me having to read the headlines to her because after the last cataract operation she can't see to read. Sometimes it feels like I spent the first half of my life taking care of children and the second half looking after Mama and Henry. Most days are all right. But some days, well, I think I'm going to scream if I don't get away from those two. But then Henry will be off all day, and by nightfall I'll start to miss him so, can't wait to see that old head coming through the door. And when Mama goes to stay with my sister every year, why I'm so glad to see her go. But then in a couple of days I start to miss her, wish I could take back all my rushed words and being so impatient. You see, it's not a hermit's life I want. Just a few minutes here and there to put my feet up, just a half hour sometimes to myself.

So. I've bought me a piece of luggage. One of those hang-up bags. And, because of the time of year it is and how cold it gets up there, a new coat. I'd love to see some snow!

Don't they have ferries still, out to Staten Island? I'd like to do that. Go to Times Square. A couple of times I've been to places that I've seen for years in photographs, and they're never the same. They're always better. I think it might be like that in New York City. All these years watching them carrying on at New Year's in Times Square. But what's it really like? That's what I'm wondering.

We've worked hard all these years, me and Henry. Too hard. It's time we let up some, enjoyed ourselves. I'm ready to kick up my heels a little.

And you know what? He doesn't know it yet, but so is Henry.

Henry: 1987

It's true what you hear about how they bound the feet of Chinese women back when. I saw some of them when I was over there. Saw how they walked on those little feet like they were walking on toy blocks, like they might fall off of them, like they were walking on something that hard. It hurt, you could tell. It hurt to look at them too.

One time I took a rag and wrapped it around my hand, wondered what it would be like to keep it there. Wondered how it would feel if I let my fist grow hard and little like one of those women's feet. They say they used to get sores and those rags would be full of blood and pus, that you could hear the women scream when they untied them sometimes. It was supposed to be a thing of beauty, is what they said, to have a little foot. They made fun of women with big feet, even the other women did. "What ugly big feet she has," someone would say, and a girl would go wrap herself back up. Pretty feet. Maybe that's what they thought it was about. But when you wrap up somebody like that, it's to keep them from going somewhere, because how you going to walk anywhere when you've got a four-inch foot with pus oozing out?

I used to want to go places by myself. Without CoraRuth or the children. Just break out every once in a while and go camping or something. I'm not saying running away or anything like that. Just wanted maybe two, three days by myself. A couple of nights out in the dark, waking up on a cold morning, watching my breath hang in the air, frying some fish in an old skillet.

Sometimes a man can just get lost; one day he looks up and says, Where am I? Sometimes that happens to me. I go over to

193

the mall with Cora, and I see these children with their purple hair and a row of earrings in their earlobes, and I think, Where in the world am I? Who are these people? And this is here in South Carolina. What do you reckon it's like in some places?

Children don't play outside anymore, I've noticed. Cora and her sister were talking the other month when she came to visit about how you never hear about children getting impetigo now. Our children got it, and we scrubbed up their legs with phisoHex, that white soap in that tall green container. Painted their sores with medicine. But Cora says no one ever gets it anymore because of all the medicines today, and better hygiene. Hygiene nothing. If children still played out in a yard all day, they'd get something too. But children just watch TV and walk around in the malls. Looks like all that air conditioning would kill them.

A man can get lost even in his own house. Last week I came home, parked the truck, and walked up to my own back door like I always do. But there was plastic covering the screens on the porch and the door wouldn't open. I figured CoraRuth must have latched it from inside, so I knocked. "Cora! You want to open up?" And here she comes, running out on the screened porch and tells me to go around front. I asked her what the devil was she talking about, just go ahead and unlatch the door. And she says: "I can't, Henry. It's nailed shut."

It seems what happened is that Cora was sitting down that morning after feeding her birds, just drinking a cup of coffee, staring at one of those cages, and suddenly it hits her that it's not right to keep them caged up like that. Now this is after the woman's been keeping birds twenty-some years. And on a Monday morning in November she decides that it's wrong. But she doesn't want to just let them go; says they'd all be dead within the hour. She's always let them fly around out on that porch in the summertime, but now she's decided that's where they're living forever. She tacks up three thicknesses of plastic all around on that big screened-in porch so the birds aren't in a draft, and she nails the back door shut so nobody will forget and go out that way and accidentally let one out. She hangs up some tree branches here and there so those dern parakeets'll think they're in the great outdoors, and she says she'll let them stay out there until over time they all die off naturally, and then she's not ever buying any more.

How do you ever know a person? is what I'm wondering. How do you feel safe in the world if you can't expect to come home and open up your own back door?

That's not all. Cora's one of those women that started graying early, I guess when she was still just in her twenties. It started in the front, at the temples, and moved to the back in this long, slow wave so that over the years you kind of forgot it was happening. It just seemed natural that CoraRuth had turned mostly gray except for this little circle of black around her neck. But the other day I come home, and I almost walked right out of my own kitchen. Right there standing in front of the stove is not that same gray head I've been seeing every day for all these years, but some dern blonde. I stepped backwards.

"How do you like it?" she says, this big grin on her face. Cora's the type that if she's pleased with herself, she's about as bad as a hyena at holding it in. She puts her hand up to her head. "Frivolous Fawn," she says.

"Who?"

"It's not a who. It's the color. Frivolous Fawn. So what do you think?"

I figured she'd just as soon not know what I was thinking, so I took up my newspaper and sat down.

"It washes right out," she says. "If I want to, I can shampoo it out in half a minute."

Well, I reckon she don't want to. It's been two weeks now, and if anything Cora's getting lighter instead of darker.

I'd just like to know what in the world is happening. My daughter is up in New York living in some crazy man's apartment, my back porch is full of bird dookie, and every night before I realize it, I've crawled into bed next to a Frivolous Fawn.

Last night I was out there on the porch trying to clean up some of that mess, and I ran across one of the Atlanta papers Will or Lucas or one of them left up here. And there on the front page of the City/State section was a story about a pregnant woman getting shot in the belly, and how the bullet had gone through the baby's head and out his neck. They were both in the hospital, that woman and her baby, both hooked up to wires but expected to make it. Next there's this story about a thirty-seven-year-old policeman who on the day he sends his bullet-proof vest out to get altered, gets shot in the chest and dies. Him with a little Vietnamese wife and two children. Then there's this story about a man who goes into a hamburger place and holds all the employees hostage, says his name is Nugget, and they've been using his name to sell little fried-chicken pieces without his permission. Says someone's going to have to pay. So all afternoon he holds the place hostage, and while he's doing it he orders himself two or three boxes of chicken nuggets and an order of fries. That's all on one page. All down in Atlanta, where I figured things were bad enough. But now Eleanor's up in New York, and there's no telling what goes on in a place like that if right down here in the South you've got unborn babies getting shot in the head and people running into a restaurant holding folks hostage.

Everybody's got a secret.

I didn't always think that was so. I mean, years ago, when CoraRuth and me were both so busy with hardly a minute to ourselves without one of the children or her mother or one of the employees asking something of us, I never thought to think what she was thinking. I figured I knew her through and through. But now that there's more time and more help and a little more money, I see there are sides to CoraRuth that are just now hitting air.

You've never seen a worker like that woman. When the children were little, she went day and night, sewed little fancy dresses for the girls, and kept this place spick-and-span. I'm not saying she never complained or that I never saw a look on her face that said, Why isn't there ever any more money? But she worked every bit as hard as I did in her own area and she could squeeze an extra cent out of every nickel. She also had my supper on the table every night when I came home, and when I went back out every night to check on things again, she might look at me real hard, but she never said anything.

But now she's full of talk and full of questions. *Henry, what are you thinking?* Dern it, CoraRuth, sometimes I'm not thinking at all, I'm just resting my brain. But she's still probing. Used to be she'd let me alone if I fell asleep in front of the TV, told the children to hush because I needed my rest. But now she starts poking at my leg with her shoe: *Wake up, Henry, you're snoring.* And supper. Cora says she's had her fill of cooking, says we need to watch our calories anyway, and on the nights she gets home from sticking her head under the hood of a car, she microwaves diet TV dinners that have these flat green things in there, *snow peas*, she says, and a little piece of chicken that fills you up about as well as an oak leaf would. By seven o'clock I'm back in the kitchen fixing myself peanut butter and crackers.

I started drawing out some plans for finally adding on, enlarging the kitchen like she's always wanted, putting in one of those greenhouse windows that she talks about. But when I show her the plans, she acts like I've shown her something in the *TV Guide* that she's already seen. No, sir, she doesn't want anything to do with the fancy kitchen. She's decided we ought to sell the place and build us a smaller house closer to town. This is where our children were reared, I told her. So what? Living here isn't going to help us remember it any better, she says.

And now her latest thing is she wants to fly up to New York to visit Eleanor. Says we ought to see that city. What's happened to the woman?

The Great Wall of China. I've been there. Nearly two thousand miles long and over two thousand years old. It's one of the wonders of the world, they say. I guess so. All those men that it took to build it, one out of every family. They gave us a tour when I was over there in the service. Me and some of the others took pictures of each one of us walking up a section of it. It's wider than you'd think, and higher. They say there's enough rocks in that wall to make a circle around the earth at the equator. They say maybe half a million men died making the thing. I've walked on it, put my weight down on those flat rocks with maybe a thousand poor old dead Chinamen lying right there underneath me.

Eleanor said one time that if she ever makes any money she's going to take me back to China. I don't think I want to go. I've seen it. And it seems to me that if a place hadn't changed in all those thousands of years, it isn't going to change much more in forty. I don't figure there would be any more broke-up bodies buried under that wall today than there was yesterday.

I do think. Sometimes when I'm lying back in my chair hearing the news, with my eyes closed, I'm thinking about all of it. I've always been responsible. We may have had rough times, but I never let a child go hungry or stay sick any longer than it took to get one of them to the doctor. I've always been strong for CoraRuth. I've always let her think we could go on through anything. I've always saved my tears for Diane until I could get outside by myself and no one would see me.

Most people think that wall in China was built to keep people out. But once you've been there you can see that it might also have been to keep people in. In some places the Chinese have pulled so many rocks out of it that there's hardly any wall left. Peasants built their houses out of it and their barns and I don't know what else.

If I start letting people take a thought here and a thought there, maybe there won't be anything left of me, either. CoraRuth might see that part of my heart's gone already, chiseled out and buried there with Diane. That other parts of it got carried off in bad seasons, in years when I thought we should just sell out. That parts of it got took when I realized I wasn't ever going to be a rich man or a famous man or someone who could take her to all those things and places we talked about and saw in pictures.

People have been getting lost all over the course of time, it seems like. Some of them got shoveled over like those Chinamen, maybe some of them when they were still taking a breath. I prefer when I'm dead. That's why I keep my thoughts mortared together deep inside my skull, so all that's happened don't come tumbling out and bury me alive.

I'll say something else now about CoraRuth: she's got spirit. No matter how bad things did get, she always believed a pot of gold was going to land right in the middle of our kitchen table. She still does. Last month they were having a contest at the Burger King, gave out these little tickets every time you bought anything. You scratched through one of those silver things to find your number, and when you did maybe you'd won a free

Coca-Cola or a free Whopper or maybe fifty thousand dollars. It took me a while to figure out what she was up to. After church she'd say, "Henry, I don't believe I can wait till we get home to have a cup of coffee." Then the next day she might say, "I've been craving one of those fish sandwiches lately." Pretty soon I realized that woman was swinging by the Burger King sometimes twice a day, waiting at the drive-through window for nothing but a Coca-Cola and then going back that afternoon and picking up our supper. If I was with her, we'd both have to go inside and order separate, so we'd have two chances instead of one. Of course all she ever won was a cheeseburger and a Whaler, but she didn't lose faith in the possibility of the fifty thousand. She had planned where every last cent was going, how much she was going to give to the children.

Another time they had this thing going at the grocery store. Every time you shopped you got this ticket, and if they drew your lucky number, you could win a side of beef. Cora calls me over at the canning house one day, says to come right home, she's won it. So I go running home, clean out the back of the station wagon, help her make room in the freezer, and we throw a couple of coolers in her car and rush off to town. You should have seen that gal. She goes strutting in there with her lucky number held out and says to one of the cashiers, "I've come for my side of beef." She's about to pop. They take us over to the manager, and he says, "Yes, ma'am. Come right on back here." All the way to the meat counter, she keeps turning around looking at me, grinning, and with this look on her face that says, *See!* We get back there, and the man is gone for a while, and then he comes out and hands her this package about the size of a shoebox wrapped in white freezer paper. Cora looks at him, then says, "Should we drive around to the rear to pick up the rest?" He tells her no, that's all there is. And poor old Cora says, "When you called you said I won the side of beef." Oh, no, ma'am, he tells her; she won third prize. Somebody else got that cow. Second place won ten porterhouse steaks, and she won this here boneless rump roast.

Well, the girl's a good sport, I have to say. She was mad as a hornet at first, and I didn't dare say a thing. But halfway home, she starting laughing. We both laughed hard about it then, and I didn't go back to the canning house that afternoon.

Cora and I got us a little nap in before Lucas got home from school, and that night we had us a good pot-roast supper. She likes telling that story on herself, laughs right along as well as anybody. I have to say, though, that she did start shopping somewhere else after that. Said the store didn't run enough coupons in the Thursday paper.

You wouldn't believe all the contest entries she has mailed in over the years: recipes she'd send in to the Pillsbury Bake-off; names she'd give to new cleaning products; all those things in women's magazines. Tell you the truth, I haven't given CoraRuth enough credit. I used to laugh at all those contests; I thought it was silly. But now I see it shows CoraRuth's a fighter. If you keep mailing in those things, it means you believe in possibility. It means you've still got hope in the future.

She doesn't know I know this, but she's mailing a dollar every week to a cousin who lives in Florida. And she's given the cousin six lucky numbers for her to play in the state lottery. The cousin sends back the Lotto ticket every week, so Cora will know she did it. I overheard them talking on the phone one time was how I learned about it. When it got up to forty-five million that one time, she sent down two dollars; I know because I saw the tickets hidden in her Bible. I was against it at first. It just seemed like another one of those silly things she does, something with as much chance as my striking oil here on our property. But now I've decided I'm all for it. I really am. I'd give anything to see old Cora win something besides a pot roast and a hamburger. I'd love to see her face, too, when she tells me about it.

The two worst years of my life was '63 and '74.

That first year, that was the year we lost Diane. It was also the year I had what they called a bleeding ulcer, and I'd only been home a few days from the hospital when Diane and a little girlfriend of hers was playing up at the end of the driveway. I'd gone out that morning to check on the trees, but I guess I was trying to get back to work too early because I was so weak I had to come home. CoraRuth had fixed me a sandwich and I was sitting up on the porch keeping an eye on the girls and trying to read the *Farm Bulletin*. I called to them a couple of times to keep away from the road, and they always sang back,

"We will!" I guess I dozed off for a minute, just closed my eyes, when I heard a horn and tires squealing up at the road. I ran off the porch, fell down all four steps, and tore a hole in my pants leg before I reached them. A ball had rolled in the road, that was all, and the driver had honked and swerved to miss the ball. But it was because I was so scared that it was something other than what it was that I yanked Diane up and spanked her. I never hit the kids. (One time with Eleanor, when she wet her pants, I did pull off my belt and just slapped at her britches, but she cried like she was beat and I never once touched the child again. And Lucas, I probably popped his butt a time or two when he was growing up, but I never spanked our children the way some folks do. Not like Grandmother Parton did, when she'd tell me to go outside and pick my own switch and then pull the leaves off and swat the back of my legs with that piece of wire privet till welts covered the skin.) No, I never did anything like that, except that one time. I was so weak from running and being scared and from hitting that little thing and then from trying to get her to hush crying that I could hardly make it back to the porch. All I had wanted was for her to be safe, but I don't remember if I really explained that.

I've never had what you'd call a best friend. I played with the others when I was a kid, but I never paired off with one boy the way you sometimes see them do. Then I played ball, and I got along fine on a team. But there was never any one person I hung around with and told things to. And after we moved up here, we were always so busy with the orchards that I never had time to make a friend. I've never been a talker. It's always been CoraRuth who buzzes around at church and school and does our socializing for us.

But there was this fellow that came along that year before our accident and started working for me. That man, Benjamin, would work till he dropped. He was the first one I ever saw that could keep up with me: out before light in the morning and working right on through till dark. And I didn't have to tell him every little thing; he dove right in and did it himself. Sometimes even did things I had never even showed him or asked him to do. There for a few months, we had sort of a rhythm going, working most days side by side. I made him my foreman, paid him more than I ever paid, and we fixed him up in a little trailer out back. CoraRuth made checked curtains for the windows and put new sheets and a spread on the bed, gave him a couple of plates and a coffee cup from one of her mother's old sets of dishes. He moved in there, and I guess I thought he was going to be permanent. He seemed to like the work, too, and I started thinking that if we ever moved off to some of the places I sometimes had a mind to move to, I'd sell the place to Ben. He was like me, not normally a talker. But at night after we finished work and was walking back up to the house, we'd discuss a thing or two. What was happening in the world. Kennedy and Khrushchev. Baseball. He was the kind of fellow you could depend on, and I believe I could have told him things if I had wanted to.

But then Ben, he just lit out. It must have been while me and Cora were still in the hospital, because when we got home, he was gone. That trailer had been empty a few weeks, I guessed from looking at it. He left it neat as a pin, just the way it was when Cora had it all cleaned up for him to move into, all the towels and sheets washed and folded. I thought there might have been a note or something, but there wasn't. Not a line.

That same year was the year Kennedy got shot. Every once in a while they'll show one of those news clips of him and Jackie and Connally riding through Dallas, and I tell you, it still tears me up. That day was Cora's mother's birthday. A neighbor had brought in a cake. But none of us could eat a thing. We just sat there staring at the television. Yeah, that was the worst year. The year it just seemed like everything went dark.

Nineteen seventy-four was a bad one too. That was the year Eleanor had that little girl that was born dead. It was also the year we never really had a winter. As early as February, forsythia and quince was blooming. It felt like May, with temperatures in the seventies. Peaches can't make it with weather like that. They've got to have enough cold days without a bad frost, or you can lose the crop. That's what happened to us. We nearly lost the whole thing. There weren't enough peaches there for a person to sell on the side of the road. I don't guess we would have made it if I hadn't taken on extra work. I added on a room to this fellow's house and helped another one build a barn. I put in a swimming pool for this lawyer in Spartanburg and painted a couple of houses. It was good weather for construction, but it was a killer if you were trying to grow peaches. Then that summer Nixon waved good-bye and he and Pat got on that helicopter. That was a bad one, '74. Not a dime in the bank and Lucas not far from going to college, crooks in the White House, and Eleanor and Jay headed for trouble.

Sometimes it feels like hope is born dead. At least it's been that way a time or two in my life. Times when all I saw was darkness, and not just right around me, but all out in the world. Times when it was hard to keep making myself get up at six-thirty every morning and keep taking one step after another. There have been times, too, when Cora and I have been no help to each other. When each of our own hurts have been so bad that we had no strength to reach out a hand to ease the other.

I have to say though that Cora and I have been married so long, and seen so much together, that I don't believe I know how to live without her. I didn't know that till just recently.

I wonder if she feels the same way. I study her and it seems like she's itching to live something different. There's this thing about New York now. She leaves encyclopedias open at certain places like the Statue of Liberty. The Empire State Building. Wall Street. Maybe she thinks she'll spark up my interest and have me saying, Yes, please. But I don't have no interest in that place or on getting on one of those planes to see it. Why can't a man stay home? Why can't he gather his family around him and keep them there so nothing can ever happen to any of them?

Well, Cora says she's going. With or without me, she's heading out. She's bought a new coat and some walking boots, and she's on the phone with Eleanor every few days asking her about things. Cora likes the simple life, I always thought, same as me. But now, now I don't know what's up with that woman.

I wake up in the middle of the night like I do, and I roll over and I see the back of that head, that new hair, and I can't help saying to myself, "CoraRuth, what are you thinking?"

I've mentioned before that I was a catcher with the Atlanta Crackers. Some folks maybe think that's an easy position, being catcher. But let me tell you, my knees are shot. Squat and stand, squat and stand; up and down like that a thousand times in every game. Your eye always on the lookout for someone stealing home, for someone landing in your lap.

I guess everybody wonders *what if,* from time to time. I sure have wondered how it all would have turned out if I'd stayed with the Crackers instead of coming up here and catching the things I did. *Bad weather*—that comes at you like something straight from the pitcher sometimes, hard and fast and slamming right in your mitt. But other times it comes up from behind you, unexpected; sometimes you catch it and sometimes you don't. Catch a pile of overdue bills; throw 'em back. Catch and throw, catch and throw, give your signals to the pitcher, up and down, up and down, get a ball in the teeth, keep an eye on the runner, watch the game.

So CoraRuth wants to get on a Delta airplane and fly up there to walk fifty miles of concrete and make sure a bunch of smart-mouthed Yankees give her the right change. Isn't she thinking? Doesn't she see that maybe if we'd never left Georgia in the first place and come up here there wouldn't ever have been anyone to run head on into that Buick and take our girl?

Curve balls coming at you. Umpires making the wrong calls. You got to pull your mask down, Cora, balance on your toes, dig in, watch for bad luck running at you. Here it comes. Here it comes. Keep your mitt up. Cover home.

Fitz: 1987

"**W**ho'll bid half a hundred?
Half a hundred? Half a hundred? Fifty? Do I hear fifty? Who'll
give fifty? Twenty. I've got twenty, who'll go thirty? Thirty?
Thirty? I've got twenty, who'll go thirty? Yes! Thirty now, who'll
go forty? Forty? Forty? *Thirty-five.* Thirty-five, forty. Forty?
Forty? Forty? *Think I would, think I would.* Forty? Forty? **Last**
time. Forty? Sold to the lady in back for thirty-five."

I'm good at this, it's in my blood.

I have a way of holding on, steely-eyed, waiting, while the
other guy is squirming and wondering if it's worth it to up the
bid one more time. My way is to jump in at the last moment,
right after everyone's energy has boiled over and the bidding
is cooling off again. Sometimes I wait too late, and I lose it.
Sometimes I jump too early and the other guy's not as tired as
I thought and maybe I pay too much. But most times I'm on
the money, and I get what I'm after.

I always sit in the back so I've got a good view of everything
and know who's bumping who. The thrill of the auction. I did
it one time, and I was hooked. Maybe it's like gambling—playing
poker or putting your quarter in one of those machines in
Nevada—I don't know, I've never done it. But I like this, especially when the bidding's going so fast the poor auctioneer's
tongue is twisting and turning over the bids with such speed
you figure he'll get tangled up in his own language. So fast the
bidder's cards are flipping and flying, and people are having
trouble keeping track of what it is they've bid. I can always tell
when it's the owner who opens a bid: it opens too high and
nobody else goes much higher; sometimes I toss up my card
when things stall, just so some old boy won't get stuck with his

own chest of drawers. Of course it's me who gets stuck from time to time, but it doesn't matter.

When I finally decided on Ben, I opened the bidding high. I gave it one good shot, tall numbers.

I didn't even shrink into myself the way I have done on occasion. I stood the full length of who I am, a good head taller than the man.

He'd been coming into my shop for years looking for old magazines. *Life*s mostly, and later *Popular Photography*. He had a little notebook and under each year had listed all the issues of *Life* he was missing. Except he didn't say "issues" or "editions." He said, "I'm missing weeks." And I had the feeling he was. Missing whole weeks out of his life. Maybe entire years.

So much inventory comes and goes through my shop that I can size the worth of something in no time. I know when a piece of furniture has had a bad refinishing job, and I can spot patch jobs with new wood, cracks in veneer, replaced handles and doors. I know when someone is trying to push a number off on me as an antique and there's not one dovetail in any drawer.

It wasn't a hasty decision. I'd been looking Ben over good since the beginning. I knew what he wanted, learned how to make him laugh.

Every time I pulled out issues I had that he was looking for, and I told him I'd keep trying to find the others. I watched my timing, controlled the pounding inside me, steadied my gaze, and at the perfect moment on the perfect day of the perfect year, I said, "I'm having chicken and dumplings for supper."

There is a cleft in his chin big enough to fill with a teaspoon's worth of wood putty. The cleft closed and opened. He was staring at me hard.

Think I would, think I would.

I upped my own bid: "Followed by banana pudding."

"I like banana pudding," he said.

The first (the only) time I ever took Jay, my son, to an auction, he acted like he was with another person. I'd flick my card in the air, or slice horizontally with it to cut a bid in half, and he'd look at me like I spoke Spanish but had never bothered to tell him about it. How'd you learn to do that? he wanted to know. He had trouble keeping up with the bidding.

When you raise a child, spend almost every minute of every day with him, you think it will always be that way. But now, there are not just days, but weeks of his life I know nothing about, friends he holds dear I've never even seen. How can that be? I sometimes wonder. When he was in Vietnam, I got letters, but they gave no information really, not about what it was truly like over there, only about wanting to come home, thanking me for the sherry cake and cookies, telling how large the roaches were, how one night he woke up and one had eaten a hole in his toe. But I never knew anything else. All those days and dark nights there, living side by side with people he probably will never see again. There was one boy, his best friend over there, who came to Jay and Eleanor's wedding; and Jay went to his. But I haven't heard his name in years.

There are all these sweet young men who work next door, boys really, tall and long-limbed, some of them frail. Boys whose families have disowned them. They come to me to talk. I want to pick them up and hold them. My son is the one their families would take in as their own. My son, who finds it so difficult to be with me.

Jay and I are lost from one another. I tried hard there for a while, for us to be closer. That's just it, though, I think I tried too hard. Tried to be too cheery, and too proper, and too motherly. And then by the time I let up and started being myself, it was too late because by then he had no way of knowing me. And what he saw, I could see, only embarrassed him. Like my hair. I wear it long and in a braid.

When Dan was alive, and even for years afterward, I went to the hairdresser once a week just as I had gone with his mother. Everyone went back then and had their hair washed and set weekly and trimmed at least once a month. You went so regularly that you got to know the other women who came on your day. Mine and Mother Ballard's day was Tuesday. I never fit in with those other women, even when I was twenty-one and sitting next to Dan's small, kind mother, both of us with our white gloves on and planning where we'd go to lunch later.

Why did I keep going so long? Habit, I'm supposing. Otherwise, why *would* I keep doing something that made me feel so awkward? The whole time I lived in that house, I don't think I rearranged but two pieces of furniture. The day I moved out, things were almost the same as Mrs. Ballard had them on the day I moved in. And after Dan died, I even kept using our same checks: Mr. Daniel K. Ballard, Mrs. Daniel K. Ballard. I don't think it was so much that I was a weak person, but I always felt there, in that house, that things weren't mine to be changing. Maybe even with Jay, that's what happened. I kept on treating him the same as the Ballards had always treated one another, like they were only cordial acquaintances having dinner out together.

Sometimes you don't even know what you've been living until you can take a step away and out. I had no idea. Not until I moved into my little shop. It wasn't all at once, not just in a day; but little by little, over a few weeks, I began feeling as if I were the young girl again who used to work at the portrait studio when I still lived with Nannie and my mother. (I was the one they let position the children, getting the hems of the dresses situated just right, their curls in the perfect places, the only one who could get the little ones to stop crying and start laughing.)

I found an old sleigh bed at auction and put it in what used to be the storage area upstairs above my store, right in the middle of the room. I found a handyman who put in a tiny kitchen and a bath in the back. I washed those tall, wide windows at the front of the building and pushed a sofa and an assortment of chairs against them. I nailed a horseshoe over my door and put nothing over my windows.

All the furniture that had been Dan's parents I left in the house and told Jay to take what he wanted; the rest went in an estate sale a few days before the new owners moved into the house. Once the furniture was gone, it felt as if all that heavy cherry and mahogany had been strapped to my back for thirty years. I was almost stooped over with it, I had been carrying it for so long.

That first week after I moved out, I called up the beauty parlor where I'd been going (the very same one Mrs. Ballard had been going to all those years) and canceled my Tuesday appointment. I told them I'd have to reschedule. But I didn't. I suppose I looked a wreck when I first started letting my hair grow out; I didn't know how to take care of it. I just washed it every few days and brushed it out and then started pulling it back as it got long. Then one day a girl came into the store with her hair in braided pigtails, and I remembered how Nannie used to plait my hair when I was little. So I started wearing it in a long braid down my back, with the color as gray as February weather.

I hate for Jay that he's embarrassed. I remember how it was when Dan first came to our little house, with Nannie in her bedroom shoes, and Mama in her housedress, an old pink shift, pulling covered bowls out of the refrigerator and putting them cold and sweaty on the kitchen table, trying to get Dan to eat something. How I tried to hurry us out of there. But the embarrassment was nothing like the guilt I felt later. To be embarrassed of those two women! I'm ashamed even now that I ever felt that. And that's why I worry about Jay Ballard. He has tried to fix me up with men in the past, but I never went with any of them. It's not that I haven't had thoughts, wanted affection. But I never was pulled by anyone until this short man, who had long ears and a hole in his chin and claimed to be missing weeks, walked into my shop.

I had something in particular he wanted immediately. A September 6, 1948, edition of *Life*.

Nineteen forty-eight was the year Jay was born, a year I thought I'd always remember. But when Ben was digging through the stacks of other magazines, I looked through that issue of *Life* and saw all kinds of things I had forgotten. The way people dressed, the hairdos, the Ipana toothpaste, Little Lulu selling Kleenex, Red Goose shoes.

It's those advertisements that really tell you how things were, even more than that series *Life* had going on the history of Western culture. "You'll be happier with a Hoover." Read that ad, and you get the feeling they're not just talking about clean carpets.

I'd forgotten how after the war my mother and so many of the other women lost their jobs when the men came home from the service. Those GIs had to support their families, people said. Mother had to support me and Nannie, too, but she still lost her job as a foreman at the pencil factory and had to become a Fuller Brush girl, selling rouge door-to-door. It was just makeup she sold—men sold the brushes—and she had to buy her own bag of samples and pay two cents for each tube of lipstick she gave away. When they stopped having Fullerettes, Mother got a job at Rich's downtown, selling other kinds of cosmetics. I guess when things change so much like that, you do need a Hoover, or something, to make you happy.

Missing weeks out of a life; we've all done it.

I wonder what I used to think about when I lived in that big house, having people wash my hair and mop my floors. I must not have been able to see anything past the windows. But when I moved into my store, all the world opened up. And I saw the world was in trouble.

Had I not been reading newspapers? Watching the TV? How had I missed not seeing how dark the rivers had gotten, and the air? How we were boring large holes in a layer of the atmosphere that was there to keep the earth from burning to pieces?

Everything I saw, and I was seeing everything, was in a mess. That's when I realized I didn't have time to get my hair done anymore. There was too much to do, making up for all that lost time. I read about the garbage dumps, how they were filling up so quickly. How pretty soon we weren't going to have room for one more sleeper sofa or Coca-Cola can in any landfill in the country. How we were cutting down all our trees to make paper, while newspapers were getting tossed into the backs of garbage trucks every day and the planet was getting hotter.

It seemed to me that supply-side economics wasn't working, that we had a surplus of *stuff* in the world and a shortage of smart thinking. That's when I saw I was in the right business. In a shop like mine, full of mostly secondhand goods and some antiques, you can help control the flow of garbage. If I'm at an auction, and I see a box full of old glass, I can toss up my bidding card and get it. And then I can take it over to the recycling place on Memorial Drive so something else can be made of it. I'm not talking about a bowl or jar with historical or artistic value, but just *stuff*, stuff that someone's liable to take out in the world and add to the clutter. We don't need it.

That's why I do what I do. The rest of it, the old furniture
and whatnot, they're just here as my cover, so my son and other
people won't think I've lost my marbles.

Poor Jay, he nearly dies when he sees me picking paper and
glass up off the sidewalks.

I've made a habit, you see, of not getting into a car unless
I have to. I take MARTA trains and buses when I need to go
a distance, and the rest of the time I get there by walking. And
when you spend a lot of time on your feet outdoors, you see
all kinds of garbage: empty Mountain Dew bottles, beer cans,
liquor bottles, hamburger wrappers, sections of the newspaper
flapping. I've seen strange things, too: pairs of shoes, an alarm
clock, a set of dentures. At the bus stops you see umbrellas and
books and rain hats. I started noticing that not many people
come back for these sorts of things. Several days in a row, I'd
see the same whiskey bottle on the same corner, the same Pepsi
Free can next to the trash can at the MARTA station.

Somebody had to do something about it. And that's when
I started collecting trash off the streets. I started with a paper
sack, but it tore and busted before I got home the first day out.
Then I used a plastic garbage bag with a drawstring, but that
got too heavy, too, and wasn't large enough. So I borrowed (on
a permanent basis) one of the grocery carts from the Kroger.
And a couple of times a week, I trek around and pick up matter.

I also keep a plastic bag in my pocket, for when I don't
have the cart and I spot something. If it's something I think
someone can use, like shoes or an umbrella, I take it to the
Kidney Foundation or the Salvation Army. The other stuff, like
the set of dentures (how do you lose something like that?),
anything that can't be recycled in one way or another, I put in
the garbage.

I have my helpers. I read somewhere about this group of young
people who help protect people on the subways in New York,
and I thought, Well, if young people are doing good, what
about old people? So I started asking around, checking to see
if senior citizens were interested in the environment. The numbers are the same as they would be in any other group of people:
some are and some aren't. But the ones who are, are dedicated.

Most of them feel the way I do: that at our age, what else is there to do that's this important? We might leave a wad of money to our children if we can, but what will it matter if they can't drink the water?

Jay says I've become a zealot, that I look foolish. Maybe so. But except for his feelings, what do I care? All over town I've got friends picking up trash. There's an old man in Morningside who rides something like a big tricycle; he has a wagon hitched to the back of it, where he throws all the glass and aluminum he gathers. There's another one—a woman—who has a little cart that her sheltie pulls behind her. There are others like us all over, with bags and buggies and grandchildren's red wagons. Once a month Eleanor comes with her truck and collects everything from all of us, and she and I take it to the recycling centers.

The revenue we get goes into the treasury of OPPO. Old People Protecting the Ozone. Jay just laughs. Well, who else is going to do anything about it? And besides, I was spinning everywhere, going in circles, not sure how to get anything done when there was so much to do. They were pulling eels that already looked cooked out of the Baltic Sea. Children were being born deformed in Eastern Europe because of all the metal pollution in the ground and air. If it was like that there, in older countries, wouldn't it be like that here before too long? Wouldn't fish soon die in the Great Lakes or in Mobile Bay? Might not Jay's children or grandchildren someday be born with deformities? I've never been much of a sleeper, but it got to where, because of all I was learning, I could hardly close my eyes at night.

My friend Carl, the one with the tricycle, he read this article about how every time you break a piece of Styrofoam or spray something from an aerosol can, you're helping to destroy the ozone layer. So Carl and I and some others began boycotting fast foods and other products that come in Styrofoam containers. We started using only stick or roll-on deodorants. But we soon figured out nobody gave a darn whether or not a handful of old people didn't buy a couple of fish sandwiches because they came boxed in Styrofoam. And it was going to take more than our just not buying spray cans to get some attention.

It was my idea to picket. We started at the Kroger (even though I *was* using one of their grocery carts) and held up signs

that called for them to stop selling Styrofoam products or anything that came in that kind of packaging; we demanded they
take all aerosol sprays off their shelves. "Protect the ozone!" we
yelled. "Return to old-fashioned egg cartons!" we hollered.

I've sat in on all kinds of demonstrations in the last few
years: I've protested Iceland's killing of whales; marched outside plants that are blowing toxic fumes out their smokestacks
and dumping poison chemicals into streams; written congress-
men and senators and governors; marched at the State Capitol
and outside the Savannah River Plant in South Carolina. But
it's OPPO that is my baby.

That hole in the ozone, it's only over Antarctica now. But
what if it spreads? What if we all end up like those eels, coming
into the world looking like we've already been broiled?

There've been hints from Jay that I'm spending his inher-
itance. So what came from the sale of the house, I've given to
him. And I set aside some more money that I've promised
myself never to spend, that will only be his. But I figure the
rest is mine to spend however I see best.

Ben. He picks up garbage with me. From the first time we went
out walking, he never said a thing. Not, *Why are you doing this*?
Not, *What does it matter*? I rattled on, the same way I do with
Jay, but he understood.

I had forgotten how it feels to touch. I'm not speaking
sexually, necessarily; I'm just talking about feeling another person's skin. He doesn't mean it, but you can get more affection
from a lamppost than you can from Jay. Sometimes I see a baby
and I think I could drink it up. I see a child and I ache to hold
him. I've cuddled and petted my dogs until they're spoiled
rotten. Pets are fine, but it's not the same. Part of the way we
are made, and this is important, includes the need to touch the
skin of other human beings.

Benjamin knows how to hold a woman's hand. He takes it
and gives it a squeeze; then he turns it over, runs his fingers
over the palm, and holds it like he's holding the most precious
thing in the world.

How we find other persons is one of the things I've become
curious about. How in all the world you can run across a person
who doesn't require tremendous explanation. Maybe you've got

some mileage on you, but you've still got plenty of good left in you, too; and maybe you sometimes have to be recycled into something different, a different shape or size maybe, maybe even a whole different person. But if you're handled correctly, you can still be of some use to somebody.

I have always been realistic about how I look. Other women have their fine lines, like a Queen Anne chair. And others are intricate and complicated and fancy like a piece of high Victorian furniture. Me—I am serviceable and dependable, as plain as an old Mission Oak hall tree or chest of drawers.

I heard that H. L. Mencken once said that if you wanted to do something nice for him after he was gone, you could smile at a homely girl. I guess old Mencken is happy.

I've eaten so many meals out since I've been living alone that I've developed an aversion to good restaurants; new paint and linen napkins make me lose all my drive. The places I like best are the ones with family food—sweet creamed corn, turkey and dressing, pork chops and gravy, macaroni and cheese, mashed potatoes. They're not easy to find, though, not in Atlanta. This is a fast city, and a prosperous one; and prosperity, I've noticed, sweeps away a lot of the services for regular people.

Almost every day I find that another landmark has disappeared—a service station, an office building, a drugstore—sides of hills are blasted away, old highways torn apart and twisted like steel. Wonderful old apartment buildings are razed without even the saving of a doorjamb or a piece of crown molding. And within no time, it seems, huge new buildings are dropped down into three-story-deep foundations. Sometimes it's a building so tall that the houses on the residential streets near it it are left in the shade all day where they used to be drenched in sunlight. If what was being torn down was replaced by something modern, I might be able to understand it. But most of the houses and apartment buildings and even office condominiums aren't contemporary at all. They're Colonial Williamsburg bricks or copies of old plantation homes, Savannah-style homes with porticoes and porches. They're tearing down everything that is old and replacing it with a replica of something even older. That tells you something: that you've got a place not sure of itself; embarrassed by what it was, and with no idea about what it wants to be.

I know all this building and rebuilding must be good for the economy, but it feels as if everything I like—all the old things—are being disposed of like fifty-five-year-old men who are retired early because they're a drain on the company.

At one of our meetings, old Carl passed around a newsletter from Greenpeace. I looked at that word. That was what I'd been hunting for years, on drives up in the woods of Tate, in Mrs. Ballard's formal garden. Green peace. It was never there, not until I started walking around this city with this certain man.

I have started cooking for me and Ben. We dine in most nights, mostly on those things I mentioned: pork chops, mashed potatoes, gravy, turkey and dressing, chicken pies. Family foods. They're supposed to kill us. Maybe a few months ago, cholesterol might have had a chance with my heart. But not now.

At night after dinner, we take walks. Or sometimes we get on a bus and ride around to different parts of the city. Grant Park, Inman Park, the West End. Some of the areas aren't safe. There are thugs who get on with us and stare. But there must be something in our eyes, because they duck their heads and look in another direction and never make a move toward me or Ben.

We go to these auctions together, too, and sometimes I come away with whole cartons and trunks full of magazines. I'm finding weeks for Ben in every year. Nineteen forty-nine, 1950, '51, '52.

I hold my card in my lap, wait for the right moment.

Think I would, think I would.

I make my bid, and win.

Eleanor: 1987

A person can lose her center. And when she does, it has the same net effect of a compass that's lost true north. It can happen to anyone, not just people who sleep on cold concrete underground or live under newspapers. I came here believing that if I could get away from the people I love, I might be able to pull in, find center, hold the magnetic needle steady.

And I have worked hard, spent these weeks at Carroll's easel, filled notebooks with sketches, gone to every museum this city will let me into.

I paint all day long, as long as there is light. And when the light is gone, I prime canvases, nail together stretcher boards. Some days I forget to eat until late afternoon, sometimes not at all, and I go to bed weak and shaky, not even realizing until morning what is wrong. Often I don't leave the loft for two or three days in a row, and I eat whatever sits in the cabinets or refrigerator: crackers, raw nuts, dry cereal, a shriveling orange. Other days I eat three meals or more, fantasizing about where I'll go for lunch or dinner. Sometimes I stay up half the night, looking at a painting, sketching.

Carroll left me names of people who might be available to model. I have painted four of these people, two of them twice. Most are artists themselves, but they need money and so sit in awkward positions for me by the hour. I place them in front of the windows, with the Manhattan Bridge and rusty water towers that roost on the tops of nearby buildings in the background. Or I put them at the windows that look south with a view of the spiky monoliths of the financial district. But my favorite backdrop is out the windows at the rear of the loft, where the old Police Building is under renovation. There's a big green tarpaulin covering the dome, and the building looks as if it has been roped and caught. I paint so long that the models complain, and sometimes they don't come back for a couple of days. When they don't show, I bring home things I find on my walks over on Mulberry Street and in Chinatown: baskets, cloth, tins and bottles, fish, vegetables, edible things I can't name. Or I spend hours at the museums, and I stay so late that often the guards tell me I have to go, and when I walk outside it's so dark that I have to find a cab instead of taking the train. Everything I see, I imagine painting. My eyes follow telephone lines, subway tracks, escalators to their farthest points, and what I take note of is linear perspective. I pass a hundred faces, a thousand, and I see that many different colors and complexions. There is a face here for everywhere in the world.

I have nearly enough pictures for a show. Large pictures, good ones; people and objects reflected in windows and other glass. I bought a six- by six-foot mirror and had it brought up in the freight elevator, and everything I paint, I paint as I see it through some reflection. Mirror Series, the paintings are called. Mirror Series #3: "Red Snapper, Reflected." Mirror Series #7: "Manhattan Bridge Reflection." And so on. It is true, I believe; the work *is* good. But I was crazy to think I could pull in. I don't think less, I think more. And not just about my family, but everyone.

Carroll left me a long list of Do's and Don'ts stuck to the refrigerator. Top of the list (right after Don't go into subway johns): Don't look straight at people. But how can you not do that, in this city?

Often I forget where I'm going I look so hard. Often I have to sit down and have a cup of coffee because looking has worn me to a frazzle.

Last week: I don't pay attention on my way to the museum (I am watching this Hispanic woman trying to breast-feed her baby on the train without anyone seeing her, and I take the subway one exit too far. I get off at Eighty-sixth Street instead of Seventy-seventh, and there is a woman sitting on the steps of the station as I walk out; she holds a sign that says: PREGNANT AND HOMELESS. I can't determine how old she is; maybe a kid, maybe as old as I am. I give her a dollar and think about her all during my lunch, all during the time I make notes and pencil sketches of a John Singer Sargent at the Met.

A study has been done that shows there are fewer cases of spinal deformities in the babies of women who take maternity vitamins three to six months before conception. I myself have a prescription for these pills. The next day I take the subway too far on purpose. She is there and I give her five dollars and a bottle of vitamins for pregnant and lactating women. She looks at me as if I'm an idiot, which maybe I am, and stuffs the pills in her pocket.

Maybe it's a scam, the sign and the part about being pregnant, maybe even about being homeless. But maybe it isn't. Maybe she'll throw the pills away, or sell them for drugs, or maybe she'll swallow them whenever she gets hungry.

I don't go anywhere—not even around the corner for a carton of juice or a bag of coffee—without extra change in my pocket. There are homeless people in Atlanta, but maybe I don't see them. Here I see them everywhere, sleeping in doorways, behind dumpsters, in the middle of the sidewalk, old people and young ones, like this maybe-pregnant girl. One man has sat next to the steps at the health food store around the corner since the day I arrived. He never moves, not when it's raining, or snowing, not when the sidewalk is full of people coming and going with their organic vegetables and little plastic sacks of couscous. He burrows under newspapers, the way you see rodents doing. What difference will a quarter make? Or half a dollar? No difference; but I can't go by without giving him and her and all of them something. Some don't look back, don't say anything, just maybe kick the trash and curl into themselves a little more. But others, they look back, and when they see you're looking, too, it startles them. That girl, she looked and looked and looked right through me.

A circle of keys, color-coded, like children's toys. Yellow opens a sequence of doors that lead from the street to the lobby and from the lobby to the hall. Blue is used inside the dark little elevator to make it stop at the ninth floor. The elevator bangs to a stop on nine, and green opens the door that leads through the long maze of Sheetrock walls: dingy, marked-on, tall. Numbered doors dot the maze as it winds through the heart and rear of the building. At the end of the hall, the last door, two more keys: orange for the Corbin lock, red for the dead bolt that protects my friend's apartment.

I think of ways to keep my parents (who claim they are coming to visit) from ever seeing the place where I live. In South Carolina, at their home, doors are never locked. Once, when they were getting ready to drive down to Atlanta to visit me, Mama realized there was no house key at all. There are burglars in South Carolina and perverts and murdering thieves. But apparently their numbers are fewer than steady church-goers, and we have always slept there with doors unlocked and windows open.

Every morning here, no matter how early I wake, there is so much traffic down on the street below, so many horns blowing that in South Carolina you would think there was a fire or a parade. At one time this was an industrial part of the city, and this building was owned by a company that manufactured hats. On the ground floor at the back of the building, where I take my garbage every few days, there used to be a loading dock. I think about what might have been delivered there: thread, fabric, boxes, feathers, heavy black machines. When I walk barefooted on the bleached pine floors in my friend's loft, I think about what must have gone on here before: young first- and second-generation American women bent over rows of sewing machines like you see in sweatshops in the movies. I try to imagine their words—Chinese, Spanish, Italian, Polish, Russian, Gaelic, Yiddish—patched together to form some language they all understand. I try to picture how it must be when they go to their homes at night, each with a set of parents, grandparents maybe, bringing something with them from the heart of so many different countries. The smells alone, from all the kinds of food (cabbage cooking, garlic, sausage, beets, tomatoes, mutton): I try to conjure those. I try to imagine what they're wearing, while they make rich women's hats. I think about the women who work for Henry, who eat their sandwiches out under his trees, who speak an English that would sound foreign here, whose food might sound and taste and smell almost ethnic in Manhattan.

It feels as if there is a generation missing. Mama still fries slices of sweet potato in a black skillet and cooks turnip greens. Henry would never, not ever, vote for a black man, or a woman—not if the woman was white or black or polka-dotted. Right now, he is probably bumping over ruts in his pickup truck, and I ride subways and live in a ten-story building where there is a freight elevator across from my bed, where I never smell grass.

Those women who maybe worked here: their parents and grandparents laid down wooden farm tools in China, left poor little villages in Italy and Spain and lightless cities all over Eastern Europe. They came here, perhaps stood inside this building, stood right here, where I make my meals. They must have needed those children and grandchildren to keep them from going crazy. They must have needed each other too. If there were such a thing as Southern immigrants, I wonder, would they have a Little Carolina here, or a Georgia Town? Maybe a two- or three-block section of the city, where, if you walked down the sidewalks, you wouldn't hear Italian or Chinese but you'd hear housewives yelling out the windows to each other, "Hey, y'all," and smell the reek of turnip greens cooking on the tops of their stoves.

The cab driver who drove me here from the airport was an Iranian, although he seemed not to want me to know that. The waiter who served my lunch yesterday spoke English to me, Greek to the cook, and Spanish to the priest who joked at the other end of the counter. The laboring people here speak more languages than the educated lawyers down on the south end of the island or the minked women who push five-hundred-dollar prams near the park and museum.

The women who work for Henry, they know languages too. The language of babies and mucus and blood. The language of hands. Ancient languages that connect everything to everything like marrow in their bones.

Those immigrants: just people running. What you learn is that you can't shake where you're from.

Fitz used to say: *Look outward.* I thought I did.

Henry used to tell me stories. Easter Island: our favorite one. The short ears and the long ears competed with each other, knocked down each other's statues, warred against one another,

Henry said. And when they had cut down all their trees, to carve their statues and move them and build their huts and make their weapons, there were no materials left to build boats with to get off the island, nothing left to grow coconuts and other things to eat. They were stranded on the most isolated piece of land in the world, with no new ways to feed or house or protect themselves. So some of the statues turned red—from all the blood that spilled in fighting and cannibalism, it is guessed.

To Fitz, this is an environmental lesson: *We'll be just like them, stuck on a place that we've ruined.*

To Henry, it's another place to dream about: *Let's go there someday, 'Nor.*

To me, it's just a gift from Henry.

When Carroll called to say he was going to Europe for two or three months and did I know anyone who might sublet his loft, he didn't mean me. I had never thought of me, either, not until he said it.

"How much?" I asked.

It was nearly fifteen hundred a month. I did quick math. I had close to eight thousand in the bank saved from the last few portraits. I could stay two months, maybe three, depending on the cost of models and supplies and other expenses, including food and my airfare there and back. I said I'd take it.

"You?" Then he asked what was going on, was there trouble between me and Will? Everyone thinks that, Mama, Henry, everyone. Even Fitz gave me an eyeball full of *What's wrong?*

But Will, he practically applauded. "That's great!" he said. Yet even Will walked around me those last few days before I left like I was ill or dying, like I was never coming home.

I think I must have done the same. Because getting *ready* to leave, or be left, is the hardest part of going. For three months I knew I was coming up here, and two or three times a week I almost chickened out, almost dialed Carroll to tell him I couldn't take the loft. I'd think, This is stupid, why would I leave my home and the person I love. I'd think how wasteful it was, when I had a perfectly fine place to paint at home. But Carroll was depending on me for the rent, and I hadn't given him enough time to find someone else. And, like Will said, I'd already bought my ticket.

The night before I left Atlanta, hours after we had gone to bed, Will pulled his hand up between my legs and left it there. It stayed still, not a movement, until I went damp and rolled to him.

Sometimes at night, when I am not so tired, I think about his hands on me and about mine on him: two little pouches like sacks of grain inside my hands, between my fingers. About him slick and hard and deep inside me. I ache when I remember. But mostly I miss the sight of him in the morning, his coming home at night, the comfort of his conversation. And yet when he tells me he is thinking about flying up here soon, I try to change the subject.

I hadn't flown in so long that I had forgotten how sad and beautiful the earth can look from the air, how there's a certain position from where you can see Atlanta and it looks like Oz. But transportation of most kinds bewilders me, and flight in particular is tough because it doesn't allow for transition: you've crossed over all those miles and people and landed in New York before you've digested the breakfast you ate in Georgia, before the smell of your husband's aftershave is off your neck. I hadn't had time to stop feeling terrible about leaving Will when we were already circling Manhattan, touching down at LaGuardia, and I was riding in the cab of a man from Iran.

When he pulled up outside Carroll's building, I thought I'd given him the wrong address or maybe been hijacked. "No, it's Broadway," I said, "between Broome and Grand." I gave him the street number again, and he gestured at the building. It was broad daylight, 1:15 in the afternoon, and the place was black. Not just the sky, but the air, the building, the streets, the trash, the clothes on the people. I couldn't think what I was doing here, in a place that looked the way I thought cities would look after the bomb had been dropped. For a minute I just sat in the cab thinking about how I could mail Carroll his money, how I could simply tell this man to turn his buggy around, and I'd go home right then, on the very next flight, and everyone would be glad. But the cab driver told me the amount of the fare again, and stuck out his hand.

I had all those keys, and the letter Carroll had sent about which one opened what. I got out with my suitcases and my bag of supplies and stood on the sidewalk and looked up.

It's funny how you can look up and it appears as if the sky is moving, when it's really you who are going somewhere. I try to think about that sometimes. I get a fix on a white line of vapor drawn by some jumbo jet, and I try to make that vapor trail stay still and make myself feel how I'm the one rotating with the earth. But it's hard to do, the way it is sometimes when you're riding along and for a second or two it feels as if it's the scenery that's flying by instead of you.

When I looked back down, the cab was gone, and I was on this dark square of earth, traveling with it.

I can't get the girl in the subway station out of my mind. And the night after I give her the pills, I dream about one of Cora's birds. I am nine or ten, and I want one of the parakeets for my own. Cora says, "All right, but if it's yours, you're the one responsible." I take one of the old cages out of the basement and clean it and line it with paper, and I stick my hand in the large cage and pull my bird out, feel it warm and tense beneath my fingers. For several weeks I take good care of the bird, rename it, feed it every day, give it fresh water, put in a little porcelain bowl for its bath. But one day I stay over at a friend's; and the next day I forget about the bird, and the next. Cora never says a word, and it's not until Monday when I am leaving for school that I remember. The bird is lying on the bottom of the cage, a green and blue heap. I look around to see if anyone is watching. I thump the bars of the cage, but there is no movement. I take out the two little empty glass feeders, and fill one with water and one with food. But that afternoon when I come home, the bird is still lying on the bottom of the cage and the food and water are untouched. Cora knows, I guess knew all along, and she gives me an empty shoebox and a shovel. And never says a word, because she doesn't have to. I dream about that dead bird, the incriminating glass feeders, my guilty act of refilling them. Someone is watching. The bird lies on the bottom of the cage, and the girl lies at the bottom of the grimy wet stairs.

She is still there, a few days later. Same sign, same clothes, a hat between her feet where people drop coins. She is slumped over, maybe sleeping, and it is difficult to tell how large or how small she is because of the old car coat she is wearing and the layers of clothes underneath it.

I stand in front of the hat and clear my throat. She doesn't notice. I don't know how to do this, without being offensive and without embarrassing her and making us both feel stupid. I think about bending near her to speak, but I'm afraid that would appear patronizing. I clear my throat again and stand there, tall, clean, fed, and say, "Would you like to get something to eat?"

She looks up at me, tired, angry, maybe in some kind of pain. "You got something to eat, leave it."

I stammer, shake my head. "I thought you might like to go somewhere warm. Get out of here."

"What do you want?" she says, accusing.

"Nothing," I tell her, but I know that isn't true. What I want is for her not to be there, for me not to have to look at her cold and huddled and hungry and putting out her hand for money.

She knows it's not true either, but she shrugs, pulls herself up, wads the hat and money and sticks it under her coat. "Sure, why not? Let's go have a party."

I find a place where I don't think they'll throw us out, and she orders two hamburgers, potatoes and gravy, french fries, and a beer. The beer is gone before the food comes, and she looks around nervously, still angry. She drinks another one with the food. Her hands are terrible, the nails used for what I guess nails were intended: tools, survival. But my hands look bad, too, I realize when I see her looking at them. The thumb and little finger on my right hand are discolored from using them when I paint. And there is cadmium yellow and aquamarine and vermilion under all my nails. But no subway grime.

She takes bites out of the food like she's punishing it instead of feeding herself. She looks around at the other diners but not at me. Only when she pushes away from the table does she turn to me. She looks straight at me again, like she did the first time, like she knows something secret about me, and says, "I need a couple of dollars."

I am living temporarily in the toughest place I know, the easiest place to say I'm an artist. Every day I am slightly terrified of one thing or another. I have never eaten so many meals alone or sat by myself in so many restaurants. My heart used to sink at the sight of people like me, but not anymore. The surprise is, I am happy like this, watching other people, eavesdropping on conversations. Maybe they are as happy as I am to learn they can be without the people they love and not disappear into the stool and counter.

Potato pancakes overlap one another on the plate and resemble brown doilies. The spinach omelet looms high and as stiff as an overwhipped yellow cloud.

It is two o'clock in the afternoon and this is my first meal of the day. The little black-headed waiter pours my second cup of decaf while he takes someone else's order. I sit at the counter in this thimble-sized coffee shop at the corner of Seventy-ninth and Madison, my favorite place to go when I take the subway to the Metropolitan. This is my second day in a row at this counter, and the roof of my mouth is still ragged from the rye toast of yesterday's egg salad.

I have tried to paint this man, Niko, my waiter. But he works every day, Monday through Sunday, during the hours when there is good light in the loft. I try to coax him, tell him I'll pay double what I pay other models, but he just laughs and slams down my coffee. There are only twelve stools at the counter, seven tables. I have to sketch while I eat because I want to stay friends and not have them shoo me out the way they do some of the old women who dawdle over crusts of bread while a clump of impatient customers huddle at the door.

When I am ready to leave, he wraps up the sandwich I have ordered for the girl. I took food to her yesterday too: a bag of apples, two bananas. She grabbed the food from me and looked back down between her feet, like she had never seen me.

Today I give her the bag with the sandwich, a hard-boiled egg, another banana. She takes it like before, but this time I say, "Do you have a place to stay when the baby comes?"

She looks at me as if she's reading all the guilt that has ever registered in my eyes. "What's this to you?" she says.

I start to sit beside her, then decide to stay where I am because of the look she gives me. "I want to help, if I can."

She pulls her coat around her. It is freezing outside and raining. She stares back at the ground. I am in the way, I see, of others who might want to throw some change. I move toward the entrance of the subway, but she yells after me. "I'll tell you what you want," she says. People look at her as they rush by. "You want to hear my story so you can nod and point your finger. Then you want to give me a buck and a banana and have me disappear like all your other problems.

"You want to help? You show me a way to pay for a roof and a bed and somebody to take care of my kid so I can keep a job. Until then, don't come around here expecting me to say thank you."

Some people look at me, but most just walk straight ahead, in a hurry to get where they're going. She's right; everything she has said since the very first has been right. I do want to know what happened, I do want to know her story, and do want her to go away, well and warm and ready to deliver a healthy baby. I move back toward her, but keep my distance.

"Okay," I say. "I'll give you some work." I tell her she can stay with me temporarily, until I go home, and that maybe I can help her learn some skills. This is almost laughable even to me, since I have so few skills of my own. But I think maybe I can teach her enough about what I do that she could be an artist's assistant or work in an artist supply store the way Will's sister does. I write down Carroll's address and my name and tell her to come tomorrow after I've had time to get things ready.

She looks at the address, folds the paper, and shoves it in her pocket. She doesn't trust any of it, not the offer or the address or me.

I buy an inflatable mattress and a pump and carry them home. At the front of the apartment, farthest away from where I paint, I inflate the mattress and cover it with sheets and a blanket. I move around the small amount of furniture Carroll has to give her privacy.

I try to think how she will react when I tell her I want her to model. I don't want her to think I'm making fun or taking advantage of her. I won't paint her the way she is, and won't try to paint her some way she isn't. I'll just paint her face, her hands, the shape of her body. And so I buy the most nondescript clothes I can find: a black T-shirt and jeans. I also buy her clean underwear and a new jacket. The shoes will have to come later when I know her size.

All night I think about calling Will, to tell him what I'm doing. But it would only worry him and he'd try to get me not to do it. The next morning I bring in food: fresh fruit and vegetables, some cheese, a chicken. I try to work, but I can't. I recheck the bed a hundred times, to see if it is comfortable. I touch the little pile of clothes. I plan how I'll show her to prime canvas and nail together the stretcher boards. I think about those fingers and the way she smelled that day over the potatoes and hamburger.

I gave her no time, so I shouldn't expect her at any certain hour. But still I pace and hesitate to go out, afraid I will miss her. It begins to get dark, and the lights from the buildings down in the financial district blink and flicker: city stars. She's not coming, I know. I sit at Carroll's long pine table, watching the lights, realizing how foolish I've been, how stupid. Why should she come? To make me feel better? There used to be a jingle on the radio for a company in Atlanta: "Call the Glass Doctor," it went, "he'll fix your panes." That jingle plays over and over in my head, a broken record, and I feel like a fool. I also feel selfish and arrogant. And I want to go home.

And then the buzzer sounds from downstairs. At first I'm not even sure what it is, I've had so few visitors, only a delivery man and the models. But then I remember the sound and I rush over to the intercom and tell her to come through the lobby to the elevator, and I'll bring her up. I imagine her pushing against the heavy door as I press the button that will release the lock. When I'm sure I've given her enough time to get inside the elevator, I press the button that brings it to the ninth floor. I quickly go down the hall to wait for her. I am standing out in the dirty corridor, and I watch, nervous, as the elevator bangs to a stop and the door opens. She kicks a bag out in front of her, a suitcase. Then she walks forward. A girl in her twenties. Bony, tall, with oily hair. "I'm sorry I didn't call," she says.

And of course it isn't the girl from the subway at all, but Will's sister, Marilyn, who picks up the bag and waits for me to lead her to the last door.

Marilyn: 1987

⁓

I rode up on the train. Got on
at Brookwood Station in Atlanta and didn't get out of my seat
until almost Virginia. We stopped places all along the way, but
I was afraid to move. Afraid someone would get my seat, or
I'd get lost and never make it back to the correct car and find
where I was supposed to be. Twenty-nine years old and afraid
to move from one car to another on the Seaboard.

It was the newspaper picture of that woman, her black
hair—bangs like a straight-hanging curtain just above those
eyes—that carried me north. New Jersey, the papers said, was
where the trial was going on. They didn't show pictures of the
child much, for security reasons, I guess. But the father, they
showed him. Pock-marked and serious. But I wasn't sure about
sincere. My knowledge of fathers is such that I don't always
trust looks. Jackie's father, or the one I'm guessing, walked up
to me only once after I got back from Abbie's. He asked,
"How've you been?" but stood back like he was afraid I might
tell him something. Other boys stayed away too for a while.
Maybe they talked; maybe they knew. Which has always been
fine with me, because sometimes I've wished the whole world
knew.

They can't even agree on a name, these two couples. So
the newspapers sometimes give both, the name the mother gave
the baby at birth and the one the father and his wife use.

When I first heard about the trial, I wasn't even sure what
surrogate meant. So I looked it up, but it still didn't make sense.
Either Mr. Webster or those newspaper people have it wrong,
because the definition in the dictionary says, "to put in the place
of another." How could that mother take anyone's place, when
she was the one who carried the child? It looks to me as if it's

the man's wife who is the surrogate, since she was the one who took the place of the mother after the baby was born.

Sometimes I find articles in magazines giving advice to parents. Things such as what to do when children use poor grammar, about how you aren't supposed to correct them, but instead repeat the sentence and use the right words. *He don't have no good toys. Oh, he doesn't have any good toys?* Other things, such as using positive reinforcement, treating them with respect. Also, when to get what shots, things to ask the doctor. The right kind of vitamins, how much time he should spend playing outdoors. Proper shoes. How to know if he's doing well in school. All this information I'm getting, and I don't know where to send it. What if that woman who has Jackie doesn't read these things, his surrogate mother?

I took the train all the way to Penn Station. I got off there and it was like something I saw in a movie one time, this giant ocean wave that flips over a cruise ship the size of a city block as if it's nothing more than a piece of foam rubber.

That's the way it looked to me, all those people running, crowding together to catch other trains, getting on subways. A giant wave of people. It smelled like urine and wet metal in there, and for the longest time I just stood back, thinking that if I moved a foot forward I'd be sucked under and washed away.

I hadn't planned to call on Eleanor, but it was all those breakers and rollers of people and I couldn't get my breath. Will had given me her address and phone number several weeks before but had said, Now don't bother her, she's trying to work.

I took a step away from the wall and rode the swell up to the street. Outside people were holding up their hands, shouting, getting cabs. It was almost dark and had started snowing. I couldn't remember what my plan had been before, how I thought I was going to get to New Jersey. I stepped off the curb, raised my hand, and one of those fast-moving cars rolled right to me.

When I pressed the button beside the apartment number where Eleanor was supposed to be, static came through the square speaker on the wall almost immediately. "Yes!" a voice said.

And I said, "Eleanor?"

"You're here," she said. And before I had a chance to say anything more, she was talking as if she already knew it was me. She said, "When you hear the buzzer, come on through the doors and get on the elevator. Press nine and it'll bring you right up."

It was just as if she had been expecting me and wasn't angry at all like I had thought she would be. I went through the tiny lobby, with its chipped marble and broken tile. There had been a ceramic mural on the wall at one time, something that looked like the Easter parade with women dressed up in all kinds of hats. But half the little pieces were missing and some of the women had no eyes or mouths and some had plaster sitting on their heads where the bonnets should have been. The place looked dark and shabby, not like anything I had imagined Eleanor living in. And the elevator was black and so small that I could hardly get my one suitcase in; it was dirty and dusty, the kind of place a janitor might keep cleaning supplies in, or hide and take his lunch. It made a jolt and a jump and slowly started moving upward.

On the ride, I kept wondering how Eleanor knew, if maybe she had seen me on the street from a window, or maybe Will had found out I was gone and had told her to be on the lookout.

She had been expecting someone all right, but it sure wasn't me. When the elevator door opened, she looked behind me, as if she thought the correct person might be there. But when she saw there was nobody else, she said, "It's you."

I nodded that it was.

"I was expecting someone else."

And then she picked up my bag and started carrying it down the hall without asking me anything. She only turned around once and said, "I don't even know her *name*."

"Marilyn," I said, wondering if she had gone crazy from living in this weird place.

"What?" she said.

"My name is Marilyn."

She just shook her head and said, "I was expecting someone else."

* * *

Eleanor's paintings were everywhere, huge paintings that took up almost every wall. They were mostly paintings of people, and what appeared in the background behind them was exactly what I was seeing out the windows: rooftops, water towers, smokestacks, bridges, skylights, fire escapes, other people's highest windows. Whereas I had come from underground, this place where Eleanor stayed was the top part of a city. It felt safer here, drier, high enough that even the tallest waves couldn't reach me.

I put down my bag and took a seat at a table. There was a narrow kitchen and a counter with stools, and halfway back was an area that was sectioned off with that bubbly kind of glass; the bedroom, it looked like. All the way in the very back, against a row of windows, was her easel. But up near the front, near the door, was an air mattress and sheets and blankets, all set up as if it had just been made ready for a visitor.

I had been looking so hard that I had forgotten about Eleanor.

"What are you doing here, Marilyn?" she said when I turned to her.

"I was on my way to New Jersey." It sounded so stupid.

"New Jersey. For what?"

The reason was ridiculous now even to me, traveling all these miles to get a good look at someone I'd only read about in the newspapers? "It's kind of a long story," I said.

"And were you planning to go on there tonight?"

"I guess so," I said. I couldn't remember.

"Because I don't have room for you here."

I glanced over at the air mattress on the floor. She knew where I was looking. "You see, someone else is supposed to be coming. Someone I've promised a place to stay."

I nodded.

"If I'd known you were coming."

"Sure, I understand." But I couldn't get off the chair. I was thinking about going back down in that elevator and opening those doors. On the sidewalk in front of her building was a hole the size of a piano, a place that was inadequately roped off and where you could hear drilling below. If I went down there, I'd fall in and drown.

"It's just that I didn't make arrangements."

I nodded again, reached for my suitcase and tried to lift it. But she touched my hand, settled the bag on the floor.

"No, put it down. You can stay. Of course you can stay. God, what am I thinking?"

That was a good question. *I* sure couldn't tell. For the next hour or so, she hardly said a word, just paced and fidgeted and once went down to the street saying she was going to see if someone had left a message.

Finally she said, "Are you hungry?"

I hadn't thought about it until she said it, but I was starving. I was also exhausted. I had barely slept on the train and now I felt heavy and weary. She said something about Chinese food and then said, "I'll just leave a note, in case she shows up."

I still didn't know who *she* was, this other person my sister-in-law was expecting. I was only glad she wasn't there yet and that I had a good chance of being the one who was going to sleep on that blue air mattress.

We walked to the end of her street and over a couple of blocks. The snow had stopped, but the streets were wet, the sidewalks icy in places. The farther we got from Eleanor's street, the more people changed: from black-clothed white people to quick-lipped Orientals. The music changed, too, and what people were selling. There were little glass fans and dolls with slanted eyes and pigtails in store windows, *Playboy*-type calendars with photographs only of Oriental women. Despite the ice and the weather, people were moving fast, even Eleanor, and I stayed as close to her as I was able, sometimes having to jump off the sidewalk and as quickly as I could run around crowds so I wouldn't lose her.

The restaurant we went to was full of mostly Chinese people sitting at large, round tables. The place was hot after how cold it had been outdoors, and when I took off my coat I felt I was steaming. There was real steam everywhere, too, escaping from covered dishes, from the door that led to the kitchen, from bowls of clear soup, and even, it seemed, from the mouths of the waiters.

We ordered Chinese beer and something that Eleanor picked off the menu. The first sips of the beer went straight to my head and made my arms and legs feel dense and weighted.

I kept watching other people's plates pass back and forth from the kitchen, and because I was so hungry, I kept trying to fill myself up by drinking.

At the table next to us was a couple with two small children. One was about three and the other just a baby. When we first sat down, the baby was fretting, putting its hands in a glass of water, splashing around and pulling out little fistfuls of ice. The glass turned over and water spilled across the plastic tablecloth and dripped into the lap of the mother. She jerked the glass away, and the baby started screaming.

I noticed that Eleanor was watching, too, and that our having something to pay attention to helped fill in the space where conversation should have been.

The father put his glass of water in front of the baby and the hand went in again. The mother said, "Bastard," to the man and removed the hand and the water. She took her paper napkin and rubbed roughly at the baby's nose, which was leaking.

The baby was crying, trying to shake his head out of her grip. Pieces of food, a chopstick, a spoon were flying. And the parents were talking so sharply to one another that they caused more disturbance than the baby. The other child had started crying, too, maybe from being confused or scared. The father was trying to stop the older child now, trying to get him to take spoonfuls of rice, to drink his water.

Other people were staring, too, not just us. And a waiter was trying to wipe up the spilled water and hand the mother another glass and napkin. The baby had stopped by now, but the other child, the other boy was wailing. Nothing would stop him. Not food or cajoling or threatening.

Eleanor and I exchanged glances, almost recognition. We both wanted to do something, I could tell. Other people were returning to their food, trying not to pay attention. We drank our beer, but the child's wailing made me feel hollow and ill.

The father had an arm around the older boy's chair and was leaning toward him, trying to reason. For a second I thought maybe it was going to work, but then he saw his mother and started up again. She put down the spoon she had been feeding the baby with, scraped back her chair, and with two long strides was around the table and beside him. She jerked the boy up and shook him. His head was snatched back and forth like a rag on a stick.

Both mine and Eleanor's eyes were bulging. Others were watching, too, as the family left, but they tried to hide their stares and would turn to each other and start talking.

I couldn't talk though or move, until Eleanor tossed a wad of money to the center of the table and said, "Come on."

We were walking fast, though stiff-kneed and cautious because of the ice; but we were keeping time with one another. We hadn't said a word to each other for two blocks, not until Eleanor stopped at a corner and looked over at me. "Which way do you think they went?" I asked. She shook her head, but looked at me differently than she ever had. For nearly half an hour we searched, all up and down Chinatown, down narrow automobile-packed streets. People were still outside stores, hawking strange-shaped exotic vegetables, buying strangled ducks and chickens off hooks and hangers.

The beer and the exercise had made me forget how cold it was. It had started snowing again, large, heavy flakes that smacked against our faces like wet lint. We stood on the sidewalk beside a crate of wide yellowish leaves that an old Oriental woman had been snatching off heads of cabbage. There was a decaying smell and a dull, thick scent of fish and seawater. I had felt slightly drunk inside that hot restaurant, but I was dead sober out in the cold and saw that what we had done was as stupid as my plans for going to New Jersey. What did we think we were going to do if we caught up with the family? Grab the children and run?

Eleanor must have been thinking the same thing because she said, "Let's go home, it's freezing."

She put wedges of yellow cheese on a plate and brought out bowls of grapes and apples. From under the sink she pulled out a six-pack of dark beer that belonged to the man who was leasing her the apartment. The beer was hot and peppery-tasting, but it was good. I wasn't hungry anymore, just tired and tipsy.

There were two slung-back canvas chairs that faced a wall of windows. We sank into them and drank the beer in the dark, looking out on the lights in all the buildings. "Those are city stars," Eleanor said. "They come out every night, even when it's cloudy and snowing. Sometimes I try to find constellations."

I took a long pull on the long-necked bottle and looked where she was pointing. "The Manhattan Milky Way," I said.

"Yeah. That's good."

I looked at some of those stars one by one, just electricity pouring through windows, and I wondered how many light-years away the people behind one window were from the people behind the next window. Light-years had to be invented, I remembered learning in school, because there were distances so great that the old numbers, with their armload of zeroes, wouldn't work. I could understand it, distances that hard to measure.

"There's the Little Dipper," she said.

"Where?"

She pointed to a squat building that stood between two tall towers. "Yeah, I see it. Right down there."

"I saw Uranus once," I said. "When my class went on a field trip to the planetarium. It was brighter than you'd think."

She walked to the kitchen, wobbly I thought, and brought back the rest of the beers. We drank them all, the whole six-pack. They fell hard against the walls of my empty stomach, then splashed up and sloshed my brain.

I was still on stars and planets, trying to remember their order of distances from Earth, when Eleanor said, "What in the world were you going to New Jersey for?"

Maybe it was the beers; or maybe the lights and the city and the crying children would have made me tell her. But I told it all. About the New Jersey couple and the woman they hired to have their baby. About going to Abbie's and about Jackie. About how I used to try to find him.

The words tumbled out like coins out of one of those gambling machines. Like they had been piling up there for years, just waiting for someone to put in the right amount and hang on the handle.

She told me things, too, about her baby daughter. About trying to have another child with Will. About why she had come up here, so she could think and work and get away from people. It seemed as if the talking went on forever, something I drifted in and out of like netting, not sure if I'd been asleep for only a few seconds or for an hour.

I don't remember who said the last words or how I made it to that air mattress. But that's where I was the next day at noon. When I woke up, the sun was out and Eleanor was at the back of the apartment, scratching on canvas.

What she does is beautiful. Making faces come alive with unlikely bits of color. Making veins in arms and necks look as if they're full and pulsing. I could never do that, put purple and brown and white together and make motion and gesture.

I straightened the little area where I had slept and put yesterday's clothes in the suitcase after I dressed. The night before, Eleanor had softened, even seemed to like me. But that was because of the beer, I decided, working on her and me. I'd get on out, find the next train that was going south.

But when Eleanor saw me watching her, she said, "How about letting me paint you? It appears that the model I was counting on isn't coming."

I was in no hurry, not to get back to Atlanta or my job, if they were still holding it for me. I could wait the number of days it would take for her to do a painting.

She put me in front of a window with one of those big bridges out in the distance behind me. Then she wheeled a huge mirror near us and looked not at me exactly, but at what she saw in the mirror.

The surprising thing was that there was enough of me to fill up one of those big canvases. I had thought most of the painting would end up being blank spaces where all my parts —arms and legs and hands and head—should have been. That the painting would only be of what was out the window and in the room, and that I'd end up like one of those negative reliefs I'd seen in Eleanor's art books or like one of those half-gone faces down in the tiled lobby.

But the miracle was that I was there, whole. A real-life person. And what was in the face surprised me even more. It was sad, maybe, and tired, but it wasn't dumb and empty like I had imagined. It was someone you might not mind knowing.

"You're good," I told her on the day she said it was finished.

She shrugged her shoulders.

"No, I mean it. You're really good."

"I don't know. Most of the time I doubt it. Most of the time I don't even think it matters. You see, in the scheme of things it really doesn't. Not when you compare it to what people do who save lives and deliver babies and feed the hungry and build houses."

I had been listening hard to this kind of talk for a couple of days, and I had noticed a thing or two. One, that Eleanor never painted herself in front of that mirror. And two, that as strange as it sounded, maybe she was a lot like me, thinking there wasn't enough of her to fill up the length and width of one of those large pieces of canvas.

I remembered something. She had all these books in there that I had been looking at when we took breaks during the day so I could work the kinks out of my legs and arms and neck muscles. Books on the history of art, big wide coffee-table books full of paintings. I picked up one of those books, turned to a page near the beginning, and said, "Look at this." It was a photograph of a painting in some cave over in France. Thousands of years old, the book said, thousands and thousands of years before Christ.

"It says here that these paintings were always found far back into the caves, yards from the entrances. So, the experts, they say that means the drawings weren't there for merely decorative purposes. That they're deep in the cave because the artists thought the drawings had some magical powers.

"But you know what I've been thinking? That that's a bunch of hooey, that those experts don't know what they're talking about. And those artists were just like you, afraid what they were doing was worthless, or at least not as important as what everyone else was doing up in the front of the cave, carving up an animal, cooking some meat, sewing some skins together. So this artist, a girl maybe, she goes way in the back and paints so no one will know what she's doing."

I had Eleanor's attention like I had had it that night looking at her stars. I kept on, telling her what I'd read just as if I knew something.

"It also says that possibly the cavemen painted because they believed putting an image of an animal on the wall gave them power over the animal when they were hunting. But you know, maybe that's not it at all. This person who did the painting, maybe she just liked to draw. Maybe she was good at it. And she couldn't not do it, even if somebody told her it was dumb. So she snuck back there and drew those bison and deer and cows and horses in secret." Eleanor looked at me strange. "Well, that's just what I've been thinking," I said, knowing I'd talked too much, feeling stupid.

"That makes sense. What else were you thinking?"

She meant it. She really wanted to know. "Well, that when you think about it on a day-to-day basis, those up in the front of the cave, the ones cooking and sewing and the ones who had hunted, what they were doing did seem the most important. I mean, you sure would think that if you were the one cold and hungry. But what's left of what they did? The ones who did the big jobs?"

The thing that kills me is that almost no one is half as bad as you might think in the beginning. You just have to figure out what's got a hold of them. I think fear sometimes has a hold of Eleanor, just like it has me. Depression's gotten a hold of me from time to time, too, right by the neck, like one of those dripping ducks down in Chinatown. That and sadness.

Olin. I've figured out that what has had a hold of Olin all these years is smallness, a feeling that he wasn't anybody. That that's what makes him raise up a hand and push people down. I think everybody's had some sweetness in them at some time or another, right after they were born, or right before. But some different thing gets a hold of all of us and squeezes us by our different parts. Sometimes sweetness just gets squeezed out. Even murderers and bearded dictators, maybe it's the devil that gets a hold of them and twists up their insides so badly that everything that crawls out of them is a snake full of meanness.

Eleanor started a self-portrait before I left. That was something, watching her stare straight ahead, not caring how she made herself look, but making sure she had all the elements—nose, eyebrow, wrinkle, that hand holding a painted rag and brushes just right.

The day I was getting ready to go home, she stood in front

of the picture she had painted of me and said she wanted to include it in a show if she had one, but that after the show was over, I could have the painting.

I walked over and stood close to where she was standing and stared where she was staring. I looked at me hard. I was a face you could talk to if you'd let me listen. I was life-sized, taking up space that I had thought was empty.

I was relieved to know there was something to me, but I didn't want me. Maybe someone else would. Someone who would pay Eleanor money to hang me over a couch or mantel, and then come home at night and look at me and wonder who I was.

Eleanor: 1987

W̶ho would have guessed about
Henry?

And who would have guessed about Fitz and that tight-lipped little boarder of mine, Mr. Bolt?

I can't say which came as more of a shock to me, the first or the latter. Both were steps off a path. But then, if you thought honestly about it, they really weren't. They were the very steps both Henry and Fitz might have taken if unsuspected turns and curves hadn't come upon them in the day-to-day of their lives up to that point.

First, Henry.

CoraRuth was all set to head north to visit me, said she was bringing Henry if she had to snatch him up by his replaced molars. Over the past months, and maybe even years (although it had happened so slowly and gradually that it had taken time for us to notice it), Henry had turned superstitious. But not just someone who wouldn't walk under a ladder or who backed off at the sight of a black cat.

Some of it I witnessed myself, and some I heard second-hand from Mama. For example. If he ate a cheeseburger on the same day he got sorry news from the tax people, he just stopped eating cheeseburgers; never ordered one again, took them right off his personal menu. If he had a flat on the way into town one morning, he no longer took the same route. Not ever. He'd drive five miles out of the way to avoid the possibility of trouble. He got to where he retraced every step that ended safely: he wore a path from the house to the garage that criss-crossed the yard like a string of X's.

But CoraRuth said it wasn't until the day she couldn't get into their bedroom that she realized how bad things had gotten. What happened is that when she tried to open the door, she heard the old porcelain knob drop to the floor on the other side. She tried to fiddle with it herself for a while, knowing how Daddy can be with wrenches and screwdrivers; but when she still couldn't get it open, she called Henry.

He ended up having to pry a bedroom window loose and crawl through it to put the old doorknob back on on the other side. But when he opened the door, instead of walking out in the hall and joining CoraRuth, he backed out of the room and crawled backwards out of that same window.

Superstition. It had Henry by the chest and shoulders. And it made you understand why he couldn't get on a plane and fly to such a big, unknown city.

I didn't hear from CoraRuth for several days, nearly that entire November week that Will's sister was staying with me. And then I got her call. I expected her to say that either she had finally talked him into it, or she was coming by herself. Either way, I had planned for it. In the beginning, the thought of Mama and Henry in New York scared me half to death. I couldn't imagine them there in the first place, and I didn't know what it would do to my concentration. But by the time I got Mama's call, I was ready for them both, anxious to see them, excited about showing them places. Every time I've gone anywhere, I've spent the biggest part of my enjoyable moments thinking about those two. When Will and I were in Europe on our honeymoon, chock-full of guilt about seeing all the things Henry used to show me in the encyclopedias (Big Ben, the Eiffel Tower, the Colosseum, the *Forum*!), I called home three times, my voice and theirs crossing back and forth like bubbles inside those cables under the sea.

Well, this is the surprise. Neither one of them was coming. When CoraRuth called, she said, "Honey, something's happened."

There it was. Disaster. My insides caved in on me. I tried to brace myself for something awful, but I knew that moment that I never could.

"What is it?" I said.

"It's Henry."

I knew it: Henry. The minute I let up on worry, the worst had come, just as I had always suspected. And I was up in New York by myself, without Will or anyone to help me face it.

Mama cleared her throat and said, "He's bought a Waffle Hut, honey."

"Excuse me?"

"I know it, it's crazy. He came home a few days ago and just handed over the deed to the franchise like it was the most ordinary thing in the world. I said, 'Henry, what can you be thinking?' He said he was thinking what he'd been thinking for years, about how he'd like to own one of those things. That he'd manage it hands-on, be there to greet people when they came in the door, maybe even help out at the griddle. Can you imagine? Henry, who can't broil a piece of meat without scorching his knuckles?"

Mama continued. "I thought he'd completely gone off the deep end at first. You read about things like that, people just snapping. He's got a notebook full of daily specials. Got this idea for a chili sandwich."

I was trying to gather it all in, this new man, this changed Henry.

"What do you think?" Cora asked me. "Do *you* think it's crazy?"

Hell no, I thought. Frying eggs was a sight better than climbing backwards out of bedroom windows.

He already had a contract on the orchards and the canning house, she told me. And later on they'd probably sell the house and the rest of the property.

"I think it's probably a good thing too," she said. "I even considered working right there with him. Making it a mom-and-pop place, kind of cozy. It's the only Waffle Hut between Spartanburg and Greenville, and if it's handled right, we could make a killing."

I smiled. Good old CoraRuth. Henry might not have known it, but he was handing her a little slice of heaven on a greasy spatula. Mama had always wanted to get her hands in business. She liked commerce, the passing of dollars. Not because it was money, but because it was exciting. Like getting all the U's in Scrabble, like making fifty-seven points with just two letters.

But CoraRuth surprised me again. "Now, though, I've decided this is Henry's thing," Mama said. "Maybe we've already been working too close together all these years. And the last thing I want in the world is something to do with a kitchen. So I'm going to keep working with my Powder Puff Mechanics. Maybe even go to work at one of those driving schools. Lord knows there are too many people on the road like Henry."

I smiled again. It wasn't disaster at all. It was a hut full of good fortune. Two firmly made, heartfelt decisions.

While I had turned my head, Henry had taken a step off that railroad track of superstition. He had found the path he should have been on all along and was heading back toward the person that used to be himself. And maybe so was Mama.

My next big jolt was Fitz and Ben.

I had gotten one quick letter from her since I'd been away. And at the bottom there was this one line: *Good news! I have found a fellow.*

A couple of times I had tried to call her at night to see what this was about, but both times there'd been no answer, and I became so busy with Marilyn and finishing up all my work that I completely forgot about it. Then came Will's call, on the very same day I'd talked to Mama. He said, "I don't guess you've been watching the news." I told him no, of course not; he knew there wasn't a TV in Carroll's apartment. Then he said what caused my insides to quake again. "There's been some trouble down here. It's about Fitz, Eleanor."

So: I'd been right all along. Henry and CoraRuth had been let off the hook, but bad luck had up and snared the last person I had ever expected it to.

"She's been arrested," Will said.

"What!"

"It's all over the news, in the papers. She and that group of hers held a demonstration at a Styrofoam manufacturing plant, and when the police arrived, they refused to vacate the premises. Fitz was the last one they hauled off. It took three big cops to lift her up and get her in the paddy wagon."

"*What!*" I was a broken record; after two shocks in one day, there wasn't a new word in my brain. "Our Fitz?" I said. "Fitz Ballard?"

"Jay was out of town so I had to post bail." The seriousness had left Will's voice now, and I noticed glee.

"And there's more. Guess who her partner in crime was?"

I couldn't have made a guess. "Just tell me," I said.

"Bolt."

"Who?"

"Ben. Our boarder. Mr. Bolt."

It was too much. Fitz getting arrested, Will posting bail. But what did Benjamin Bolt have to do with any of it?

"I don't understand."

"*He's* the one she's been seeing."

Will was right, it made all the papers. As soon as we got off the phone, I was down at the newsstand. And there it was in the lower right-hand corner on the front page of the biggest paper in the country: ELDERLY ACTIVISTS STAGE SIT-IN AT GEORGIA PLANT. Under that, a smaller headline: 6 ARRESTED AS ENVIRON-MENTALISTS PROTEST MANUFACTURE OF STYROFOAM.

Fitz was described as the ringleader and given credit for planning the demonstration and the group's decision to stay put when the police requested that they leave. "Mrs. Louise F. Ballard," the article said, "founder of Old People Protecting the Ozone (OPPO), was charged with disorderly conduct yesterday when her organization's peaceful demonstration ended in arrests."

On the jump page, where the story continued, there was a photograph of Fitz sitting Indian-style, grinning from ear to ear and surrounded by policemen. And to her right was Mr. Bolt in profile, running from the scene, but with a protest sign still in his hand. The caption said: MRS. LOUISE BALLARD, EL-DERLY ENVIRONMENTALIST, AND UNIDENTIFIED PARTICIPANT DUR-ING YESTERDAY'S DEMONSTRATION.

When I finally got through to Fitz, she was as chipper as ever. "Can you believe all the press we've gotten?" she said. "It's terrific."

"But are you all right?"

"Oh, shoot, I'm fine. Of course Jay's not too pleased about it. Thinks I belong in a sanitarium."

Then I asked her about Mr. Bolt. "Why didn't you tell me it was him?" I asked her.

"I didn't have a clue he was your boarder till Will saw his picture in the newspaper and told me. He just said he had a garage apartment somewhere; I didn't know it was yours."

Will had told me that no one had seen Ben since just before all the arrests. "He lit out like a sore-tailed cat, and no one has seen hide nor hair," he said. "And he's vacated his apartment, apparently snuck in during the middle of the night and ran off in the dark with his clothes and a few personal items."

When I asked Fitz about this, she said, "Oh, he's just had a bad fright," she said. "He'll be back though, once all the dust has settled."

I didn't have trouble imagining Fitz getting arrested or even enjoying it. The real surprise to me was her being attracted to that little dried-up bit of a man. Fitz is built like a tanker, tall and broad. Not a fat woman, but one Gram would describe as having big bones. In the pictures taken at my and Jay's wedding, dressed in a light blue organdy dress, she had jdwarfed CoraRuth so, who was dressed in yellow chiffon, that when they stood side by side, she made Mama look as inconsequential as a canary.

I had seen pictures of Jay's father, a large, important-looking man like those tall CEOs I had painted portraits of. That's what I had expected of Fitz, with her height, if she ever picked again. But Ben? That quiet man who lived behind my house and gave me his rent each month in ten-dollar bills?

But, like Henry, it makes sense when you think about it. That would be like her, to fall for the last person anyone would expect, the one no one else would touch, the way she did sometimes with what everyone else thought was a bad piece of furniture. A piece she knew needed only a little cleaning up, some Minwax maybe, gentle rubbing. At Christmas time I'd seen her pick the worst tree on the lot because she was afraid no one else would take it, and the tree would have been cut down for nothing. Ben, Fitz's roughed-up little rooster. Suddenly it wasn't so hard to imagine.

The morning after Marilyn arrived in New York, while she was still sleeping, I rode the Green Line uptown to the Eighty-sixth Street exit. The girl wasn't there. I waited, huddled on the same steps where she had caught people's coins, but she never showed.

CoraRuth used to take canned goods to the migrants who worked for us, gave them our old clothes, paid for shoes and diapers for their babies. That girl could be one of their daughters, still moving, still searching for what they call the American Dream, although I can't see what's so typically American about it—the right to have a home.

Mama said once, "I'll never get their faces out of my mind."

Everyone we've ever known, we take them with us all the time. Even people we've never known, all those who lived before us. I care about them all. The people who made those beautiful curious marks deep in caves. The people I saw on the streets in New York, with their sad, desperate signs on the subways and in tunnels underground, huddling under newspapers, over heating grates.

There is never any getting away, really, from the people you love. I went to New York to escape my family and their pull on me. But even before they started arriving and calling, they were always with me. Sometimes their faces were more real to me, so many miles away, than when I'd been with them.

But the thing is, I can't keep Henry or Mama or Will or Fitz or any of them safe, any more than Henry's careful steps could keep him away from bad luck and inclement weather.

I found the book Marilyn had been looking at, the one with cave drawings in it. There was one with a negative hand imprint. I wished I could be where it was so I could stick out my hand and touch it. People have been making pictures forever, and maybe Marilyn was right: not because it gave them magical powers, but because they had to. Maybe it's that simple. *I'm* simple, just a person with giraffe eyes.

Maybe I'm no good at what I'm doing and maybe this new series of mine will be a flop. But I'll still keep painting. Maybe I'll go back to the Waffle Hut, do a series of paintings on Kitty and the other girls. Then go on up to South Carolina and see what kind of waitresses Henry has got. Do a life-sized painting of him suited up in one of those orange uniforms, playing short-order king over a griddle of hash browns.

* * *

The week after Marilyn left, I felt terrible. It was the flu, I guess, because I was achy and so tired that all I wanted to do was sleep. But I had a plane to catch in two days and all my things to pack, the paintings to take care of, the place to put back together the way Carroll had left it.

I was sweeping up and dusting, when I had to take a break and I sat down on one of the wide windowsills. It was one of the windows on the north side of the building, a view that had been less interesting than the others. I looked over at the rusty water towers, at the white boxy letters on a building a block away. While I was looking, my fingers were touching deep grooves in the sill. I looked down. It was a name I'd been touching, something I hadn't seen before. Josephine Feodosevich. The letters were jagged and clumsy, but completely distinct.

My mind was racing: perhaps the name belonged to one of the girls I had imagined working there years before, sewing up hats. Perhaps she took one of those industrial needles and scratched her name on the sill one hot August day when the windows were up. Or maybe she did it over months or years, a letter at a time, when no one was looking.

It was like the drawings in the caves. Someone had had to record something, leave part of themselves behind. My heart went out to this Josephine, whoever she had been.

There are holes in every life, in every family. In our family, there is the one where my sister used to be and where my infant daughter should have been. There are also holes where people were taken from us in other ways: Will and his Kate, me and Jay, Marilyn and her baby. Those empty spaces where lives used to be do not go away. Not ever. And some people don't ever recover. Like Jay. The losses that had come to him as a boy or a teenager or a man had done him in. He seemed lost somehow, and I had a feeling he always would be. And Marilyn. I had been wrong about her for years. She wasn't stupid or spineless as I had thought. But she was lost, too, as lost as that child of hers she probably would never find.

But Mama and Henry were going to be okay, I realized. A time or two the life had been kicked right out of them, and the years had beat them both around like they were rag dolls. But they were strong.

And so was I. I ran my fingers slowly over the letters of

Josephine Feodosevich. If I ever had a daughter, I decided, I'd give her this name. I'd pick it up off the sill, where its owner had left it for me, and I'd pass it on. I thought about Will. Will, who had more energy than any ten normal men. Who, maybe more than any of the rest of us, had the need to leave his mark. Will who, miraculously, loved *me*, the one I had always thought of as the worst Christmas tree on the lot. I was so much like Henry, superstitious, afraid everything was always my fault, afraid of things that might never happen. I was tired of being that way. But I had spent so much of my life, so much of my energy, worrying about people, it was difficult to think about changing. What would I do with my time? Who would I be? It was scary.

It was also time to go home. I missed my husband and wanted to see him. There was so much to talk about, so many things to get settled. It had always seemed as if loving people was my one big talent, the one thing that came easily. But loving people was hard work, and it was still going to take the greatest part of my energy. The key was learning how to do it without getting lost. I didn't fully possess that key yet, but I was trying.

It was the week before Christmas when I left Carroll's loft. People are happy in New York during the holidays, and the city felt welcoming and gracious and even more energetic than usual. I had taken care of the paintings and my supplies, and all that was left to get to the airport was me and my suitcase. I put it on Carroll's bed, along with my airline ticket and the money I'd need for cab fare and tips. All the rest of the money that was left from what I'd brought with me, I stuck in an envelope in my coat pocket and rode the elevator downstairs.

I walked across Broome Street to Mott, through Little Italy and down into Chinatown. I listened to all the different music, the different words, the language. I smelled the food, looked at every color my eye would ever know. I loved this place. All of it, its griminess, its trash, its incredible collage of people.

I walked back up Broadway to SoHo. My neighborhood. There were people there who knew me, who spoke to me when I walked in the store for lettuce and coffee. I passed all the galleries I loved. Leo Castelli and the others on Broadway, Mary Boone, Nancy Hoffman; Paula Cooper over on Wooster.

Then I walked back down Houston Street, turned left toward home, and made a last stop at the health food store. He was there, the man who had been sleeping there since I first arrived weeks before. The sun was out but it was cold, and he was curled under a rat's nest of newspapers. All of him was the same color, the papers, the filthy clothes, his dirty skin.

I handed him the envelope with the money. Nearly six hundred dollars. Perhaps it would get him passage to someplace safer or warmer. Or help him get cleaned up so he could get a job. Or maybe it would buy him warmth, a new coat, some blankets. Maybe it would buy him nothing more than an endlessly flowing bottle of burning liquid. Maybe it would become kindling for a crazy man's fire. It didn't matter. It was only money.

When I left, the plane tipped its wings like a hawk and circled Manhattan. I could see the park. A rectangle of green in a forest of buildings. All those people.

The plane leveled, tipped again, and leveled once more. I crossed my arms over myself and settled in for the swift ride home, taking millions of pictures with me, ones that would comfort me and haunt me forever.

Ben: 1988

Everybody that is here has run from something: hard winters, Castro, parents, overbearing children. They all look pulled-up and plopped-down. Most of them got houses, but not that many got homes. They aren't happy either, most of the ones that I see. They yell at each other from cars, scream at each other in grocery stores. I go in the shops and the young cashiers don't like to talk English to me, they all seem so angry.

Dead of winter and eighty degrees. People don't care about their shoes. Wear straw sandals and canvas sneakers, let their leather go scuffed and dusty. The sand is gray-white and blinding. I didn't pick it, Miami. It was just where the bus was headed.

I dream that I've gone back and explained it all. How scared I was seeing everybody getting arrested. Afraid of being locked away myself. I tell her it was hearing those things on the news: wealthy Atlanta woman; widow of rich insurance executive; former Druid Hills resident. That picture they showed of that big house where she used to live. A mansion.

What would a woman with all that want with a man who rubbed shoe leather, who had brown Kiwi polish deep in the lines of his hands? Bald head. Bad eyes. No future.

I tell her no one ever done what she did, reach out and touch me. How she made a part of me work again, a part I had thought might not move because nobody but me had used it in thirty years.

I tell her I've got heartache. Heartlove. Evelyn, out in the world like one of those kidnapped children that's dead or lost but without me ever knowing. Her face as a baby.

That old dog.

Her, Fitz, warm and soft. Telling me things. Listening.

Holding my hand while we ride the bus. While we sit at the airport and watch those big jets circling. Everybody going places.

I pull her to me, hold her. Hear her breathing. Smell her hair. She laughs. I say, "Fitz, I'm not never going."

But there's no Fitz there. No breathing, no hair. It's only a dream and I'm holding on to no one.

I pick up my feet from the hot pavement. Carry my things in these brown bags. A wad of clothes. This one certain magazine. These few pictures. I take step after step, like I always have. Keep walking.

But what I see is it's north I'm headed. Back up the sunshine road. My legs are saying to me, Ben, give it one last try. My arm and thumb go out, and strangers give me rides. They talk, and I sit and nod and tap my foot: go faster! The mile markers ticking off like time. I sit and nod, and deep inside me, so quiet only one person living can hear it, I say, Coming towards you. Coming home.

My tongue don't speak those words, though, when I get there. And my legs won't take me across the street. I sit on the bench watching people pass back and forth under that bell at her door. I hole up there and watch for Fitz, and when I see her I do the old trick. I pull the big tall woman up into my Minolta, and late at night I look at that face I caught and I tell it, Sorry, Sorry, and wish that it were mine.